THE BLOOD OF GOD

IN THE SHADOW OF SIN: BOOK THREE

BY
ALAN HARRISON

Cover design by MiblArt
Map by Cornelia Yoder

ISBN 9781838132842 (paperback):
ISBN 9781838132859 (ebook):

I

For those who fight anyway

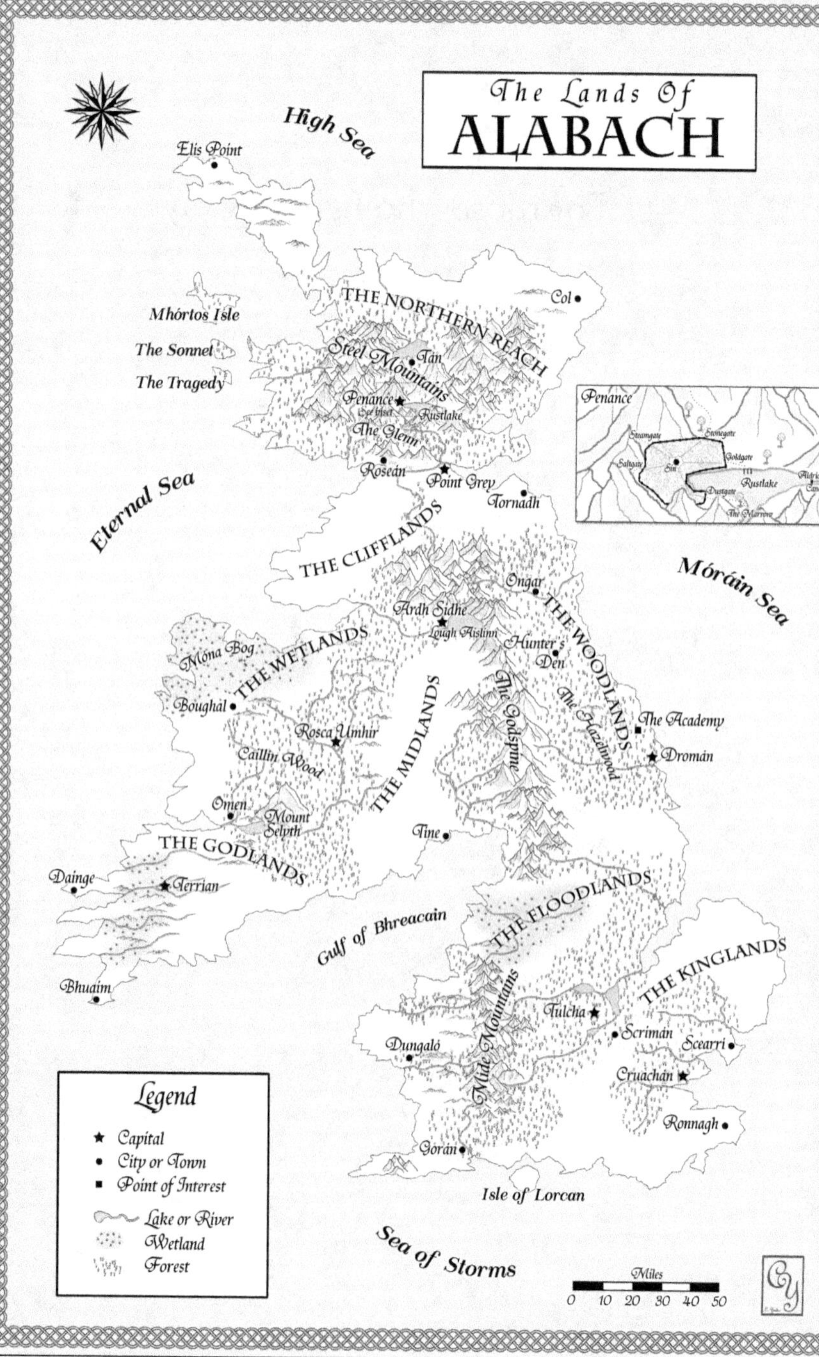

The Lands Of
ALABACH
High Sea
Elis Point
THE NORTHERN REACH
Col
Mhórtos Isle
The Sonnet
The Tragedy
Steel Mountains
Tán
Penance
The Inlet
Rustlake
The Glenn
Roseán
Point Grey
Tornadh
Eternal Sea
THE CLIFFLANDS
Móráin Sea
Ongar
Ardh Sidhe
Lough Aislinn
THE WOODLANDS
Hunter's Den
Móna Bog
THE WETLANDS
Boughal
Rosca Umhir
THE MIDLANDS
The Godspine
The Hazelwood
The Academy
Dromán
Caillin Wood
Omen
Mount Selyth
Tine
THE GODLANDS
Dainge
Terrian
Gulf of Bhreacain
THE FLOODLANDS
Bhuaim
THE KINGLANDS
Tulcha
Scrimán
Scearri
Dungaló
Cruachán
Ronnagh
Góran
Isle of Lorcan
Sea of Storms
Penance
Strangate
Stonegate
Saltgate
Goldgate
Sin
Rustlake
Dustgate
The Marren
Aldrich Canal
Legend
Capital
City or Town
Point of Interest
Lake or River
Wetland
Forest
Miles
0   10   20   30   40   50

CONTENTS

Prologue: The Coward's War 1

Chapter 1: In the Eyes of Seletoth 20

Chapter 2: The Last Carríga 33

Chapter 3: What is Right 40

Chapter 4: What Must Be Done 49

Chapter 5: From His Lips 63

Chapter 6: The Majestic 78

Chapter 7: In the Light of the Lady 91

Chapter 8: The Light Fades 102

Chapter 9: The Grey Plague 121

Chapter 10: The Blood of God 130

Chapter 11: Incarnate 145

Chapter 12: Hunter's Den 145

Chapter 13: The White Rose 190

Chapter 14: God's Spine 202

Chapter 15: Scarlet Robes 220

Chapter 16: The Silverback's Reach 230

Chapter 17: As It Was Written 253

Chapter 18: At Mount Selyth's Peak 262

Chapter 19: Heresy 280

Chapter 20: The Truth 295

Chapter 21: Omniscience 307

Chapter 22: Our New World 316

Epilogue: Journal of Padraig Tuathil 340

Guide to Alabach, Her Places, and Her People 344

PROLOGUE:
THE COWARD'S WAR

Earthmaster Seán held his tongue. It wasn't something he was used to doing. From the classrooms of the Academy to the council hall of the Triad, and even within the inner circles of the Silverback's dissident movement, Seán had always spoken his mind, caring little for who he contradicted.

But tonight, in the throne room of Keep Carríga, standing before the Earl of the Midlands, he kept his thoughts to himself. Even as the undead horde slew the townsfolk of Rosca Umhír outside and threw their bodies against the castle walls, Seán remained silent.

I am a visitor, he reminded himself. *It is not my place to question his lordship, no matter how questionable his actions may be.*

"Sire, please you must reconsider!" cried the crystallographer who had brought the dire news that Ardh Sidhe to the north had fallen. "We cannot assume help is on the way."

"I assume nothing!" said Earl Carríga, with a voice that once commanded an army of a thousand strong. Several of his councilmen and advisors shrank back in fear. "How *dare* you seek refuge in my keep, then demand I open my doors to let in those... creatures!"

To Seán's surprise, the crystallographer stood his ground. "But the townsfolk, your highness. If fighting back against this enemy is not an option, then please, lower the drawbridge for them."

"The town is already lost," said Earl Carríga. "We are all who remain."

A concerned mutter ran through the room. Indeed, the faint sounds of screaming and shouting amidst the slaughter outside implied the very opposite.

Pathetic, thought Seán. *A whole life cultivating an image of a war-leader, only to die sitting on his arse as his castle is breached.*

Seán sighed. He too would likely die alongside the fool.

Only a few short days ago, everything was in place. Seán had arrived at Rosca Umhír to be Earl Carríga's arcane advisor, and the Silverback's rebellion was days from being set in motion. The Simian's plan was a simple one: Nicole and her Reapers would take Point Grey, holding the Clifflands as Argyll gave his demands to the Crown. Fair demands, in Seán's eyes. First to establish an independent Simian state throughout the Northern Reach of Alabach, and second to destroy the wicked Church of the Trinity, redistributing the opulent wealth of the Basilica of Penance to the needy.

In the event that King Diarmuid did not capitulate, choosing instead to engage with the separatist forces in Point Grey, the Silverback had another plan.

Though a plan no more, now that a different enemy threatened the kingdom.

Seán looked up to a great stained-glass window that stood behind the earl's throne. It bore the image of King Móráin the First during his alleged "apotheosis," with his bright, golden wings that blinded the Simian natives with their radiance. More lies of the Church, conceived to shield the world from the Truth, just as the garish stained-glass image obscured the flames of the burning city outside.

None had spoken up since the earl's last outburst. Across the room, two noblemen in robes hung their heads in silence, while a younger man prayed in frantic whispers, hands clasped. The others formed tight huddles, weeping quietly together.

Hopeless, thought Seán, his fingers slowly forming a fist. *How did it all become so....*

A knock boomed through the room, causing many to jump in fright. It came from the entrance to the throne room, where a mighty oaken door sealed those within from the horrors unfolding without.

When the knock came a second time, one guard set aside his pike to open the door slightly. It seemed that he was ready to dismiss whoever was on the other side, but once the door was ajar, it abruptly burst inward.

A women strode in, a mass of dark plate-mail clinking with each of her steps. She held a great helm under one arm, with a swan crest atop its head, its wings outstretched, its golden bill open as if shrieking.

"Father," she said, taking a knee. "Our marksmen are fatigued and ineffective against this enemy. I sought to lead a vanguard out across the drawbridge. Light cavalry to clear the way for armoured knights. Lord-Lieutenant Torloch said he could rally those guarding the halls to join, but none will act without your command."

Earl Carríga leaned forward, eyes open and wide, as if scarcely believing what he could see.

"And no command shall be given," he rasped. "The royal guard and the city guard and the Lord-Lieutenant's knights have all been ordered to guard this keep. They shall do nothing else."

The armoured woman stood, mouth ajar. Seán knew her as Lady Aislinn Carríga, though she looked like no lady tonight. She was the last heir of the Carríga dynasty, with Sir Bearach dead and Cathal in Penance, soon to join him.

"Father, they're slaughtering our people freely out there! Lord-Lieutenant Torloch was readying his men to ride out, but someone raised the drawbridge."

"I gave the order to raise it," said Earl Carríga. "And anyone who dares leave shall be hung as a deserter."

"Deserter?!" Aislinn cried. "If anyone is deserting their post, Father, it's you."

"Treason!" roared the earl. "How *dare* you stand before me, wearing my son's armour like a play-acting child!"

"My brother would never hide while innocents are in danger. It's only a matter of time before the dead are upon us too. Why are you so content in waiting for that time to come?"

"Because Keep Carriga has never been breached," said the earl. "These walls have thrown back worse enemies in the past. This dead horde have brought no siege engines or towers to take this castle. So here we shall stay!"

Aislinn's mouth quivered, unable to find the words to respond. She turned her back to her father and left the throne room, her stride more confident than her entrance.

After the guards closed the door gently behind her, the room went back into its mild stir, as if nothing had happened.

Seán glanced up at the earl.

Keep Carriga has never been breached because Keep Carriga has never seen real war. And no castle in the kingdom has seen a war quite like this.

Seán smiled, seeing the irony that even if this horde never came, Keep Carriga would have seen a fate far worse than a siege.

This was part of the Silverback's master plan, to be executed after Point Grey was taken by the Reapers. Once the Crown's forces were focused north, Seán was to retrieve a small device from a safe house within Rosca Umhir. This device, invented by the genius of Chief Engineer Nicole, was said to be capable of destroying an entire castle with a single blast. Meanwhile, other loyal dissidents would do the same to other castles throughout the kingdom.

And that was how the Silverback would wage his war. One big display in Point Grey to draw King Diarmuid's full attention northwards. Then His Grace would receive word that Keep Carríga of the Midlands was destroyed without siege. The Crown could respond in one of two ways: by pulling out of the Clifflands entirely, or splitting their forces. Either way, another castle elsewhere in the kingdom would be blown to rubble, without any visible cause. And the Silverback would make it clear that these attacks would not stop unless the Crown met his demands.

A coward's war, mused Seán. *But an effective one.* Indeed, what force could possibly stop a tactic like this?

Though despite all the planning and preparations Seán, the Silverback, and all the other dissidents had made these past twelve moons, the dead rising from their graves had never been considered.

So, when Seán had received a short wave from Penance some days ago that, no, the Silverback was not responsible for this undead scourge, the fire in his heart went out.

All we can do now is wait.

For a moment, Seán's mind drifted outside of the throne room, across the burning moat and through the city streets. If the dissident safe house was still intact, perhaps Nicole's device would still be there. Seán cursed himself. If only he had the foresight to bring it. Then, if the dead were to storm the walls with their full might, he could use it to destroy the castle and everyone inside. Sure, it would see him dead, but what better death was there than wiping out much of this enemy at the same time?

Seán shook his head. It was a futile thought. Of course, things would be different if he had brought the weapon with him. Things would be different too if he had never joined the Silverback, or if he had just ignored his Seeing of Seletoth.

"Seletoth," he whispered, clasping his hands together. *The One and True*, he thought, not daring to say that part aloud. "Hear us. Help us."

He had always kept his faith to himself, acting the part of loyal mage and servant of the Church. His Earthmaster's robes were earned not only through hard work and study, but through careful politicking and positioning with the brothers of the Academy and the nobility of the many courts of Alabach. And that required him keep his beliefs a secret. How much easier it would have been, to have just murdered his old tutor, like the young Pyromancer Fionn had done back in Penance to become Firemaster? Seán found himself smiling, wondering how Fionn was faring now within the Triad, dealing with all the chaos that had erupted throughout the Seachtú. The dead had taken Point Grey and Ardh Sidhe, and it was only a matter of time before they tried to take Dromán too. Hopefully the mages there could fight them back, but if not... would Penance, or even Cruachan come next?

Seán leaned against a stone wall, exhaling deeply. The others in the hall whispered among themselves, pacing backwards and forwards while the earl sat in silence, staring blankly ahead.

Contemplating what you've done? thought Seán. *Regretting condemning your whole city to death?*

"Look!" came a voice from across the room. A noblewoman pointed towards a narrow window overlooking the northern castle walls. "The drawbridge, it's opening!"

Many in the hall shrieked. Seán darted over. The great drawbridge was indeed lowering, like the jaw of a great beast, light spilling forth from its mouth.

Across the moat, the undead soldiers sacking and burning the north ward of Rosca Umhír stopped their butchery. One by one, their attention turned towards the descending mass of steel and wood and chains.

As the drawbridge met the far side of the moat, the undead gathered to cross it. Some wights had the appearance of simple farmhands, waving tools of their trade overhead. Others were soldiers, wearing the colours of Point Grey or Ardh Sidhe. Perhaps they once fought the horde, falling only to serve the enemy that felled them.

Will the same fate await us, should we perish too?

"They're coming!" cried a young man to Seán's side. "Why would they lower it? Why would they let them in?"

Suddenly, a large figure came bursting from the light of the keep. A warhorse, clad in thick armour, galloped across the bridge. Thunderous hooves pounded against the oak. As it approached the few undead soldiers crossing, the steed's rider lowered a lance. And they accelerated, rider and horse moving as one.

With a crash, they collided with the undead. One soldier met the lance head-first. Another fell, trampled under the destrier's hooves, while the rest were knocked aside from the impact, falling with muffled splashes into the black water below. The knight circled back to finish the rest, wielding the warhorse as a weapon just as much as the lance that struck down all who stood before them.

The rider paused and held up their lance. Fires from the burning city glimmered against its tip. The crest upon the knight's head shimmered too; a black swan, with two wings outspread.

"Cathal Carríga!" cried one of the councilmen. "The Black Swan of Rosca Umhír has returned to save us!"

"Not Cathal," said Seán. He threw a glance towards the earl. "Lady Aislinn."

The earl did not respond. He leaned his head against one hand: a balled fist pressed against his temple. His eyes, glazed over and staring, were fixated towards the window where the scene was unfolding.

Seán looked back outside again. Aislinn still pointed her lance high and forward; a signal for cavalry to charge. But no charge came. More undead nearby began to take notice, plodding and stumbling towards her.

Aislinn lowered her lance and rode into the burning city. And the drawbridge began to rise behind her.

"No!" cried Seán. He turned towards the earl. "She's out there alone! Send out the foreriders, the infantry, whatever you have!"

"A noble death she chose herself," said the earl, shaking his head. "Her father shall die a coward tonight, but she shall do so a hero. A fool, of course, but a hero nonetheless."

"What is *wrong* with you?" said Seán. "It's a siege we're unlikely to survive, but you insist on giving up without a fight!"

"I thought the king would save us...." muttered the earl. "Dromán and Cruachan still stand, with forces enough to throw the enemy back. I wanted to spare my life, my men... my family."

Tears welled in the earl's eyes. Seán swore under his breath, then looked to the battle outside. The undead were crowding into the North Ward now, with Lady Carríga nowhere to be seen beneath the broken, decaying bodies that filled the streets.

Such a waste. Unbridled bravery makes many a martyr.

He looked on as more undead swarmed the area, crawling over the rubble of broken buildings and shattered cobblestones.

To go out without a plan, dying for nothing more than an empty statement. His mind went back to the ridiculous idea he had earlier, of using Nicole's weapon to blow Keep Carríga to the

Holy Hell, taking half the horde with it. That, at least, would be a sacrifice worth a damn.

But the weapon was hidden away in a cache, in a safe house in the South Ward; an old store house, derelict and bordered up.

The horde continued to surge in the streets; possibly the bulk of them had come here now, drawn by Aislinn's act of defiance. The would-be-knight was still nowhere to be seen.

Then, the most peculiarly thought crossed Seán's mind. He glanced behind him, past the sobbing earl in his throne, towards the stained-glass effigy of the false god-king.

Southwards.

She's drawn their attention, he realised. *I may not have another chance.*

He broke into a sprint across the throne room.

I'll make her sacrifice count.

He raised both hands as he passed the bewildered earl, pointing towards the window.

Sand cast in flames. He forced his power into the glass. *Ancient stone, crushed to dust and forged anew.*

With a screech, the stained-glass window shattered. And amidst the broken fragments of azure and gold that burst forth, Earthmaster Seán leapt into the night.

Everything slowed as he fell through the air, four stories separating him from the black waters of the moat. Ignoring the gasps and shouts from those back up in the throne room, Seán focused his attention on the shards of glass, pulling on their elementary components. Silicon and iron of rocks and stone, shattered to sand, then boiled to glass. But there was more. Other minerals that gave it colour. As Seán plummeted to the ground, studies once long forgotten began to return to the surface of his mind.

Metal oxides... one for each colour.

The power of his soul reached for cobalt oxide, comprising the blue fragments that had formed the sky of the image before he shattered it. Copper oxide had given the hills of the northern reach their vibrant greens. The golden skin, hair, and wings of Móráin had come from gold itself.

Enough gold used here to house a family, thought Seán, focusing on each element within the shards that surrounded him as he fell.

Once he had a grasp on each, a slight tug on the power of his soul pulled each piece of glass beneath him. There, he shaped them under his feet, rounding their edges like a bowl. As the moat rushed up to meet him, Seán pulled on the cobblestones of a street across the water. These were much easier to grasp, far closer to their fundamental form than the stained glass. Abruptly, dozens of individual cobblestones flew up towards him, forming a crooked slope from the bank of the moat to an empty space just beneath his feet.

Seán narrowed his eyes, bracing himself for impact. The glass platform beneath his feet shrieked as it struck the stone, but Seán's Geomancy held it together. He held both hands out wide to help keep balance, though most of his balance came too from his magic, adding and subtracting weight from either side of the flat glass slab as it skidded along the cobblestone slope.

Of course, the fundamental laws of force prevented a Geomancer from outright levitating or flying upon a platform of stone or metal or glass beneath their feet. An exertion of force in one direction required that same exertion in the opposite direction, which Geomancy was unable to provide.

But Geomancy could be used to decelerate a descent, as Earthmaster Seán did here. He pulled the glass platform upwards, adding to its friction against the cobblestone slope, all while maintaining perfect balance. Deftly, he slid to the edge of the moat, jumping from the glass platform before it shattered against the ground.

He hit the ground in a roll, his old muscles and bones aching with the impact.

Been a while since I tried that, he thought, standing through a dull throb in his legs. He turned and let the stones of the platform fall into the water.

As predicted, there were no undead here. Without wasting more time, Seán gathered himself, and ran southwards, through the broken streets of Rosca Umhír.

Heart pounding and lungs heaving, Seán sprinted past crumbling remnants of what once was a quiet, residential part of the city. He made his way through Blide Street with little hassle. Here, a long, winding back-road took him past dozens of two-up-two-down terraced houses, many of which were shattered and crumbling. And all of which were vacant.

Far too late, thought Seán, as he ran. *Fool, I am. I should have done something sooner than this.*

He turned a corner to see a group of figures standing in the middle of Bracken Street. Skeletons, clutching spears and rounded shields. Even without eyes, one turned and seemed to *see* Seán. The figures shrieked with unholy voices. Together, they charged.

The Earthmaster planted a foot into the ground and focused his power into the cobblestones around him. With gritted teeth and a strong tug, a dozen came free. They floated before him, silently, as the undead came running.

Then Seán dashed forward, pushing the wall of stones with him. He forced his soul into them, then thrust one towards the wight that came at him first, striking its head and knocking it prone. He extended both hands outwards, causing the stones to twist around him. He roared with effort as he met the other undead, forcing each stone towards any that came near. Projectiles met undead faces and bony necks, cracking them with each collision.

When each stone was spent, he reached out and found them again, pulling them back towards him, spinning them around his body. The undead themselves gave no indication that they were put off by this, unrelenting in their efforts to continue their attack.

And Seán was unrelenting in his response.

Gradually, he made his way through the street, his senses sharpened on his surroundings. The stone buildings here had been ruined recently, though not by these wights. When a small handful of the undead remained standing before him, Seán quickened his pace. But somewhere behind him, towards the centre of the city, more guttural cries rang out. He glanced over his shoulder to see a stream of wights pour out from an adjacent alley; hundreds of dead eyes locked on his own.

Seán took a deep breath and focused on the shambling remnants of a nearby tenement building.

Granite, he thought, letting his soul grope along every inch of the building. *Born from the molten fires that rage beneath the earth.* The stone here one once formed a massive batholith, far into the Northern Reach. Its surface was laced with tiny specks of feldspar and quartz. Each sung a different note as Seán's soul poured over them.

Once he had a firm grip on the entire structure, and once the advancing horde were positioned perfectly adjacent to it, Seán surged his power and pulled the building into the street, crushing the advancing bodies with a loud rumble and a burst of dust.

The undead answered this with silence, and no more followed.

Exhausted, Seán ran onwards, trying to reconstruct the broken buildings with his memories. There once was a cobbler store here, run by an elderly gentleman who moonlighted as a locksmith. Further on, a smouldering mass of stone marked where a healer's clinic once stood.

Finally, around a slight right bend, past a row of hedges miraculously still intact after all that they had seen, Seán found himself standing before the dissident safehouse. It was a squat, single-story building with a single window and a single door boarded up.

All that marked this building as out of the ordinary was a very faint etching above the door, visible only to those who were looking for it. One circle within another circle, with two lines forming a V underneath.

Seán never knew what the symbol actually meant. It was some rune of some Simian or criminal language he knew little about. All he knew was that this shape marked where the cache was hidden. And that was all he needed to know.

I'll take it back to the keep, he thought. *I'll take it back and kill every last one of them.*

He reached out to touch the wooden boards across the door, then looked around to see if he was still alone.

Behind him, he saw a single figure, standing alone in the street.

A young girl, with black hair mottled with blood and a cloak made from black feathers.

"You're powerful," she said, stepping towards Seán. "Stronger that the other Geomancers...."

"Who are you?" said Seán. "What are you doing here?"

"You must be an Earthmaster. My undead didn't stand a chance against you."

"*Your* undead? Are you...? Did you...?"

"I brought them, yes," she said. She made a movement with her fingers, gesturing towards the stones of the road beneath her feet. "I'm looking for souls like yours. Mages and Masters. Gods and half-gods." With a flick of her wrist, the cobblestones around her rose. "I liked the trick you did, with the rocks, circling around you. Do they teach that at the Academy?"

"Who are you?" repeated Seán, narrowing his eyes.

As if responding, the stones around the girl shot towards Seán. On instinct, he raised his hands, forcing them back with his own power. But the force that drove them towards him was far stronger than anything he could hope to counter.

How? thought Seán, as the stones struck him. Two hit his chest, winding him. Another struck a shin, shattering the bone and crumbling him to the ground.

He gritted his teeth through the pain, trying to figure out what was happening. If this magic was the girl's alone, she was stronger than an entire army of battlemages. But how was that possible?

And the undead... she named them her own.

She walked over to him, two more stones floating over her head. As soon as Seán saw the girl's eyes—cold and numb to the death she had wrought—he knew that she meant to kill him.

"Wait!" he wheezed, desperately thinking of a plan. "You said you seek more mages. I... I know where you can find them."

The girl paused and smiled. If something so wicked could even be called a smile.

He pretended to be trying to find of the words to say, but Seán's mind was elsewhere, frantically thinking through the pain that seared his body.

Few know of the weapon. If I die here, it could be lost. He tried to reach out into the safehouse for it, but the pain hampered his grasp on his power. Then, another idea came to him. He turned his attention to the stone beneath him: cobblestones still. These were basalt, formed from the fiery blood of the earth cooling above ground. With the little power he could muster, Seán pressed his soul into the stones, making cracks form along them.

"Tell me," said the girl. She struck one of the stones down at Seán, cracking it against his shoulder.

The Earthmaster howled in pain, but he continued to work those cracks through the stones beneath him. He kept his eyes fixated on hers and mouthed some words without meaning, stalling for time.

"Speak!" she cried. "Speak now, or I'll kill you slowly."

As Seán formed the last crack in the stone, completing his work, he smiled. "The mages of the Academy, my dear. They'll hunt you down, and they'll crush you like a worm."

The girl laughed, lifting both stones up again. She threw them down to deliver the killing blow.

Seán's last thoughts were with the cracks he had left in the road. It was the best he could do, and he hoped it was enough. The faint symbol etched over the storehouse was far too faded to be found by anyone who wasn't looking for it, after all. His last thoughts were a prayer to Seletoth, that the marking he had left as cracks in the road—two concentric circles and a V underneath—would be enough.

Chapter 1:
In the Eyes of Seletoth

I write this against the advice of my Church, for I do not believe truths as important as these should be forgotten. It is my wish that once completed, this record is locked away so none may ever look upon its pages. But I do not wish for it to be lost. The truths of our existence, no matter how terrible, should never be lost.

The Truth, by King Móráin I, AC55

***

Across the Arch-Canon's study, a portrait of Seletoth hung on the wall. The oil-painted deity held a staff in one hand, the other raised overhead in a fist. Like most artists' depictions of the Lord, here He took the form of a bearded patriarch with a stance as strong as his gaze. Seletoth stood over the ruined Simian tower that He had named Sin, in a city that He would later name Penance.

If the Godslayer returns, thought Farris, *there'll be nothing left to name.* He folded and unfolded his legs as he sat upon the cushioned recliner. Arch-Canon Cathbad was late.

The Simian glanced back up at the portrait, meeting Lord Seletoth's eyes. Framed in gold, the great portrait would have formed the centrepiece of the back wall if it hadn't been for the extravagant door adjacent to it. With silver inlays and cushioned, oaken wood studded with precious stones, the door seemed to encompass all the arrogant wealth of the Church. Arrogance further emphasised when the door swung open.

Arch-Canon Cathbad strode into the study, the tails of his red-silk robe dangling across the immaculate floor. A golden stole lay upon his shoulders, with the three rings of the Trinity displayed at both ends. The man himself wasn't quite as exquisite as his vestments, with pale lips like a crooked gash across his jaundiced face. Black circles surrounded his eyes, but they held a look as austere as that depicted on the portrait behind him.

Without a saying a word, Cathbad stood before Farris and raised a hand towards him, fingers curled into a half-fist. On one finger was a ring: a thick golden band with a large white stone set in its crown. Like the Arch-Canon's stole, the stone bore an engraving of the three interlocking circles of the Trinity.

Farris stared at the ring, unsure what was expected of him. He grew even more confused when the Arch-Canon slowly moved it towards Farris's face.

"It's, um, very nice," said Farris, moving the pontiff's hand away.

Arch-Canon Cathbad scowled, then took a seat, shaking his head and muttering to himself.

I knew this was a terrible idea, thought Farris. *They should have sent someone else in my place. Anyone else.*

"Farris Silvertongue," said Cathbad, emphasising each syllable. For a man so frail, his voice had a certain strength that surprised the Simian. "I've heard a lot about you."

"And I, you," said Farris, supressing a smile. He had played this game before, back in the courts of Cruachan.

The Arch-Canon shifted his seat. "You were imprisoned here in the Basilica less than a moon ago, but you escaped. Now you've been sent here to speak to me, as if an equal. Why shouldn't I have my men throw you back into a cell?"

"Firstly," began Farris, leaning forward. "You lost half of your Churchguard the night the undead horde came. Secondly, those that survived did so because I convinced them to abandon their posts. If anything, they owe their lives to me."

Farris paused, giving Cathbad the chance to dwell on what he had said. Once a faint shade of red appeared upon those pale cheeks, Farris spoke again.

"And finally, I am here on behalf of Argyll the Silverback, representing the Triad. And their forces are presently stronger than your own."

"The Triad is no longer," said Cathbad, raising a dismissive hand. "Borris is dead, and both Argyll and Cathal Carriga hang onto life by less than a thread."

"Yet they still live," said Farris. "As the Tower still stands."

This led to a lull, which Farris dared not break. He had no experience negotiating, for his strength lay in deceit over diplomacy. This much he had argued back in the House of the Triad, before Nicole and the others flew south. It was General-Commander Plackart who had first suggested Farris talk to the Arch-Canon, but it was Nicole who had convinced him.

Our future is uncertain, she had said, *and in the coming days we'll all have to play roles we are not comfortable with.* Sure, with the Triad in tatters, only the owners of Penance's lands and armies had any kind of power. But that was a frail, transient power pulled by a dozen different hands in a dozen different directions. And the seams were already starting to tear.

"So, you represent the dying Triad," said Cathbad. "And you feel the need to meet me face-to-face despite your contempt for the Church." He folded his arms. "Why?"

Farris chose his words carefully.

"You are well aware we are in a time of crisis, my Lord." He wasn't entirely sure whether or not this was the correct title. "The undead have been defeated, but the one who led them now possesses power never witnessed before. If we are to stand a chance against her, we'll need the combined strength of the Church and the Triad. We wish to use the Skyfleet to its fullest potential. And only the Church can help us with that."

"Of course," said Cathbad. His wry smile told that this was more of a confirmation of Farris's need for help, rather than an affirmative.

Every airship in Penance relied on the use of blue focus-crystals to fly. Since the gas that kept ships afloat was highly flammable, and the power that propelled them came from the heat of fires within, only crystals infused with the icy magic of hydromancy could ensure the former never came into contact with the latter. However, all things magic were under the remit of the Church, and they maintained tight control over all air travel in Alabach.

"Furthermore," said Farris, shifting in his seat, "we request the Churchguard to join the Triad's army."

The Arch-Canon sat forward. "But as you put it, the Churchguard would no longer listen to me. So why are you even asking?"

This time, Farris smiled openly. "This is only a formality, really."

The Arch-Canon stood and strolled to a nearby window. From it, the remains of the Tower of Sin were visible, the crooked, broken structure the central point of the city.

"We must know her motives before we can hope to fight her," said Cathbad. "Has the Triad anything to say to that matter?"

Farris held his tongue. *Not yet. That is a card best played if straits grow dire.*

"A small portion of Triad's army has assembled in Dromán," Farris said, avoiding the question. "We have fortified the ruined city and made camp within the Academy." This much was a lie, for the Triad's soldiers had instead made camp on the outskirts of the Dromán, protecting the ancient structure that lay beneath the ground.

Cathbad frowned. "How strong are your forces? Surely there were many casualties in the wake of the horde."

"Five hundred, but we're presently only capable of flying half of them. With the use of your focus-crystals, we can get all of them to Dromán by nightfall tomorrow."

"And if we were to add the Churchguard, we would bring that number to well over a thousand. A thousand trained soldiers against a single girl."

"Yes," said Farris. "But I fear it won't be enough."

The Arch-Canon had no response to this. In truth, the Triad's army would be augmented with Nicole's technology: Armour made from Simian-steel that no Geomancer could hope to bend. Flames untouchable by any Pyromancer. Firearms with a hundred times the power of a crossbow. Enough power to hold back even an army of mages.

But what about a god?

"And do the fanatics make up much of your number?" asked Cathbad with a sneer.

"Yes," said Farris. "The Sons of Seletoth played a significant role in defending the city. Their valour is as unwavering as their faith."

"There is no faith in heresy. They've disregarded our teachings in favour of their own. They deny the grace of the Trinity and paint their own effigy of the Lord."

Farris smirked. "Their *effigy* has grown in popularity since the night the horde came. One of their central tenets has been that only Seletoth, their One True God, holds the power of the Trinity, and the Lady and the King are mere mortals. King Diarmuid's death has added some strength to this view."

Cathbad paused. He opened his mouth slightly, mouthing words before he spoke them. Eventually, he asked, "Have you ever heard of Divine Penetrance."

"Yes," said Farris. "I once believed in it too. I saw enough proof to convince me the king possessed the gift of immortality, but witnessing his death first-hand changed that. In a world where the dead rise and the gods fall, I don't know what to believe any more."

"Of course," said the Arch-Canon. "These are testing times for us all." He turned his attention back to the window looking out over the city. "Tell me, you've worked by King Diarmuid's side. Have you ever entertained the possibility that he has an heir? That the gift was passed onto another?"

"No," said Farris. "King Diarmuid was fond of brothels back in his youth, and even more so in his later days, but he never fathered a son. Your men made sure of that."

Cathbad clasped his hands together, interlocking thin fingers with thin fingers. "How so?"

Farris stood. "You know well 'how so!' You had the Wraiths of Seletoth track any woman Diarmuid lay with, murdering those who fell victim to his seed. I've read the reports; dozens died because you were too afraid to say to your king, 'No!'"

"If I know more than I let on, Farris, then you know far, far less. These 'Wraiths,' as you call them, are no different to the Sons of Seletoth: nothing more than mortal men who chose to serve the Lord in a manner different to me or you."

Farris inhaled deeply. *He thinks this will get to me.*

"I've spoken to one of the Sons about his Seeing," said Farris. "He told me that he felt Seletoth's infinite power and learned that He does not love us. Does this adhere to the teachings of the Church?"

The smile faded from Cathbad's face. "Of course not. The Lord created the earth and Her fruits and loves each of His creations like a parent does a child. The Sons' iconoclasm is nothing more than a baseless attack on our faith."

"Then why does the Church not share this same love for the people of Alabach?" Farris's voice was rising. "Families starve outside your walls while you walk on carpets paved with enough gold to save them." He gestured to the portrait of Seletoth. "Doesn't your god want you to help His children?"

The Arch-canon closed his eyes. "That is not our purpose. We uphold the moral and intellectual fabric of society, and we have allocated our resources to best let us achieve that."

"I'm sure there are many in Penance who'd prefer food and shelter than whatever the Holy Hell that's supposed to mean."

Cathbad shook his head and sighed. "Farris Silvertongue, you must not assume you can do a better job bearing the burdens of those who rule. How easy it must be, to sit across from me and claim you could feed and shelter the poor—all the poor—if you only you were in my place. Yes, the riches of our establishment would be yours in that case to do as you please. But they too come with the responsibility of ensuring the continuity of the Church. If you truly understood the purpose of our work, you'd quickly see that opening the Basilica doors and spreading its wealth across the land without a plan would be reckless and irresponsible."

"But it would be the right thing to do."

Cathbad smiled. "Perhaps. But often what the people want is not the same as what they need."

Farris bared his teeth. "And what is it they need more than food and shelter? If you saw what I've seen growing up in the Dustworks, you'd do whatever you could to help."

"Ah," said Cathbad. "But if you knew what I know about the will of our Lord, you'd understand why we cannot."

Farris didn't respond. *Oh, but I know quite a bit about that already.*

The Arch-Canon returned to his seat. "Back to the matter at hand, what makes you think the girl will travel south?"

"The scouts of the Triad have been spread across the Clifflands in the wake of the attack on Penance." Farris paused. He could have lied there and then and said they saw her, but he hesitated.

As if sensing this weakness, Cathbad pressed further. "But she has already destroyed Dromán with her horde, correct? She marched her army through the Academy grounds and took a thousand battlemages into her ranks. I don't believe she'd leave any behind, so why go back?"

Farris narrowed his eyes.

He knows, he realised. *He just wants me to admit it.* He considered Cathbad for another moment. The man's expression was unreadable, like grey stone. *Let's see what reaction this gets.*

"We have found the tomb of the Lady Meadhbh," Farris began. He kept his voice low and calm. "It is located near Dromán. Santos and King Diarmuid uncovered it a year ago when they were building the underground railway. Shortly after the horde was defeated here, we parlayed with the Lady Meadhbh Herself."

Farris paused. Although Cathbad's expression remained unchanged, his eyes no longer seemed so dark. Instead, they stared back at Farris with something between wonder and fear.

Oh dear. Perhaps he didn't know after all.

"She told us of the lies of the Church," Farris continued. "That Seletoth did not create the heavens and the earth, or the flora and fauna that inhabit them. All He created was the Human race, and only they are bound to the Tapestry of Fate."

"This is known," whispered Cathbad. "Though not by many. What else did She say?"

"Meadhbh alluded to something She called 'the Truth.' Some secret that the Church was established to protect. Some piece of knowledge that drove many mad once they witnessed it. She believes that Morrigan has caught a glimpse of this Truth and will do whatever it takes to learn more. When she does, destroying Seletoth and ending all life will be the only reasonable response."

Farris's words seemed to weaken Cathbad. The old man placed a trembling hand against his wrinkled neck, grimacing as he rubbed his skin.

"This is what I feared the most," he muttered, looking away. "The power to see what truths the gods show to us is indeed a gift, but often comes with the curse of being unable to unsee them..." He slowly met Farris's eyes. "Tell me, what was it like to be face to face with a god?"

Farris considered the question. The Arch-Canon's demeanour now seemed closer to what one would expect of a man of his age, without the robe and the stole.

"It was... horrible. All my life, I did not believe in power greater than my own. I did not believe something so terrible, yet so beautiful, could exist."

"Your reaction is understandable," said Cathbad. "Not many have experienced what you have, and even fewer are capable of carrying on afterwards. They say that those who tend to Seletoth Himself on the peak of Mount Selyth are not even allowed to look upon His face."

"They say…" repeated Farris. "I get the impression you know more than you let on."

The Arch-Canon smiled weakly. "Farris Silvertongue, that is the most sensible thing you've said since this meeting began. Let's say I give you what you need to fly the Triad's army south, and a few hundred of my own to join them. What next?"

"We'll fortify the entrance to Meadhbh's Tomb and scout the area. We'll protect the Lady will all of our might."

"And are you willing to do whatever it takes?"

"Yes," said Farris, slowly. He recalled Morrigan's form after she killed King Diarmuid. The two great black-feathered wings that unfurled from her body. Argyll sprinting towards her. Morrigan throwing him from the Tower of Sin…. "There is nothing more important right now than stopping Morrigan. Nothing."

The Arch-Canon smiled. "I'll see to it that an adequate number of ships harboured at Sin are fitted with focus-crystals. Though we will only allow for enough to see them to Dromán and back. And those blasphemous long-distance ships will remain grounded here. Furthermore, I'll have a small portion of our remaining Churchguard assembled at dawn."

Farris nodded. *Two half measures. More than enough to count this as a win.*

Cathbad rose to his feet. "All that's left to be asked now Farris, is will you be ready to join them in this fight?"

"No," said Farris, extending a hand. "But I won't let that stop me."

"An admirable attitude. But what if you are called to lead them? Dog-headed determination alone is not enough to be a ruler. If that time comes, will you be able to tell the difference between what is right, and what must be done?"

Farris did not answer, and Cathbad did not wait for a reply. With a sweep of his robes, the Arch-canon turned to leave. But it wasn't the splendour of his garments that kept Farris's attention as he left, nor was it the confidence in his stride. The harsh eyes of Lord Seletoth stared down at the Simian from the portrait across the room, as if having already cast judgment on his actions.

"Not yet," muttered Farris, "We're just getting started."

CHAPTER 2:
THE LAST CARRÍGA

The city of Penance still lingers between joy and despair. Many citizens continue to celebrate their so-called victory over the horde, but they do not know what this victory implies. They do not understand what happened up there in the Tower of Sin. None saw the look on the Silverback's face as he slid a dagger across King Diarmuid's neck, nor did they witness the birth of a new god. No, something potentially more powerful than any god, if the Lady is correct.

I jumped on the opportunity to leave Penance with the Chief Engineer, to fly south tomorrow and begin fortifying the Dromán outpost. Before we left, the Chief Engineer convinced Farris to petition the Churchguard to help us. As much as I hate to admit it, the Simian does have a way with words, but I doubt he'll be able to convince the Arch-Canon. He'd have a better chance of purging all the poison from the Glenn.

Journal of Padraig Tuathil, 13th Day under the Moon of Nes, AC404

***

The body of Cathal Carríga stared unblinking at the ceiling through eyes in sunken sockets. Although a lad not much past twenty years, he had the appearance of a man who had seen four times that. Of a man who had lived a long, and healthy life.

Fionn bowed his head as grieving thoughts ran through his mind. Thoughts that were not his own.

He would have died fighting the horde if he was able, said Sir Bearach. The dead knight's voice echoed against the back of Fionn's head. *He doesn't deserve to slip away from the world like this.*

Fionn grimaced, balling the hand that once belonged to Sir Bearach into a fist. *Nobody does.*

Across the clinic, Aislinn Carríga gazed down at her dying brother. Almost as large as a Simian, her presence alone brought the clinic into a deep, solemn silence.

Only the two healers tending to the dying man made any sound. One pulled back the sheets to take Cathal's hand into her own. Beneath yellowing translucent skin, red and blue veins slithered up the frail arm, where a slender tube entered the man's skin at his wrist. The healer deftly pulled the tube from the arm, revealing the significant length which had lain within. Fionn tried hard not to recoil with fright.

Simian medicine, mused Fionn. *Our white magic and alchemy are far simpler than their chemistry, so why keep him alive with the latter?* Not that it mattered any longer. The Silverback had promised Aislinn that her brother would be allowed pass in peace. But now, the Silverback too lay in another clinic's bed, still unconscious since the night the horde came. It was likely he'd recover, but in what state, the healers could only guess.

Fionn flexed the fingers on his left hand, his own hand. The white mages of the Triad had done a great job of healing the wound Morrigan had left behind, but they could no nothing to make his hand less grotesque, with swollen pink skin now all that lay between his index and far-finger. Those he could move but nothing more.

"How much longer?" said Aislinn, turning the heads of the two healers tending to Cathal Carriga with her tone.

"This was the only thing that kept him alive, milady," said one of the healers, now dismantling the apparatus that held the network of tubes that once gripped Cathal's body. "If you have anything you want to say, now would be the best time."

If Aislinn had heard those words, she gave no indication. The Lady of Rosca Umhir continued to stare down at her brother.

Bearach, thought Fionn. *I think... I think I should tell her. This could very well be our—*

I said no! barked the knight. *Just let her grieve for one brother at a time.*

A low murmur escaped Cathal's greying lips, though nothing close to a spoken word. Fionn had read about this before. Death rattles: the sound of a man's last breath leaving his body. But something flickered in the patient's eyes, and for the first time since Fionn had first seen him, Cathal Carríga blinked.

A lucid glint replaced Cathal's dead stare as he rolled over to face Fionn. In silence, he considered Fionn's over-sized right arm for a moment, then turned to the other side to look up at the giant of a lady that stood over him.

"Ash…" he groaned, something close to a smile creeping across his face. "Am I home?"

"Cathal," whispered Aislinn. All her stoic strength vanished as she stooped down to face her brother. "Is that really you?"

"I… I do not know," croaked Cathal. "I heard you… I thought I already passed. But now you're here. Where… where is Bearach?"

Aislinn shook her head. "I don't know. So much has happened, Cathal. There's so much to tell."

The man flinched and shook his head. "I heard talk… talk of war. Are we… fighting still?"

"No. The war is over, Cathal. We've won."

He nodded. "Good. I can hear them calling to me, Ash. The voices of Tierna Meall."

"Don't go," said Aislinn, taking Cathal's hand in her own. "You were gone for so long. They'll fix you up and—"

"No… it has come. I can hear them. I can hear Mother… Father. I can hear…."

Cathal's voice trailed off into another low moan, then he went still.

"Cathal!" cried Aislinn, placing a hand on her brother's shoulder. "Come back! Please! Don't leave me here alone. There's... there's no one left." She shook him, but Cathal Carriga did not respond.

"Aislinn..." said Fionn. "I'm sorry. I —"

"I fled home when we were attacked," she whispered. "I left Mother and Father and everyone else there behind and came here. Just so I would no longer be alone."

"And you're not alone."

"I appreciate your kindness, Fionn, but apart from you, I'm alone in a city of strangers. And I'm all that's left of Rosca Umhir. I'm all that's left to remember that great city."

"No," said Fionn. "That's not true. There's —"

Please, came Bearach's voice at the back of Fionn's mind. His anger had left, leaving only a weak plea. *Don't.*

Fionn obeyed the words of the dead knight, leaving Aislinn to deal with her loss on her own. If only Bearach would agree to have Aislinn speak to him through Fionn. Then at least he'd feel like all he had gone through had served some good. Some *purpose.* He looked down at his severed hand again. No, Fionn was just as powerless here as he was out on the battlefield at the Goldgate. Sure, he had helped turn the tide of that battle with his fire, but once Morrigan turned up, his magic was useless. To her, he was like a blade of grass trampled under the foot of a mammoth.

Without warning, the door to the clinic swung open with a slam. A figure as wide as its frame entered, taller than all within the room. With coarse, brown hair covering every inch of his body, the Simian strode towards Fionn without paying much mind to anyone else.

"Firemaster Fionn," he said, his deep voice booming through the room. "The council are meeting now, and your attendance is required."

"Ah, Farris," said Fionn. "How did your meeting with the Arch-Canon go?"

"Not as expected," said the Simian. "He's seeing that an adequate portion of the skyfleet is fitted with focus-crystals for the flight south, and he's giving us a portion of the Churchguard to bolster our numbers."

"Oh," said Fionn. *He's being sarcastic.* Even after living in Penance for more than a year, Fionn never really understood Simian humour.

"And why are the council meeting at such short notice?"

"To make preparations for the flight south," said Farris slowly, as if Fionn would have trouble understanding. "The resources of the city must now be re-allocated to sustain the Churchguard and the Triad's supply-line."

Fionn's eyes widened. He glanced over to Aislinn, who shrugged.

"Anyway," said Farris. "Your attendance is required. That's all."

As abruptly as he came, Farris left.

"Was he serious?" asked Fionn. "The Church handed their forces over to us? Old Cathbad is thinking about something other than himself for once?"

"I don't know," said Aislinn. "But I'm sure we'll see soon enough."

CHAPTER 3:
WHAT IS RIGHT

For a long time, my people were lost, wandering through the hills of Arinor without a home, or a purpose. Then the Grey Plague came, destroying any hope they had of finding somewhere to settle.

Until a young woman named Meadhbh said that Lord Seletoth had spoken to her of a land to the west. A land the Grey Plague could not touch. None believed her, until she bore a son without ever laying with a man. The father, she said, was Seletoth Himself.

And the son, of course, was me.

The Truth, by King Móráin I, AC55

***

The first meeting of the Triad since the Battle of Penance was far busier than those Farris was used to. Dozens of Simians and a handful of Humans filled the room, many standing, some leaning against the white marbled walls. Every seat was occupied, bar the three at the top of the room. Those were reserved for the Triad itself.

The nervous chatter of the crowd continued past the scheduled start time, with no leader, no real leader, to initiate the discussion.

But we have so much to discuss, thought Farris, eyeing the attendees. Like the meeting held before when the refugees of the Seachtú came to Penance, many businesses and landowners of the city stood in wait today. Without the Silverback's presence, it was General-Commander Plackart who spoke first.

"Let us begin," he growled, looking to the others as if they were his subjects. He added no more volume than usual to his voice, but still, this silenced the room. The old Simian hesitated before speaking, his scarred lips pursed in concentration.

"A victory was won in this city not seven days ago," he began. He folded his arms, heavy vambraces upon both clinking together. "But our work is not yet complete. In fact, the city's problems are now threefold. First, the walls of the Stoneworks must be repaired in case this enemy should return. Second, our remaining food provisions are waning, and redistribution of our resources must be carefully considered if we are to survive the winter. Finally, law and order has broken down across the residential districts, with looters and thieves thriving in the chaos the horde left behind."

"One of my stores was raided last night!" said one Simian merchant. Farris recognised him as Edwin the Grey. "Bandits stole away half a years' worth of stock."

Farris cut in before Plackart could respond. "Can you please elaborate for the council, what specifically you mean by 'stock?'"

"G-grain and dried foods," stammered Edwin. "Income that was fairly earned and—"

"It seems, Commander Plackart," interrupted Farris, "that of our city's three problems, the second is being resolved by the third."

"Nonsense!" cried another finely dressed Simian. "These are anarchists that have no respect for authority! They must be put down brutally before the city descends into ruin."

"These are just desperate people who need to eat," said Farris. "Surely—"

Plackart raised a hand. As another merchant spoke up, Plackart leaned in towards Farris. "Not now, lad," he whispered. "We need to find a solution that keeps us all happy, and that won't happen if you keep goading them."

"If I may," said Ruairí of the Sons of Seletoth. "Based on the current accounts of the Triad, our granaries have just half the capacity needed to see us through the winter. We will rely on the commerce of private merchants to make up the rest of that shortfall."

Farris narrowed his eyes. Ruairí seemed to have his finger on the pulses of many different arms of the Triad. Wasn't he just a priest or a leader of the Sons of Seletoth? He was close to Argyll, sure, but how did that land him the responsibilities of treasurer of the Triad?

"So that settles it," said Edwin. "If you want us to fortify the Triad's winter stores, you must send soldiers through the city streets clean up those who don't respect the law."

"The Triad's soldiers will not be available for this task," said Plackart. He adopted a blank stare and a level voice as he said this, not engaging with the other Simians directly.

This seemed to puzzle Edwin, but landowner Wheaton the Wise seemed to understand.

"Ah yes," he said. "The repairs needed for the wall. Of course, we must prioritise the safety of—"

"The Triad's army will not be utilised to rebuild," said Plackart. This caused a ripple to go through the room.

"Then what purpose will they serve?" said one voice for the crowd.

"What are our taxes going towards, if not to protect the city?"

"Skies above! Not even an answer!"

Plackart looked to Farris as the stirring in the crowd turned to shouting.

"If the Churchguard are joining us on the march south," whispered Plackart. "Then they'll need the Triad's supplies too." He glanced to Ruairi. "We'll have to empty those granaries before we leave."

Farris looked to the rest of the council. Although made up of stewards and lawmen, diplomats and treasurers, they dealt with the minutia of the running of Penance. They themselves made no decisions, no difficult decisions. That responsibility fell to those who would have occupied the three empty seats of the Triad that loomed overhead.

But in their absence, who has the right to make any decision?

Only the few who had spoken with the Lady Meadhbh truly knew the stakes they were dealing with. Of those, Padraig and Nicole were already in Dromán. Before she left, Nicole had suggested Farris negotiate with Cathbad, something he thought absurd. Then against all odds Cathbad agreed to Farris' terms. Farris never would have thought it possible, but somehow Nicole did.

Maybe she'd know what to do if she was here.

For all their talk of law and order, now the hall was in chaos. Merchants and landowners squared off against one another, while others hurled abuse at those on the council's tables. One steward quickly gathered his notes together as if hoping that would prompt the others to end the meeting.

Aislinn and Fionn sat to the opposite side of Farris. Apart from him, they were only others who here who had met Meadhbh.

"What do you suggest we do," said Farris to them. "Use what we have to repair the city and feed the people, or send everything south?"

"Maybe we can split our forces," said Aislinn. "Send some to Dromán, have the rest stay here, and keep everyone happy."

Fionn frowned. "That certainly would be the most optimal approach, but if there's a chance our full forces are not enough to fight Morrígan, what hope do we have with half?"

Farris swore, glancing over to the Silverback's empty chair, then over to Ruairí. "What would Argyll have chosen?"

Ruairí smiled, idly running a hand through his long, wavy hair. "Why, I'm sure you know him more than I do. And surely you knew the answer to that before you asked."

Farris swore under his breath. The Silverback would have done whatever was necessary, caring not for the qualms of others. But Farris still considered the businessmen of Penance. Sure, they were motivated entirely by greed, but they were right about one thing: taking all the food from Penance would be sure to leave its people to stave.

Either we starve our civilians or starve our soldiers....

No, he couldn't ask a thousand men to march without food. The cause that brought them south was more important than anything else.

The difference between what's right, and what must be done, echoed the words of Arch-Canon Cathbad. Farris shook his head.

No. I will not let anyone starve. There must be another way. There must be.

"For those of us flying to Dromán," said Fionn. "Could we rely on the land there for food? Hunting and foraging at the like?"

"That would be a risk in itself," said Plackart. "We have no idea what state the Godslayer left the Hazelwood in. And besides, we've two hundred horses and elk to feed too. Grazing will only get them so far."

Fionn had a response to this, but Farris's attention waned, and he did not hear it. For a growing fear began burning in his chest.

The people will have to starve. We'll have to leave them in the cold to freeze and to starve.

He closed his eyes.

There must be another solution. Why go through all this effort to save the people of Penance one day to just leave them to die the next?

"No army can march without a supply-line," said Plackart. He didn't add to that or provide any solution, much to Fionn's visible frustration.

"The undead horde did," said Aislinn, smiling weakly. "Morrígan didn't have to worry about logistics like this."

Farris widened his eyes as an idea formed.

"That's it," he said, standing up. All eyes turned to him. "The army of the Triad will march south, and Penance's granaries will remain untouched, as they are."

"Are you mad?" said Placket. "Did you not hear what I said?"

"I did not," said Farris, "I was listening to Aislinn." He cleared his throat, letting the silence of the room hang for a moment, just to ensure everyone was listening. "Throughout the history of Alabach, armies have pillaged settlements they set upon for the purpose of replenishing their supplies. Food stores, weapons caches, gold... but the undead horde were different. As they marched across the land and razed cities, all they sought were corpses. Corpses to add to their numbers. They had no need for food or fresh water.

"Taking this into account, we can therefore assume that, although the settlements of the Seachtú lie in ruin, they should still have ample supplies to accommodate our needs."

He turned to Plackart. "Heading towards Dromán, the first major settlement is Point Grey. We can send scouts in there to assess the situation and bring our empty supply caravans in if it's both safe and beneficial to do so."

Plackart nodded. That was all Farris needed.

"But what about these looters?" said Wheaton. "Can't anything be done to stop them?"

"If we see that Penance's remaining supplies are fairly distributed," said Ruairí, "the need to commit crime will be deterred. At least temporarily. I can stay and see that it's done."

None had any immediate objection to this, so Farris spoke before any could think of one. "Then it's settled. We'll prepare the army to fly to Dromán tomorrow and send a contingent of scouts ahead to Point Grey to see what the horde left behind."

Those on the council nodded, while the businessmen of Penance looked up at the Simian in awe. Farris smiled.

Cathbad was wrong. Why figure out the difference between what's right and what must be done, when a little ingenuity can accomplish both?

Chapter 4:
What Must Be Done

We spent the day travelling from Penance to Dromán aboard a small airship named Sovereign. An ironic name, given the age-old desire for Simians to rule themselves rather than to acknowledge our divine, supreme ruler. Alas, that ruler is no more, and the Lady Meadhbh is the closest thing we have for a leader, a true leader, in this war against the Godslayer.

We arrived at the Dromán camp just as dusk was setting in. Those who had come before had already set up a decent fortification around the railway outpost. Chief Engineer Nicole saw to that task well, with deep trenches and wooden palisades surrounding the entrance into the underground tomb.

Now, we're awaiting the rest of ships from Penance. Our soldiers need rest, but there is so much work ahead of us.

Journal of Padraig Tuathil, 13th Day under the Moon of Nes, AC404

In the hours before dawn broke the following morning, four ships sailed softly through the Rustlake in the waxing light. Farris rode in one, accompanied by Plackart and five other Triad scouts. Each wore a gold and blue tabard across chainmail armour, marking them soldiers of the Triad. The tabard was one layer too much for Farris, however. He was already beginning to sweat under his armour. He and the other Simians sat in silence on the deck as their vessel approach Aldrich Canal. Towards the back of the ship, seven elk mounts waited impatiently, grunting and snorting with their faces concealed in nosebags.

The other ships contained no passengers, only a small crew to make the round trip to Point Grey. Those ships were crammed with carts and wagons, bound together as to not rattle over whatever conditions Móráin Sea had in store. The captain of *Cornucopia*, a sturdy cargo ship, had declared the day to come would be a cold but calm one.

Despite this, Farris was not at ease. So conflicted the Council of the Triad had been in relation to the allocation of Penance's final stores, they latched on quite quickly to Farris's plan. Too quickly for Farris's liking, as this meant their situation would be all the more worse off should they fail. And to ensure the day-long round trip to Point Grey would not represent a long delay to the full army's departure from Penance, they had taken a crystallographer with them, who'd relay the message back to Penance once the supplies were secured. The mage, a middle-aged man in a green robe, paced impatiently back and forth across the deck.

The ships emerged from Aldrich Canal out into Heretic's Bay. From there, they turned south towards Moray Head, but Farris kept his gaze locked on the eastern horizon. The sun was low above it now, blocked by thick, grey clouds. He imagined what kind of lands there were out there, possibly battling a storm beneath that same sky. Although Humans came from the lands beyond the sea some four hundred years ago, none had ever dared go back. Partially out of fear of the Grey Plague—the mysterious force that drove them here in the first place, but mainly out of devotion to their faith. Alabach was a promised land, apparently. Though why would a god promise a land already occupied? And why take even further steps to keep everyone trapped there? Argyll the Silverback had often said the Simian people should leave Alabach and let the Humans have it if they were so bloody caught up in the idea of staying

"I heard you're the one who escaped the Basilica," said Plackart, clearing his throat and approaching Farris from behind. "How did you manage that?"

Farris smiled. "It didn't take too much convincing. The guards there were just as eager to leave as the prisoners. The approaching horde should take most of the credit."

But Plackart did not laugh. "Sometimes we must give ourselves credit when warranted. Few will do it for you. Many others would have died in your position, along with the other guards and prisoners of the Church."

Farris found himself lost for words. This was a rare occurrence.

"You are resourceful, Farris Silvertongue," Plackart continued. "More so than most others. You saw how the council listened to you. We were caught between a boulder and a cliff's edge this morning, forced to choose between letting the people of Penance starve or letting this Godslayer destroy the rest of the world. But you found an option that lets us address both. That is highly commendable."

Farris swallowed deeply. Plackart was a well-respected leader in the Triad's military, to hear him speak so highly about his skills was... surprising.

More so because the Silverback was never one for praise.

"Thank you," said Farris. "But I fear what happens if we fail."

Plackart smiled. "Then we'll make sure we won't."

***

The voyage took most of the day, which Farris passed with idle chat among to the other scouts. They retold stories of the Battle of Penance, as most had been stationed at the Goldgate when the dead came. One claimed to have seen Fionn, the Firemaster, leap down from the city walls down into the horde itself.

"Covered himself in a ball of fire," he said, gesturing madly as he did. "Jumped right down into the undead and burned them all to a crisp."

"I'll never forget that smell," said another. She spoke in a strained, hoarse voice. "Like burnt meat, mixed in with the stench of sweat and piss and shit."

"Sounds like the time I had to share a cabin with Davin," roared another. He laughed, throwing his arm around the first scout, whose sour face suggested his name.

Some hours after noon, the ships turned westwards, coming into Moray Head. And some time after this, the smouldering ruins of Point Grey's harbour appeared on the horizon. Farris shuddered to think that this was the same view those fleeing the city had witnessed when Morrigan attacked; numerous families crammed into fishing boats sailing away from the slaughter, towards an uncertain life of refuge in Penance.

And how many of them died when the horde came back northwards, larger and stronger than before?

No, he could not dwell on that, or on other losses the living had taken over the course of this war... if war was even the right word to use for it. All that mattered now was securing the supply-line for the Triad's army. And stopping Morrigan after that.

The ships docked at Point Grey's harbour, which was empty now given the exodus of its people some few moons ago.

"You'll stay here," said Plackart to the crystallographer, who seemed quite glad to be docked. "You're as important a part of this mission than anyone else. Do you have all you need to communicate with Penance?"

"Yes," said the crystallographer. "I've two waves ready: One confirming our success, the other our failure. This way I can send one as soon as we know our outcome."

"Excellent," said Plackart. He gestured towards the ship's crewmen, who were preparing the gang plank for embarkment. "No need to wait for the other ships. Scouts, mount up and see what we can find."

***

Farris paced slowly through the streets of Point Grey on his elk mount. He always felt invincible upon this steed—the same one that had seen him through the Battle of Penance—but he had never thought to have given it a name. He kept his gaze locked forward on the empty streets ahead of him. From memory, the market quarter of the city was ahead, which surely would have some remaining stock of cured meats and dried food that would still be fit for use.

He rode beside one of the scouts—a light-furred Simian who seemed to have a much better grasp at controlling her elk than Farris did.

Maybe I could get some formal training when this is all over, thought Farris. *And then I'll finally give this beast a name.*

As they took a left turn into the marketplace of the city, Farris's fears were finally realised.

The terror that had come to Point Grey had left the marketplace in a ruin. Mounds of red bricks that had once been buildings encircled a cobblestone square. Pieces of walls still stood, like grey, scorched spectres of what had once been there.

Farris paced through the square, trying to recreate the market from memory. Just ahead of him, a long, low roof hung over a sheltered section of the square. A discarded wheel of a wagon lay before it, with charred wood and broken spokes. This, Farris reckoned, would have been where the various green-grocers would have sold their wares.

And just behind this wall would be where they'd store them.

Farris braced himself for the inevitable sight of broken crates and barrels, their contents scattered haphazardly across the ground by the invading army... but what he saw disappointed him even more.

The backs of the walls were empty. Where stacks of crates and barrels would have been kept, ready to be sold to the people of Point Grey, there was nothing but a bare, dusty stone floor.

Farris dismounted, then crouched down to examine the ground.

Strange. The horde would have had no need for provisions like this. Farris searched for signs of any crates or barrels being broken or smashed, but he found not even a splinter on the stone.

A slow, familiar panic set in.

I was wrong, he thought, his lower jaw quivering uncontrollably. *There's nothing left here. Nothing for the Triad's men. Nothing for the people of Penance. What can we do now?*

Farris's heartbeat quickened, pounding first in his chest, then its sound resounded through his skull.

I wasted so much time... Morrigan might have killed the Lady by now. Might have taken... taken...

Farris closed his eyes tightly.

No. We can't give up. Not now. Not yet!

"Sir?"

We could hunt for game in the Hazelwood. Feed the soldiers that way. But... no...

"Farris?"

In an instant, the panic stopped, and Farris opened his eyes. The scout stood before him.

"Farris... sir?" she said. "We found something."

"Food? Provisions?"

The Simian shook her head. She pointed southwards.

"Outside the village. There's smoke coming from a barn."

Farris's heartbeat surged. *Survivors! In a place as hopeless as this?*

His face broke out into a smile. To think that some people had manged to survive both the horde and the purged land left in its wake.

Farris's smile vanished, for he realised what this truly meant.

***

The scouts regrouped at the edge of the town. They too had found very little; far less that what one would expect from a town evacuated at short notice. As General-Commander Plackart explained the situation, pointing towards the thin trail of smoke that emanated from a building about half a mile to the south, the mood changed abruptly. In silence they mounted up, and made their way across the old dirt road as dusk began to set in. This took them uphill, where several buildings loomed ahead. Two granaries flanked a large wooden barn, and just as the scout had reported, smoke poured from a stone chimney atop its wide, grey-slated roof.

"What if there's someone there?" whispered a scout behind Farris. He got no response, though Farris looked to Commander-Plackart for a reaction. The old Simian pretended not to hear, despite being well within earshot. Instead, he stared ahead; eyes focused on the first signs of life they'd come across since leaving Penance.

As they got closer, Farris could make out the smaller details of the barn. It seemed that the horde had come through here too, evidenced by flattened grass and fences surrounding the buildings. The granaries appeared to be untouched: two narrow wooden buildings raised a foot off the ground on short, stone columns. Both of their doors were shut tight. The door to the barn, on the other hand, was slightly ajar. Farris's breath caught in his throat when he heard the faint sounds of whispering from within.

Plackart gestured them to dismount, which they did in silence. The seven Simians took their weapons off their mounts—polearms and spears and longswords among them—then walked towards the barn. Farris held his halberd in his hands, his fingers wrapped tight about the shaft. Ahead of him, Plackart wore his large greatsword on his back, its hilt rocking to and fro as he walked ahead of the party.

Without a knock, or even hesitation, Plackart pushed through the door.

The barn's interior consisted mainly of a single room, with a high ceiling and large walls about the perimeter. These walls were barely visible, however, due to the stacks upon stacks of barrels, boxes, and crates piled upon each other. On the far side of the room was a stone hearth, with a meagre fire blazing within. Sitting around this was a small group of Humans, their pale faces turned towards the Simian intruders.

Farris's throat immediately went dry as he drew closer to the group. At the front, was one elderly man with an ill-fitting chainmail coif around his head and shoulders. Next to him stood a burly middle-aged man who gripped a spear in trembling hands. Behind him was a woman of a similar age, who stood before two young children, as if to shield them against the Simians who had barged into their home.

"I am General-Commander Plackart of the Triad," boomed the Simian's voice as he approached. "The army of the Triad has need of the grain and provisions of Point Grey left behind by the horde. If you—"

The middle-aged man spat on the ground. "You think you can come in here and *steal* from us? After all that's happened?"

Plackart paused. "If you were to let me finish, we have ships that can take you to Penance in return, where your needs will be looked after."

The old man stepped forward. "This farm has been in my family for generations. The stars themselves will fall before we hand it over to you rats!"

Farris grimaced. *Please. Just listen to us. Please.*

"You do not have any choice in the matter," said Plackart, gesturing to the piles of crates around them. "These supplies are surely too much for a small family and will spoil before you can put them to use. The army of the Triad however could—"

"You can't take it!" cried the middle-aged man. He moved to stand in front of his family. The spear in his hands was no longer shaking but raised towards Plackart. "Are you really going to kill a family of farmers for some food?"

Please. Let them see reason. Gods, let them see why it's so important for them to listen.

It took Farris more than a moment to realise he was praying. He was *actually* praying.

"We've fought off worse than you," said the woman. "We've protected this farm from crop blight and drought.

Infestations of weevils and mice. Even the undead army came and went, and we stood through it all."

"Exactly," said the old man. "And what's a few armoured rats compared to the mass of the undead?"

Farris closed his eyes. *Please, let them see reason. Just let them give us what we need.*

Commander Plackart took his greatsword into his hands. Its blade was as longer than the armed man was tall, and thicker than the elderly man was wide.

"We will not ask again," said Plackart. "In the name of the Triad, I command you give us control of your supplies. We wish to resolve this peacefully."

But the family stood strong.

Of course. This is their home. This is the fruits of their labour. Why would they listen to us? We are strangers... intruders... no different than the Firstborn four hundred years ago.

He closed his eyes. *There must be another way. Another solution. Perhaps we can take just half, or offer to purchase a volume or—*

A creak of wood overhead disrupted Farris's trail of thought. He opened his eyes but dared not look up. Instead, he saw the middle-aged man glance upwards for a moment, then back at Plackart.

Something's wrong. Farris shifted the grip on his halberd.

Closing his eyes again, he focused on the sound overhead. Somewhere between the beats of his pounding heart, he heard it again. A slight *creak*, like a foot upon a wooden beam.

Then came the faint sound of a sharp intake of breath. Farris bent his knees, ready now for what was to come.

A dark shape fell from the ceiling, plummeting towards Plackart's head. As soon as it came into view, however, Farris leapt, swinging his halberd towards it. With a sharp yell, the dark shape fell aside, the light of the fire revealing it as a young lad clutching a dagger in two hands. He wore a simple white shirt, stained heavily with blood pouring from his waist.

Farris glanced down at his own weapon; the axe-head covered in the blood of the boy.

"No," Farris whimpered.

The woman screamed, clutching the two children into her body. Both Humans ran towards Plackart, the younger plunging the spear towards him.

"No!" roared Farris. "We can—"

But the Commander's greatsword was already in motion. With a deft forward movement, Plackart swung the blade in a large arc, striking both men at once. The two fell, and the woman's screams were joined by those of the children.

"No!!" Farris cried. He dropped to his knees. The stone hearth was stained with blood. The body of the younger lad still twitched in the light of the fire.

"As I said," continued Plackart, as if there was no interruption. "You will be compensated and re-housed in Penance in exchange for these provisions. Do I make myself clear?"

The woman barely managed to nod her head, which was enough for Plackart to give the order to the other scouts to send news to Penance they had succeeded.

But Farris's eyes remained fixed on the body of the young lad as it went still.

Was there anything I could have said? Was there anything I could have done?

But he knew, perhaps he had always known that there was no way for this to end, other than through bloodshed. Part of him had to admit that this was the only way. As Cathbad would have said, it was just something that had to be done.

And when he found himself agreeing with the old Arch-Canon, Farris hated himself even more.

CHAPTER 5:
FROM HIS LIPS

As a child, I always knew I was different. Indeed, those who knew of the mysterious circumstance of my birth would stare and whisper in my presence. But from an early age, I could feel Seletoth's presence, as if He was an ever-present father helping to raise me. Then He began to speak to me, and from Him, I learned that I was capable of manipulating the elements of the land through magic. He showed me that this was a talent also latent in my peers.

As I taught them how to manipulate Nature and Her fruits, many others came from afar to learn too.

By the age of sixteen, I was the closest our dispersed community had to a leader.

And by seventeen, they made me king.

The Truth, by King Móráin I, AC55

***

Fionn sat in the council room of the house of the Triad. He leaned forward, forearms resting on his lap with both hands clasped. He kept the heel of his left foot raised, and his left knee jittered with anxiety.

What's taking them so long, Bearach asked. *Surely, they would have arrived by now?*

The atmosphere of the council hall indicated the others present shared the same concern as the knight. Members of the council surrounded the table, some sitting, others standing, all with eyes fixed upon the single crystallographer sitting at the far end.

The crystallographer tended to a curious apparatus roughly the size of a hand-organ. Embedded in the centre of it was a chunk of white crystal. Filaments of wire encircled the crystal and reached out to connect to the rest of the box at various spots. Through a hole on the side, the crystallographer rested one hand; the other held a Simian-inkpen, ready to relay whatever message came.

Magic in one hand, Simian technology in the other, thought Fionn. He had a rudimentary understanding of how the crystal amplifier worked, though its name was somewhat of a misnomer. At any moment now, a moment for which everyone waited with bated breath, that crystal would begin to resonate with a pattern sent from one of the ships sent out to Point Grey. Using a code known and understood by both crystallographers at either end of the communication, this would be translated into a word, phrase, or even a full report. The pattern of a resonance crystal would typically be too fast for even the most talented mage to read, but the amplifier would take the signal from the crystal and send a slower version to the crystallographer's hand via a prodding rod. With the fingers of this hand, the crystallographer would be able to speed up, slow down, or repeat specific parts of the message, all while transcribing the message with the other hand.

Fionn had always struggled in the translation part, let alone interpreting and communicating a message simultaneously. Playing with fire was a far more interesting use of magic.

Although all in the room eagerly awaited the message from Farris, the knot of anxiety in Fionn's belly had been tied by a different source. In his breast pocket, he held a letter. An unexpected letter from an unexpected source.

What would the zealot want with us? asked Sir Bearach. *And why so much secrecy?*

Fionn shared Bearach's curiosity. He had found the letter in his chamber that morning, signed by Ruairí of the Sons of Seletoth, with instructions to meet him in the Silverback's ward at dusk today. He was instructed to come alone and tell no one of this meeting.

Just go now, lad, said Sir Bearach. *The sun will set within the hour, and what use are you here?*

Fionn looked around. Of course, the crystallographer would relay news of Farris's success or failure, and the councilmen of the Triad were already aware of what actions to take either way. Fionn's eyes then met those of Chief-

Sergeant Bernice, a towering female Simian with auburn-coloured fur contrasting her dark gaze. She'd surely set out to share the message with the rest of the awaiting army, so what use had Fionn here?

He slowly stood, giving the rest of the council an opportunity to react if they wanted him to stay. When none did, he made his way to the door.

"Firemaster," said Bernice as he passed. "Do you not wish to see the outcome of Plackart's trip south?"

"I do," said Fionn, slowly. "But I have other business to attend to in the meantime."

Bernice didn't respond immediately, but Fionn could swear he saw her eyes narrow, ever so slightly.

"Don't go too far," she said. "We'll need to reassess our situation if their mission fails. Though if it were up to me, we'd fly south regardless of the outcome."

"Then the people of Penance can be thankful that it's not."

With this Fionn left, walking down the hall at a pace faster than he would typically be used to.

Glance back, lad, said Bearach. *She might be following us!*

Not likely, said Fionn, stealing a look over his shoulder anyway. Only an empty corridor lay behind. *These military types are often slower to disobey chain of command than their attitudes would imply.*

Let's hope she's like the others, then.

Fionn ascended a marble set of steps, passing a large mural of the Tower of Sin the extended from floor to ceiling. This artist's depiction showed the tower as tall it had been before the Fall, piercing the clouds farther than any other mountain in Alabach.

Was it pettiness that drove Seletoth to tear it down? wondered Sir Bearach. *Or something else?*

Fionn considered the question. Many scholars believed that Seletoth had every right to punish the Simians for their Sin, though others framed it as arrogance. The counterargument was that trying to project Human emotions unto Seletoth was folly, as we could never truly comprehend His will. And besides, He surely had a good reason for doing it.

Based on what Meadhbh had said, however, Fionn perhaps understood the Fall of Sin a little bit more.

She had said the only Humans were bound by Fate and that Simians were free to do as they wish. If the Simians who built Sin did so out of their own free will, perhaps Seletoth's destruction of it was an attempt to bring the Simians back in line with what Fate had predicted. After all, the Fall of Sin itself was seen by many Simians as a rallying point against Human rule. If not for the Fall of Sin, Penance, and indeed Alabach, would look very different.

On the next floor, Fionn walked through another corridor before arriving at a row of doors leading to several wards. He passed Cathal's old ward and stood before the door to another.

"Hello?" said Fionn, stepping inside. "Ruairí?

This ward was similar to Cathal's, with its square shape and drab interior. Its bed, however, was much larger, and in it lay Argyll the Silverback. A robust Simian, he still held the room to attention with his presence, as he always had, even when unconscious. The many tubes and instruments that tended to Cathal's state were absent here. In fact, Argyll seemed like he was only sleeping, his complexion and composition no different to how they were when he was awake.

Beside him sat Ruairí. The Son of Seletoth wore a brown waistcoat over a grey shirt. His usual necklace hung round his neck, emblazoned with the symbol of the Sons—a trio of crooked, interlocking circles. It hung heavy on a silver chain, which glimmered in the weakening light of the coming evening.

"You're early," said Ruairí, whispering, as though not to wake Argyll.

"I wasn't needed in the council hall," said Fionn. "They're just waiting to hear back from Point Grey, so they can wait without me. Besides, it seemed like you required my attention more than they did."

Ruairí sighed. "I don't require anything from you, Fionn. I just wanted to have... a chat."

Fionn frowned. "Is that so?"

So why was it important we came alone? asked Sir Bearach. *Why the secrecy?*

"And what would you like to discuss?" asked Fionn. "Anything in particular?"

Ruairí stood and strode across the room. A fur overcoat lay strewn over a chair beside the window. Next to this, was a leather pack. Ruairí squatted down next to it, and produced two cups and a bottle of wine, its colour a deep ruby.

"Bhuaím Blackberry Red," said Ruairí, cradling the bottle in both hands as he turned to face Fionn. "This was gifted to me from a friend in Terrian, right before the horde came. Could very well be the last bottle left in this frightening new world."

Ruairí unsealed the bottle and poured himself a glass. Fionn tilted his head as he watched. Something was certainly off. Ruairí usually exhibited incredible confidence as he spoke, even at the council meeting yesterday. Confidence edging on arrogance, if Fionn was to be perfectly honest. But now, Ruairí's voice seemed weaker, not just from whispering, but as if it was frail. As if he was frightened.

When his cup was full, he held out an empty one to Fionn. "What would you say to a toast? To Farris's success in Point Grey, and to yours whenever you reach Dromán."

Fionn instinctively reached out for the glass, but then paused. He turned an eye towards the unconscious Silverback, still motionless in his bed, bar the slow rise and fall of his massive chest.

What do you want? thought Fionn. This was the type of thing Farris or Argyll would have done with ease, navigating strange conversations, unravelling others' intentions while concealing their own. Fionn, had much less experience in that realm of politics, despite his time on the council.

"Sure," said Fionn. "Regardless of Farris's outcome, tomorrow will be a long day for me. So, just one for luck."

Ruairí smiled weakly and poured a glass for Fionn. He handed it to him, holding it between a delicate thumb and forefinger, as if afraid of cracking it.

Both Fionn and Ruairí raised their glasses and took a deep drink. The taste came first as a sharp burst of fruits and berries that quickly turned dry in Fionn's mouth. As he swallowed, it a left bitter impression, like scrumpy set to ferment for too long. He went to raise the cup for a second taste but met Ruairí's eyes instead.

"And to Argyll's health," Fionn said, giving another awkward salute towards the bed. "Is there any update on his condition?"

"No," said Ruairí. "The healers reckon he'll awaken by the end of this moon, but they still dare not speculate on what condition he'll be in."

This brought a lull to the conversation, as the two drank in silence.

"Was there anything in particular you wanted to ask me?" ventured Fionn. He rotated the cup in his hand, his grasp on the stem awkward with his severed third and fourth finger.

"Nothing more than looking for some insight as to what's going on." Ruairí sipped from his drink.

Fionn snorted. "You think I'd have a better idea than you? You're the Silverback's right hand after all, aiding him in all his duties with the Triad." Fionn leaned back, ready to take a triumphant quaff. "And if I understand it, in matters far more important than that too."

Ruairí's eyes narrowed. "Tell me how much you know, then."

"Garth told me most of it, on the way back from Roseán. The rumours that the Silverback has been leading a covert rebellion against the Crown and the Church are true. The Sons of Seletoth have been aiding him due to the involvement in the latter. Garth was mapping the Glenn for the Silverback, but he didn't elaborate on why. He also alluded to powerful weapons that Nicole had been working on, which I assume were the automatons and firearms we used to fight back the horde. Now, based on these, conjecture would lead me to conclude that these covert operations of the Silverback's were close enough to boiling into outright rebellion. Perhaps the massacre at the Basilica was part of it. Perhaps the death of Borris Blackhands was part of it. But as I said, that much is conjecture. And I'd wager that much is but a small portion of what you know."

Ruairí had kept a straight face during this, but after a moment, he smiled. "Such a clever lad. You and Farris would have gotten along very well had circumstances been different."

"What do you mean?" said Fionn. He had only really spoken to Farris a handful of times, and most of those times he had been using an alias. "Is he involved with the Movement too?"

Ruairí reached for the bottle to top up his cup. Then offered to do the same to Fionn's.

"As the Silverback tells it, there would be no Movement at all without Farris."

Fionn accepted the drink and turned his eyes up to Ruairí as he realised what he meant.

"Farris? Really? But he always seemed so… quiet."

"The Silverback describes him as a mastermind. Never to his face, mind you. Farris earned the name 'Silvertongue' some four years ago. Before Argyll got involved in politics, he was the leader of the Guild of Thieves here in Penance. They started off as a petty gang, slowly growing into an organised crime syndicate with all the right people in all the right pockets. They had some connections over in Cruachan, so Farris was sent to set up another operation there. Another 'Guild Chapter,' he'd call it."

"Sounds like a big task," said Fionn.

"It was. Farris set up a network of thieves and smugglers throughout the city but ran into a host of problems. The City Watch of Cruachan was already corrupt, see, but to another group—Smugglers who named themselves the Black Sail.

Farris's work was encroaching on theirs, and a war of sorts broke out. Hideouts were ransacked and burned, footpads were killed on the streets, and many of those once loyal to Farris turned their cloaks to the Black Sail, who had a much firmer grasp on the City Watch than the Guild had."

"Sounds like it was a terrible idea," said Fionn, feeling more confident with every mouthful of wine. "To have such a strong operation in Penance, why spread your resources to another city so far away, competing against others with far more experience and connections than your own?"

Ruairí laughed. "That's exactly what any intelligent Human would see, but not an intelligent Simian. Against all odds, Farris proved that the Silverback was right to trust him."

He leaned forward and dropped his voice to a giddy whisper. "Farris rounded up those that had betrayed him, and those who were planning to, and removed their heads." Fionn gasped, and after a long, dramatic pause, Ruairí continued.

"Then he went and presented them to King Diarmuid, claiming that *he alone* had routed out the Guild of Thieves. All the while, Captain Padraig Tuathil was standing beside the king, well aware that these were the Black Sail's newest converts but couldn't say a word because they had been paying him off! Farris didn't even ask for any compensation. His plan was to continue the Guild's operations in Cruachan, with everyone believing they had been completely disbanded. See, he told the King that these were the heads of the Guild's highest captains and lieutenants. Again, Tuathil knew this wasn't true, but couldn't say and word. All he could do was watch on as King Diarmuid, seeing that Farris had refused payment, went on to offer Farris *a job*."

Fionn guffawed. "He did *what?*"

"King Diarmuid had been chasing down the Black Sail for years, with Tuathil leading the charge. But since Tuathil was already bought and sold by the Sail, the king thought him incompetent. Then along comes Farris, apparently eliminating a separate criminal organisation without any hassle, and without any promise of pay. It made perfect sense, then, to hire Farris to track down the Black Sail, and put Tuathil on other duties throughout the city."

Fionn's eyes widened. "So, with that one stunt," he said, slowly, "Farris had routed out traitors of the Guild, allowed the Guild to appear disbanded in the eyes of King Diarmuid, got himself a job with the Crown to take down a rival gang, all while also making Tuathil a less valuable inside man by taking him away from their case." Fionn had been counting off each of these on his severed hand but had run out of fingers doing so.

"Tuathil was outsmarted every step of the way, and never stood a chance," said Ruairí. "Though, fate would have it that he would wind up in here in Penance by Farris's side once more."

"True, but She said that none of this was fated to happen," said Fionn, without thinking.

Ruairí stirred. "Who said this?" he snapped.

Careful, lad, said Sir Bearach. *He wasn't there, remember? Does he even know the Lady lives under Dromán?*

Fionn frowned. *His religion would dictate She doesn't live at all.*

He quickly considered his options. None who had seen the Lady had been sworn to secrecy or anything like that. Sure, the Triad's army were planning to fly out to defend Her in the morning. So Fionn reckoned surely more than just those that spoke to Her knew She existed.

"The Lady Meadhbh," said Fionn, simply. "We met Her after the Battle of Penance, in Her tomb near Dromán. That's why we're flying south. To protect the Her."

"And this is all true?" said Ruairí.

Fionn paused. "Of course. Why would—" He smiled and placed his glass down onto the ground, then folded his arms. "I see. This is why you wanted to speak to me alone. You don't believe in the Lady."

"Not as the Church teaches," said Ruairí. He turned his gaze to the floor. "Perhaps what you saw was a spirit, or an illusion."

Fionn laughed. "You're clearly an intelligent man in the know of what's going on in this city, but your faith is blinding you on this one topic. Why does even it matter what we call Her? A spirit, or a demon, or a god, or—"

"She is no god!"

Ruairí's voice rose so quickly and so sharply, it caused Fionn to jump with fright.

"How do you know?" said Fionn, his heart still racing. "I was *there*, Ruairí. She said things that nobody had any business knowing. I had never seen anything like it before."

"I have," said Ruairí, "in my Seeing of Seletoth. The teachings of the Church are hundreds of years old and comprise many conflicting scriptures and sources. Perhaps Seletoth spoke directly to King Móráin the First, but whatever He said has since been passed on and filtered through generations of men, twisted and distorted to suit their own needs. And those of the institution of the Church. The tenets of the Sons of Seletoth, on the other hand, come directly from His lips to our ears."

"Perhaps," said Fionn. "I witnessed someone having one of these Seeings, you know. My old mentor, Firemaster Conleth, right before he tried to kill me."

"I remember," said Ruairí. "You came to the Council to tell us of his death."

Fionn grimaced as the memory came back. The shrillness of Conleth's raving. The heat of the flames that tried to consume Fionn. The smell of Conleth's flesh as it burned.

"Wait..." said Fionn. "In his ranting, Conleth spoke of chaos, and disorder...."

"This much is consistent with those who have Seen," said Ruairí. "It sounds like he saw too much, though, and it broke his mind."

"No..." said Fionn. "It wasn't entirely nonsensical, looking back now. He said Penance was a cancer... a cancer on the Tapestry of Fate. I didn't think much of it at the time, but the Lady said that everyone is bound to Fate. Everyone but Simians, who can break free. She said that Morrigan was fated to end all life, but because the Simians here fought back, they disrupted the Tapestry of Fate. And now there's hope that we can win. That must be what Conleth saw! He saw that Penance, a city full of Simians, was capable of disrupting the Tapestry of Fate before they even did so!"

Ruairí didn't respond. He moved his mouth slowly, as if repeating what Fionn had said to himself. "And after that, did he say anything else?"

"Not that I can remember. His last words were 'you have no idea what you are,' whatever that means."

"No!" cried Ruairí, standing so quickly it caused his glass of wine to smash on the floor. "You must be mistaken. The Lord surely did not show him such blasphemy."

Fionn narrowed his eyes. He had never seen Ruairí act like this. In fact, he had never seen Ruairí be so... emotional. Before he could respond, however, the clinic door swung open. Lieutenant Bernice stood in its frame.

Maybe she did follow us after all, said Bearach.

"Firemaster Fionn," said the Simian. "We have received word from Plackart. The mission to Point Grey was a success. Ships full of provisions are on the way back here. We fly south at dawn."

CHAPTER 6:
THE MAJESTIC

For the years that followed, I led my people westwards, across lands unknown. We came across others, Humans just like us, and we took them into our community. We taught them about Seletoth and found that some could even learn magic too. Our numbers grew as we crossed Arinor.

In part, we were fleeing the Grey Plague. Whenever we'd attempt to settle, it was there, in the air, in the soil, killing any chance we had of surviving.

But another force was pulling us westwards. I could feel Seletoth, stronger and stronger with each league we travelled. The home He promised us was so far away, but His love guided me towards it.

And every man, woman, and child that lived followed.

The Truth, by King Móráin I, AC55

***

The army of Penance gathered in the Tower of Sin the following day. A contingent of cavalry waited outside; riders upon elk mounts waiting patiently to board *Diplomacy* and

Lionel's Grace, the largest of the two airships fitted for the journey. Most of the soldiers wore heavy armour, with long lances and halberds made from Simian-Steel. Others were lightly armoured, with chainmail over gambesons bearing the sigil of the Triad, a blue triangle on a field striped with green and white.

Inside Sin, the Sons of Seletoth were boarding *Tradewind*, *Golden Heart*, and *The Kingsmill*. Many of them wore Simian firearms slung over their shoulders—seemingly harmless tubes of steel and wood to those who had never witnessed their power. They were joined by the Churchguard, their scarlet robes and immaculate armour a stark contrast to the Sons. True to his word, Arch-Canon Cathbad had ensured their numbers rivalled those of the Triad's Army, who were boarding the *The Javelin*, *Red Sentinel*, *Horizon*, *Cumulous* and *The Majestic*. Many of these were trade vessels, emissary ships, and scouting crafts that once were fitted with their own specific instruments and equipment, now stripped bare to serve the same purpose: to bring this newly assembled army south. To aid them, another ship, *Ambassador*, was being loaded with crates and barrels of provisions to feed this army, along with timber and tools for building fortifications around the Dromán outpost. Only three ships remained docked and untouched, the gargantuan ships *Sinfall*, *The Dreadnought* and *Thunder*, just as Cathbad had demanded.

The gathering was truly a wonderous sight: Humans marching with Simians, great knights clad in the finest of armour alongside men armed only with their faith.

Fionn reckoned it would have been worthy of a bard's song if not for the terrible hangover pounding through his skull.

How much did I even drink last night? he thought, struggling to keep balance as he walked up the gangway of *The Majestic*.

He could have sworn it was no more than three glasses, but it felt like he had drunken as many flagons instead.

It was three for sure, said Sir Bearach. *I was keeping count. Ruairí drank the same, so he must be in a similar shape too.*

Fionn rubbed his eyes. He hadn't slept much the previous night; most of it was spent contorted over a chamber pot, purging the contents of both his stomach and bowels.

How old was that wine bottle?

Why does it matter? said Sir Bearach. *I thought it was supposed to get better as it aged!*

Fortunately, Fionn had woken up just in time for the ships to depart, but he felt as if he was ready to sleep for a full night. Whatever alcohol that had been present in his body was gone now, leaving only a gasping, systemic dehydration in its wake.

He walked alongside other foot-soldiers of the Triad into the open maw of the ship. Many were Simians; citizens of Penance who had taken up arms for the Triad before, but others were Humans who had fled to Penance when the horde came, serving for the city's army in exchange for the refuge it had granted them.

Among those Fionn boarded with, many threw glances at his red cloak, and the adornments that marked him as Firemaster. As he passed a young soldier, Fionn heard his named whispered, as if in reverence.

I'm not worthy of this, he thought, flexing the fingers on his severed hand. *When I came face to face with the Godslayer, she maimed me.*

"Fionn!" cried another voice. "Firemaster Fionn!"

Fionn turned around to find the source of the familiar voice. A man carrying a simple spear over one shoulder came running through the crowd.

"Ah, Cormac of Roseán," said Fionn, nodding as the man approached. "It is good to see you well."

Fionn wished he could say the same for himself; somehow speaking out loud had caused the beating in his skull to return. He quickly took a drink from his waterskin. The water on his parched lips tasted like it had been sweetened. He had to stop himself abruptly to ensure he didn't consume all he had brought with him.

"And you," said Cormac, patting Fionn on the shoulder as if they were old friends.

I suppose we have been through a lot together, said Fionn. He hadn't made any real friends since he had arrived in Penance. Just allies who he had narrowly avoided death with multiple times.

The two boarded together. The landing dock of *The Majestic* was far less majestic than that of *The Glory of Penance*: the ship Fionn and Bearach had taken from Cruachan, seemingly an eternity ago now.

This ship's interior was far narrower, with two stretching corridors towards the ship's bow and stern. Unlike *The Glory*, the ceiling was made of thick steel, held up with heavy, wooden beams. Fionn reckoned this was to separate the large ballonets filled with explosive gas overhead from the rest of the ship. This was confirmed by the many signs Fionn walked past warning the passengers aboard to avoid open flames and sparks on their journey.

Perhaps that is why they were staring at me, thought Fionn.

Following the crowd, Fionn came into a large room at the back of the ship. This was extravagantly designed, with a red velvet carpet and thick, gold embroidered curtains open to reveal large windows with filigree adornments around their frame.

The room was void of furniture, however. This was seemingly once a luxury suite to allow the nobility of Penance to travel with absolute comfort. But all comforts had been removed to allow some two hundred soldiers of the Triad to sit on the floor with their arms and armour for the duration of the journey.

"It is good to see you still fighting," said Fionn, as he took a seat on the floor beside Cormac. "Despite the horrors we witnessed at the Goldgate."

"It is in spite of them that I'm here," said Cormac. "But it's a shame the same can't be said for many others who were by my side that night."

"We lost too many good people to the horde," said Fionn. "Hopefully we can end it all in Dromán."

A group of men carrying spears walked past, one laughing a loud, shrill laugh at an unheard joke.

"It isn't just those that died who aren't with us," said Cormac, more quietly now. He leaned in towards Fionn. "Many were... recruited. By the Sons of Seletoth."

"The Sons?" said Fionn, looking around. "But aren't they here too?"

"Not all of them. With the king dead, and the Móráin line at an end, there's little reason to continue worshiping the Trinity. That fellow who was always with the Silverback came to talk to our battalion after the fighting was done. Most of them disavowed the Church and its teachings, in favour of those of the Sons."

Ruairí, said Sir Bearach.

"But not you?" said Fionn.

"I wasn't there, sure. I was down in the tunnels with you and the others, meeting the Lady Meadhbh Herself. When I came back, those in the battalion told me of their newfound faith. But of course, I couldn't renounce the existence of the Trinity."

"Because they don't believe in the Lady," said Fionn, nodding.

That's why he wanted to meet you, lad, said Sir Bearach. *It wasn't to learn about the Lady, but to recruit you.*

Of course, thought Fionn. *And he saw the folly in his attempt once I told him that the She really does exist.*

"Many of those he spoke to," continued Cormac, "left the Triad's army, opting to stay in Penance while the rest of us marched out."

"So, they're planning something?" said Fionn. "What could be more important that stopping the Godslayer?"

Cormac's gaze fell to the ground, he shook his head slightly.

"I'm sorry," said Fionn. "She's still your daughter after all."

"My daughter is dead," said Cormac. He folded his arms. "And we're going to kill the monster that has taken her place."

As the others settled into place, the room's well-kept floor was barely visible beneath all the bodies that sat on it. With a low whirr, the engines of the ship started, and among a chorus of excited voices, it slowly began to rise from the ground.

Others whooped and cheered as the ship took flight, but Fionn's stomach immediately began to stir again.

I thought we got the last of it out, said Sir Bearach.

Nausea took hold of Fionn with an overwhelming force that pushed out every other thought and feeling from his mind. He stumbled to his feet, blinking his eyes with watering lids.

"Fionn, are you okay?" said Cormac. "You've gone terribly pale."

Fionn dared not respond. He rushed out into the hall, hoping to find some suitable place to throw up. After a few steps up the corridor towards the direction of the bridge, Fionn's stomach gave way, hurling its meagre contents to the ground with a scattered splash. Between gasping breaths he threw up again, this time expelling nothing. The dry wretch came out of him with so little voluntary input, it was as if Fionn no longer had control of his body. With another heave, the muscles on his neck tensed up, and an unbearable pressure pushed against the back of his eyeballs, bringing flashing stars into his vision.

Afterwards, Fionn slumped onto the floor, gasping for air. His stomach felt somewhat settled now, but the nausea was still there.

Are you sure it was just three glasses, Bearach?

Before the dead knight could answer, another voice called out.

"Fionn, are you alright?"

He turned to see Aislinn Carríga approaching from behind. She was dressed in dark plate armour, as thick as concrete.

"Just air-sick," said Fionn. "I think I'm over the worst of it now."

Aislinn laughed. "I used to suffer a great deal too, when I was a child. I find walking helps. I'd suggest you do the same."

She crouched down to help him up. Fionn found himself amazed at the ease at which she took his weight and propped him onto his feet.

"You don't get it anymore?" said Fionn. "Air-sickness?"

"I reckon I grew out of it. But the walking definitely helps."

That much I can vouch for! said Sir Bearach. *She could barely handle a carriage ride without feeling unwell.*

It is strange though, replied Fionn. *I was completely fine aboard* The Glory of Penance.

Were you up drinking the night before then too?

No, I suppose I was more sensible back then.

"I must have grown into it," said Fionn as they walked. "Have you any other suggestions to shake it off?"

"Keep your eyes out the windows," she said. "And try to convince your mind that you're moving."

They approached a porthole looking out over the starboard of the ship. Through it, the city of Penance fell away as the ship sailed over the Steel Mountains. On the other side of the Rustlake, another, larger ship, flew past in the distance.

"But I know we're moving," said Fionn. "Why do I need to convince my mind of the same?"

Aislinn sighed. "A healer told me about the cause of travel sickness once. See, there's fluid inside our ears, and its ebb and flow give us our sense of balance. It's how we know we're right-side up or upside down. So, when you're aboard a boat or an airship moving very quickly, your ears tell your brain that you're moving."

"Makes sense," said Fionn. He had studied some amount of white magic back when he was in the Academy, and likely once knew the technical term for the fluids Aislinn mentioned. Though it was detail long forgotten now.

"But there is a problem," said Aislinn. "Even though we're travelling across the Northern Reach, we're standing still. Our ears are telling us that we're moving, but our eyes are saying the opposite. This discordant messaging into our brains causes it to come to the wrong conclusion. Not that we're aboard a moving ship, but that one of the signals is incorrect. And apparently another way that information can get garbled as read by our brains is—"

"Poison," finished Fionn. "So, when travel-sick, our brains think we've been poisoned?"

"Exactly," said Aislinn. "And our bodies know exactly what to do if they detect poison in our bellies."

Fionn glanced back at the floor where he had thrown up. Aislinn laughed.

"It's funny, some sailors would laugh and jeer at their peers that show symptoms of sea sickness, claiming that they're weak or frail. But if anything, those are the ones who are stronger than the rest, since their bodies are better equipped for dealing with poison compared to the others. Indeed, many ailments are caused by our bodies trying to protect themselves. Like someone trying to help with the wrong tools to do so."

"Kind of like us," said Fionn. "Flying out to Dromán to protect one god from another. Do you think we even stand a chance?"

"I didn't think I could escape the horde on foot," said Aislinn. "But I did. I didn't think we could fight them back at Penance, but we did. I suppose the real answer is that I don't know whether or not we stand a chance. So, we may as go and see if we do."

The ship accelerated as they crossed the Clifflands, and soon Fionn found that his air-sickness had returned. He excused himself from Aislinn, as even speaking seemed to much effort now. He spent the rest of the journey with his head pressed against the glass of the porthole, watching the baren landscape zip past below.

As the afternoon deepened, Fionn's illness did not subside. He was happy enough to linger in the one place for the rest of the journey, just praying with every passing moment that the ship would land.

Indeed, after about six hours of travel, the ship began to descend.

Are we here already? asked Sir Bearach. *I thought the journey would be closer to eight hours.*

Fionn agreed with the knight, but part of him hoped that they had reached their destination. Unfortunately, a quick glance out from the window told him they had just reached the northern border of the Hazelwood.

So why are we landing?

Fionn's body welcomed the decrease in pace as the ship slowly descended. As it landed, some people emerged into the corridor. It didn't seem that they were getting ready to disembark, so Fionn joined them. He caught some excited murmurs among them but wasn't quite sure of their context.

After the ship came to a halt, some time passed as the crew fussed themselves with the gangway door. Eventually, this opened, revealing a wooden bridge that descended down to the grassy planes below. The trees of the Hazelwood loomed ahead to the south.

But at the foot of the gangway were seven Simians upon mounts. Fionn squinted, recognising General-Commander Plackart at the head and Farris just behind. As the Simians embarked, the rest of those aboard burst into applause.

"Plackart's back!" cried one Human next to Fionn. "I wonder how Point Grey is faring."

"I don't," said another Simian. "As long as my family back home are fed, it can burn for all I care."

Plackart stepped through the door, tending to his mount that walked alongside him. The General-Commander's face was still and stoic as it always was. He didn't even acknowledge the cheers of jubilation that greeted him as he boarded.

Fionn wondered if something was wrong, if the party had come across something on their journey to or from Point Grey to trouble them so much. And when the next Simian came on behind Plackart, Fionn's suspicions were confirmed. For Farris Silvertongue came behind. His face was pale, and his eyes stared blankly ahead, wide and unfocused. As the crowd cheered again, Fionn caught Farris's glance. The Simian was agitated. His mouth was ajar, and his lips were quivering. No matter how terrible Fionn had felt during this flight, he reckoned Farris felt far worse.

CHAPTER 7:
IN THE LIGHT OF THE LADY

Against our enemies, He is our sword

Against the plague, He is our shield

In His name, this land is blessed,

For in His words, it was promised,

The One, Most True,

Lord Seletoth

Sermon of the Sons of Seletoth, from God's Blood, 1:22

***

Farris spent most of *The Majestic's* journey alone, watching the Hazelwood drift by beneath them. As the afternoon approached evening, the trees below began to thin out, though Farris was sure they hadn't even reached the Tithe; the river on which sat Dromán itself.

Much to Farris's confusion, the trees fell away entirely as the ship continued south, leaving a gaping hole of stumps in the place of the lush forestry that had come before it.

"That would be Santos's handiwork," said Plackart, approaching Farris's side. "The timber needed to build his tunnel under the ground came from here, so I'm told. The Dromán outpost lies in the centre of the cavity."

Farris didn't respond. He hadn't been able to bring himself to even speak to Plackart since they left Point Grey.

"Far simpler, things would have been," continued Plackart, "if the tunnel had been finished before all this began. We could have made the journey in half the time with twice the cargo if the trains were ready."

"And with fewer dead," said Farris. It was only when he spoke that he realised how dry his throat was. The words came out with a sting.

"It had to be done, Farris. We fought in self-defence. The lad would have buried his blade in my back if you had not reacted so quickly."

But maybe we would have deserved as much, Farris wanted to say, but thought it better to keep his mouth shut. Unfortunately, Plackart pushed the point anyway.

"We are at war, Farris, and sacrifice is as much a part of it as combat is. We gave those villagers the option to leave, and they chose to fight instead. It was their inability to sacrifice their homes, that we—"

"Don't," spat Farris. "Don't spin the fault to their side."

Plackart raised his hands. "I do not wish to. But know that they left us with no choice."

"Would you have understood, had you been in their shoes?"

"Of course. As a soldier of the Triad, I know that—"

"You're missing the point." interrupted Farris. "In their shoes, you are not a soldier. If not for your training and your military service, would you have understood?"

Plackart responded only with a scowl, his lips pursed as tight as the faded scar that crossed his left cheek.

Farris saw this as a chance to press on. "Oh, has the Triad has made you forget what it means to defend something closer to your heart than the chain of command? Have you forgotten that there's nothing worth defending more than one's home? Or perhaps you prefer the taste of King Diarmuid's boots to your—"

"Know your place, Farris Silvertongue!" roared Plackart. This caused a few eavesdroppers to jump in fright. "You will *not* speak to me in that manner while in uniform."

"Fine," said Farris. He promptly removed his chain-mail gauntlets, then grabbed his blue and gold tabard and pulled it off. He tossed both aside. "Now, where was I?"

Plackart scowled at the discarded uniform. "You were never a soldier. Just a thug who got lucky."

Part of Farris wanted to strike Plackart there and then, but he stayed his hand. He had caused enough of a scene already and maiming the General-Commander wouldn't help with the fight against Morrígan.

And deep down, he knew it wouldn't quell the fires of guilt that burned inside him.

***

Sometime later, the Triad's fortification at the Dromán outpost came into view. A makeshift moat with jagged palisades encircled a meagre-looking stone structure. Farris had seen one of these stone structures before. Several days after the Battle of Penance, Nicole had snuck himself, Cormac, Fionn, Aislinn and Padraig out from Penance via a stolen ship named *Gallant*. Without the go-ahead from the Church, the ship only had enough blue focus-crystals to take them to Ongar and back. The rest of the way they made on elk and horseback, through the railway tunnel, which they had entered via a similar outpost near Ongar.

This structure, however, was heavily fortified with a half-built trench encircling it. Many soldiers ran to and fro through the encampment, some carrying supplies, others setting up tents and pavilions. On the far side of the camp, three great airships stood harboured to a temporary air-dock made of steel. *The Majestic* joined these, between *Horizon* and *The Kingsmill*. A group of Simians tended to the craft as it landed, taking ropes and chains from the ship and fastening them to mechanisms across the dock, which tightened and pulled the ship into position.

Aboard the ship, the passengers shuffled and fussed, waiting for the gangway to be set up and the doors to open. This brought an air of excitement, but it did nothing to lighten Farris's spirits.

When the doors opened, Farris followed the flow of soldiers that spilled out into the camp. Lieutenants roared commands as those disembarking sprang straight to work.

I better find something to make myself useful, he thought, noticing Fionn and Aislinn walking out into the camp just behind him.

"Farris!" a voice cried out from up ahead. From up ahead Nicole running towards him, her shirt stained black with soot and grime.

As he saw her, Farris was overcome with a bizarre feeling. It was as if only now had the burdens and tolls of the past few days suddenly surfaced, threatening to boil over. The familiar sense of panic began to form, and Farris found his heartbeat quicken and his breathing growing short. But rather than succumb to the feeling, as he had so many times before, he ran to Nicole to embrace her. The waves of anxiety suddenly retreated, and the weight from his shoulders vanished.

"Well, I'm glad to see you too," said Nicole, laughing as she hugged him back. As he felt her warmth, Farris found that he could not bear the thought of being away from her again. In fact, it made him question how he ever managed at all with her. But this wasn't the same drive of attraction or passion he had felt with other female Simians in the past, but something new. Something that made him question all he had ever learned before, all he had ever believed, for how he could have claimed to have lived a fulfilling life before without this incredible force by his side?

Only now did he notice that he was crying, with wet eyes buried in Nicole's fur. Fortunately, none alighting from the ship paid much mind as they passed, for to a casual onlooker, they likely looked like a couple reunited.

Eventually, they pulled away from one another, but the feeling still lingered.

"So much has happened," said Farris, wiping his eyes. "I have so much to tell you."

"It will have to wait," said Nicole. "She wants to see you."

"Who?" But something in the way Nicole had emphasised the word 'She' told him the answer already.

"Meadhbh. But She didn't say why. Oh, Fionn!" she called out for the Pyromaster, passing through the dock. "I've got something for you."

She reached into a pocket and revealed two rings. Farris recognised these as flint-rings, used by Pyromancers to create sparks.

"Oh, thanks," said Fionn. "I really appreciate—wait!" He paused as she handed the rings to him. He held one up to his eye to examine them. "Are these made from your steel?"

Nicole smiled. "Yes, I heard about what happened to your fingers in Penance. This way, Morrigan won't be able to grasp them with Geomancy like she did before."

"I don't know what to say," said Fionn, beaming as he slipped the rings onto his oversized hand. "Again, thank you."

Nicole nodded, then turned back towards Farris. "We better hurry. It's rude to leave a Lady waiting, after all."

The two walked through the busy camp. Evening was setting in, and many soldiers set to work building fires all around them. Overhead, the rest of the ships that left Penance were arriving, descending towards the others at the dock. They passed two of Nicole's reapers—huge steel bodies with Simian pilots inside. They were running drills, making slow, repetitive movements as another Simian shouted orders at them.

Nicole paused as they reached the wooden door of the stone building in the centre of the camp. She pulled a long metal key from a trouser pocket and worked it inside a large brass keyhole. Sure enough, the door clicked open, revealing nothing more than a round, empty room inside.

In the centre of the room, however, was a single trap door. Nicole opened this carefully to reveal a set of steel stairs, winding downwards into darkness.

"Watch your step," said Nicole, walking across the room to take a torch from the wall. "It's a long way down."

Farris followed her into the darkness. Every step let out a metallic clang as they went, which rang out rhythmically as both descended. Round and round they went, until Nicole's footsteps were silenced by solid ground. When Farris emerged, he found himself in the familiar surroundings of the Dromán Outpost.

They stood in a wide cavern, lined with meagre shacks and structures along the walls. The railway itself dissected the outpost, two straight lines of steel linking a tunnel to the north with one to the south. On the opposite side, several soldiers stood guard, their backs facing a crooked hole in the wall.

Nicole brought Farris across the clearing, paying the guards little mind. They certainly noticed her, though, stepping aside to let her reach the hole.

Just like before, the hole led them to another set of stairs, though these stood in stark contrast to those before, made from dark stone slabs of different shapes and sizes. The set of crooked steps led them down towards a faint blue light, bringing them past dozens of strange columns bent out of shape. Where the walls met the ceiling, the angles were off, as if it were something no sane engineer would consider structurally sound.

Farris stumbled at the last step, which was far smaller than the rest. Now, the two Simians stood before the source of the blue hue: a wide altar, as odd in design as the rest of the temple.

"You have returned!" came a terrible voice. The from the light emerged a woman. Every inch of her body was beauty manifested, with smooth blue skin glowing and pulsating along with the blue light. A face so lovely it could have been carved from marble stared down at them, but the voice that escaped Her alluring lips brought nothing but terror to Farris's ears. "Those that should be dead stand before me once more."

Nicole immediately dropped to her knees, much to Farris's surprise.

"My Lady," she said. "You asked me to bring you Farris Silvertongue, and I did so without question. We are here to do whatever you bid."

"I can't promise the same," said Farris. He knew one thing was for certain; he wouldn't bow to anyone.

"You..." said Meadhbh. She took a step towards Farris. "You have spent your life denying the existence of the gods, and you have unwillingly played a pivotal role in unravelling the Tapestry of Fate. Because of you, I am still whole, and the Godslayer has not yet claimed my power."

"Morrigan," said Farris. "She has a name. I had the pleasure of meeting her once in a tavern, back before she lost her mind."

"Something you were never fated to do," said Meadhbh. "But like all Simians, the threads of fate do not bind you as tightly as Seletoth's creations. Where they have failed, you and your kind have succeeded. Chaos now replaces order, and there is hope for us all."

"I understood that much," said Farris. "So, what did you want to say to me?"

The Lady hesitated. "Even I am surprised by the efforts you have made to protect me, as vain as they may be. This may very well be the last of our days. The Godslayer has claimed the power of the Móráin line for herself, but unlike the eighteen kings that came before her, she has learned to harness the power dormant in Seletoth's bloodline. I fear she may already be unstoppable."

"We will not fail," said Nicole, rising to her feet. "We will protect you, no matter what it takes. Even if it kills us all."

"I fear it may," said Meadhbh. "For if I am slain, the powers protecting this land will die too, and all of Alabach will be consumed by the Grey Plague. Regardless of the outcome, Farris Silvertongue, I want you to you know now that I am grateful for all you have done. Even if the Lord falls, and the Age of Life is brought to an end, know that for a moment, a god bowed before a mortal."

With this, the Lady slowly went to one knee, then bowed her head towards Farris.

"Well," he said. "I appreciate—"

But his words were cut short by a low drone that rang out somewhere above them. All three looked up at the ceiling, with nothing more than those strange angles to glaring down at them.

"What was that?" said Farris, right before the noise rang out again, longer, and louder than before.

Nicole's eyes went wide. "No, not now. We're not ready yet, we've only just arrived." She gave Farris a worried look. "The enemy has been sighted. She's here."

CHAPTER 8:
THE LIGHT FADES

The journey west was difficult. With each passing day, the Grey Plague followed, threatening to catch us if we slowed. By boat, we crossed a sea to reach the land He had promised us. We named it Alabach and arrived on the southern coast.

But our welcome was not warm. The natives fought back with great ferocity and might. Intelligent creatures, they had mastered the art of metallurgy in ways we could only dream. Had we waged conventional warfare against them, we surely would have been cast back into the sea.

But with the Lord's magic on our side, we crushed their early skirmishes. We settled in the region known as the Kinglands today, and claimed the south of Alabach for ourselves.

But Seletoth still lay somewhere further north, and our journey would not be over until we found Him.

The Truth, by King Móráin I, AC 55.

Chaos erupted all over the camp as the horn's blast rang through the air. The boots of soldiers running into position thundered against the ground, drowning out cries of their superiors.

"Aislinn!" called out Fionn as he saw her mounting. "What am I do to?"

"Plackart!" she shouted back at him. She donned her helm and climbed on an armoured horse. "He's leading the vanguard."

Fionn sprinted through the camp. Soldiers scrambled from tents among cries and shouts, others frantically donned armour and tended to their weapons. Towards the edge of the camp, a large host of infantry was assembling. General-Commander Plackart walked through their ranks in gilded armour.

"Firemaster!" he roared. "Our enemy is here. We will meet her in open battle and end this once and for all." He handed Fionn a Simian-made spyglass and pointed eastwards.

Fionn looked through the eyeglass. It took a moment for his vision to focus, but once it did, a dark figure appeared at the edge of the clearing.

Unarmed and alone, Morrigan wore a feathered black cloak, just like before.

"She brought no army." said Plackart. "There's nothing but empty landscape between us and her. We end this now."

"Plackart!" came a voice. He and Fionn turned to see Farris and Nicole running towards them.

"Farris Silvertongue," sneered Plackart. "What brings you here?"

"It's a trap," said Farris, panting for breath. "It must be a trap. Why else wait until we have all arrived before revealing herself? Why even give us the chance to muster our strength? You need to call off the vanguard, you—"

"You will *not* give me orders!" growled Plackart. "After our last meeting, you should grateful you're not being charged with desertion."

"Plackart, please!" said Farris. "Just listen."

"Archers, take aim!" roared the commander, turning back towards his men. A row of marksmen standing behind him raised their bows. "Fire!"

A hundred arrows shot up to the sky, then landed about the clearing. Plackart grabbed the spyglass from Fionn's hands and looked through it.

"She's unharmed," he muttered. "And still coming towards us."

"There's no way she'd let herself be exposed like this," said Farris. "We need to reconsider."

"Infantry!" cried Plackart. He raised his greatsword in one hand over his head. "Today we repay the debt this Godslayer left us with in Penance. For every Human and Simian life she took from us. With me!"

A barrage of battle cries rose up, and the infantry charged, with Plackart at their head. Human and Simian alike, they sprinted into the clearing with spears lowered. Fionn braced himself as the rest of the soldiers ran past him. His eyes met Farris's.

"You believe me, right?" said Farris. "Surely you can see that this is a trap."

"I do," said Fionn. He clicked his flint rings together to create a spark, which quickly turned to a burning ball of fire in his hands. "But they need me, and I don't have much of a choice."

With that he turned to face the clearing, now filled with charging soldiers, and followed.

***

"Damn idiots," said Farris, kicking at the trodden grass. "It's as if they want to be killed."

"The cavalry," said Nicole. "They're just mounting now. We still have time."

With this, Farris and Nicole ran into the camp. One contingent of elk cavalry charged past into the battlefield, some twenty or so riders among them. Farris waved his hands and called out to them, but they did not slow.

"Bastards," grunted Farris.

"Captain Tuathil is over there," said Nicole, pointing. Indeed, at the southern end of the camp, Padraig was addressed another group of riders from atop a destrier.

Farris bolted towards the horses, jumping aside as two men carrying a pile of spears almost collided with him.

"Padraig!" called Farris. "If these are your men, order them to stand down until we figure out what's happening!"

Padraig glared down at Farris. "They are, but I'll do no such thing. The rest of the cavalry battalions are already taking position to flank her. We cannot desert them." He lowered his visor. "And I'll slay her myself for what she did in Cruachan."

In a moment of desperation, Farris leapt towards Padraig. The captain's mount reared, throwing its rider off balance. Farris grabbed at whatever his hands could reach, reins, saddle, arms, he wasn't sure what, but the next moment, both he and Padraig were on the ground.

Farris bared his fangs. "Temper your bloodlust for one moment and listen to reason!"

"I'll have you hanged for this!" spat Padraig. "And I didn't need another reason to see you dead!"

"It's a trap, Padraig. She's left herself exposed, alone, facing the might of the Triad. She must know that we'd ride out to kill her."

For a painful few seconds, Padraig stared up at Farris kneeling on his chest. The ground beneath them shook with the beat of hooves, indicating that another battalion of cavalry were riding out. But Padraig's soldiers had dismounted and now stood surrounding the captain and the Simian on the ground. Padraig gritted his teeth, which caused Farris to shift his weight, putting more on the captain's chest and bringing his face closer to the Human's. Farris considered what he'd do if Padraig didn't comply. Could he be justified in restraining him even more?

Eventually, Padraig spoke. "I know you to be a liar and a cheat, Farris. A spy. A thief. On most matters, I'd never trust the likes of you. But when it comes to deception, I know of no one with more experience."

Farris stepped aside as Padraig sat up to address his soldiers. "We stand down! Until we figure out what's happening."

Aislinn Carríga stood with those of the battalion, but she was facing out towards the clearing.

"Captain," she said, her voice quivering. "Look!"

***

Fionn ran as fast as he could to catch up with the vanguard. His heart pumped in his chest, as a force unlike anything he had felt before seemed to take over his body, forcing his legs to move as fast as he could, as if he were lighter than ever.

The thrill of battle runs through your veins, laughed Sir Bearach. *You have the blood of a warrior in you, lad!*

Fionn found he couldn't focus on much more than the pounding of his feet against the ground. Stumps of tree trunks raced past him as he made his way halfway across the field. Squinting through the fading evening's light, some fifty or so yards ahead of him, the vanguard met Morrigan.

A fierce gust of wind came from where she stood, knocking Fionn to the ground and throwing those closer to her up into the air. Within the swirling blast, dozens of cries and shouts rang out. Through the chaos, the young girl walked past the parting of bodies as they were tossed aside like rag dolls.

Fionn slowly stood, finding others around him doing the same. Ahead of him, another group of soldiers charged at Morrígan, dozens of pikes in a row.

The girl barely reacted. In an instant, great pillars of fire burst around her, consuming those who stood their ground.

"No," muttered Fionn. The dying men cried out; voices made shrill with agony. Fionn gritted his teeth and found his feet. He pointed his hands out towards the inferno.

It's just Pyromancy, he said to himself, finding the flames ahead of him in his fingers.

He felt the heat in his hands and let roar the fire of his own soul. Rionach's theorems and formulae ran through his head, and Fionn muttered their calculations.

But something didn't add up.

The transfer of heat through the air was *wrong,* somehow. But Fionn didn't have time to figure out why, for another swirl of fire came hurling towards him. He gritted his teeth and reached out to the flames, quelling them before they approached him.

He broke into a sprint towards the strewn bodies of dazed, disorientated soldiers. Three more swirling twisters of fire surrounded Morrigan. None dared come near her now, as she slowly walked forward, surrounded by flames that barely touched the black feathers of her cloak.

Fionn ran forward, reaching out to the flames. He roared with effort as something was preventing him from quelling these as easily as the first. Injured soldiers on the ground nearby looked up at him, eyes wide and mouths open in awe at the one person who was standing against this unstoppable force.

What's wrong? cried Sir Bearach. *Is she fighting back?*

Not quite, thought Fionn. Beads of sweat ran down his brow as he barely gained control of the flames. *It's something else.*

His energy drained from his body far quicker than he was used to. But with another grunt of effort, *there,* he gained hold of the three pillars of flame. He yelled out loud as he forced the last drops of power of his soul into them, causing them to vanish into the warm air.

You did it, lad! Well done!

Fionn fell to his knees with exhaustion, but the other soldiers, seeing this defiance, stood, and made another charge at Morrigan.

It's no use, thought Fionn. *The air... the earth... none of it feels right.* A realisation came over him. *She has full command of them all. Every particle of the soil... every drop of vapour in the air. They're hers now.*

Overhead, clouds quickly formed, centring on Morrígan. Spears and arrows shot towards her, ahead of another reckless charge led by the General-Commander himself, but each missed, as if steered away at the last minute.

Then the clouds burst, and more soldiers fell, writhing in pain. With horror, Fionn saw that it was not rain that fell from the clouds, but long icicles, sharp like knives.

Quickly, Fionn crawled away from the fight, still not strong enough to stand. An icicle struck the ground mere inches from his head.

This is folly, thought Fionn. *How many has she killed already? How many more can we spare?*

Look! cried Sir Bearach. *Between the trees, outside the clearing! The cavalry is encircling her!*

The dead knight spoke these words with glee, as if excited for the outcome. But Fionn did not share his optimism.

Other soldiers attempted to flee, but the rain of icicles widened, and more men fell.

Then, Morrígan's eyes met Fionn's.

Get up lad! roared Sir Bearach. *Run!*

With effort, Fionn shifted his weight to stand, though his muscles failed him. All he could do was watch helplessly as Morrígan strode towards him.

The girl made an elaborate gesture and a torrent of rain poured down over Fionn. He raised his hands to protect himself, but the moisture on his body quickly turned to ice, freezing him in place.

"Once more, our paths cross," said Morrigan. Her voice was that of an adolescent girl, a stark contrast to the horrors she had wrought.

Fionn's jaw was frozen shut. More moisture from the rain encircled him, encasing him in a thick layer of ice, like a crystal. Slowly, it began to rise, lifting him from the ground.

"Do you truly believe you can stop me?" she said, eyes locked on Fionn as he rose. "I want you to see what I am capable of, and I want you to despair. For even without an army of my own, I'll throw back this one, and anything else Penance can manage!"

Fionn was now some twenty feet over the ground. Up here, her destruction was clearly visible, with a wide circle of injured and dying infantry all around her. More ice poured down onto the battlefield like arrows from the heavens. Morrigan stood amidst it all.

It's over, thought Fionn. *She's toying with us, like a child would with ants.*

Look! said Sir Bearach. *They're coming!*

Fionn glanced to the far end of the battlefield. A hundred elk and horses of the Triad's cavalry came bursting from the forest: great, armoured beasts galloping through trees. Shimmering knights rode upon them, with huge lances and halberds in hand, all pointing towards Morrigan. The girl's back was turned to them, as if unaware that the might of the Triad, the strength of the Simians, the last of Humankind, all massed, converging towards her. Lieutenant Bernice led the charge, clad in heavy plate of blue steel just like her steed, a great elk, with antlers spanning the length of two fully grown Simians. Many more knights followed. They charged into this new hell Morrigan had created, but they did so without fear or hesitation.

Fionn's heart soared at the sight. Morrigan still didn't seem to notice, and all it would take would be one lance, one of those blessed, brave knights to hold fast and end all of this for once and for all.

As the riders approached, Morrigan's wings unfurled.

What Fionn had thought was a cloak was instead great, black-feathered wings emerging from Morrigan's shoulders. Once covering her body, now they stretched out, like the branches from a blackened tree. Morrigan raised her arms, and the wings beat, causing her to rise above the ground. She rose until her eyes were level with Fionn's. Far below them, the charging cavalry came to a lurching halt, some riders falling from their mounts.

"The Truth has been hidden from us," she said. "I will kill every last man, woman, and child to learn it."

A rumble came from beneath them. At the edge of the clearing, the ground appeared to shift, bulging upwards.

No, thought Fionn. *What is she doing?*

The ground shook again, this time more violently than before. Beneath the feet of the cavalry, a fissure formed. Then, like a yawning beast, the ground opened up.

Those in the centre fell right in, disappearing into the blackness below. Others tried to flee, but the cracks grew wider, until those running were consumed too.

Fionn look on helplessly as elks, horses, Humans and Simians alike shrieked, calling for help as the earth itself betrayed them. Walls of dirt rose high around the perimeter of the clearing, then moved inwards, closing in on those who had managed to outrun the crevasse.

Soon, the entire battlefield was consumed by the terrible cavity, as every soldier, knight, and animal that braved the charge against Morrigan fell into it. Now only Fionn remained, floating above the carnage, face to face with the Godslayer.

"You are nothing," she said, reaching a hand to Fionn. Slowly the ice that encased him started to melt. "The Crown, the Church, the Triad, are all fleeting things in the face of the gods themselves. But I will rise above them too."

Fionn's body was abruptly freed from the prison of ice, and he found himself helplessly tumbling towards the ground.

But the ground was not there to greet him.

Far he fell into the pit, in silence and darkness. Then with a cracking *thud*, he landed on something hard, like steel. It writhed beneath him. Voices groaned and called and cried out all around him.

Bodies. He was surrounded by bodies, helplessly lying broken in this dark chasm.

I need to get out, he thought, scrambling to stand. Only now did he notice the pain in his legs, his arms, his back. Bones were surely broken, but a growing, pounding fear in his heart made it difficult to him to pinpoint exactly where the pain was.

He looked upwards towards the light, so far away. He reached for it, in vain, for he may as well have been trying to reach for the clouds.

Then, from either side of the hole high above, dirt began to trickle down upon him.

In the air, Morrigan now floated and stared down into the mass grave. Amidst the sound of desperate screams turning hoarse with terror, her cold smile was the last thing Fionn saw before the dirt covered his face. Before the walls closed in.

And the light faded.

***

"No," muttered Farris, his knees growing weak.

By his side, Nicole remained silent. Along with the rest of the soldiers who had waited at the camp, they could do nothing but watch as the ground opened and swallowed the army that rode out to meet the girl.

"Fionn," muttered Farris. "Plackart...."

"What do we do?" asked Padraig. "How can we fight her like this?"

Concerned mutters ran through the rest of the soldiers. Some Farris recognised from the Churchguard, those who had rode out under his command.

My command, he thought. *I brought them here. To fight without plan. To lose without hope.*

Crippling anxiety shook Farris's chest once more, bringing water to his eyes. His lower jaw quivered, and another wave of terror moved up his spine.

She's coming. She's coming for the rest of us.

"We still have the Reapers," said Nicole. "We make a last stand at the temple, to protect the Lady."

"Fuck the Lady!" said Farris. "We need to protect ourselves."

"But we promised!" said Nicole. "We said we'd do it even if it cost us our lives. Even if we—"

She was cut off by a surge of flames that soared over their heads: a bolt of fire that came shooting from the battlefield, colliding with the airships of the docks.

And as the gas of the ships ignited, a huge fireball engulfed the southern side of the camp.

Farris was knocked off his feet. Disorientated and dazed, he squinted through the camp. A ship ignited and burst ahead of him, huge plumes of smoke billowing forth and spilling into the sky.

He looked up to see the bodies of the docked airships burn. Massive flames leapt from vessel to vessel, tearing through the cotton skins of the ships and leaving only the steel bodies of the rigid frames beneath. These quickly melted, losing their shape and collapsing among one another.

People fled from the inferno, as others called for water and for help.

Panicking, Farris stood. Nicole was nearby, looking up at the fires.

"The gas," she muttered. "It's burning faster than any Pyromancer could hope to replicate. More than—"

"Nicole!" rasped Farris, pulling her to her feet. "Take everyone you can and run. Get out of here. Go to the Academy and hide, just... fucking hide, and I'll come find you."

Nicole looked about her. Indeed, many who were still alive ran back and forth aimlessly. Padraig seemed to have gathered his battalion again, but he lacked the confidence he had demonstrated before the fighting began.

"But what about the Lady?" she said. "We can't leave Her."

"Don't worry about Meadhbh," said Farris. "I'm going to pay Her one last visit, then I'll meet you in the Academy. Lead everyone there. We'll be safe for a little while at least."

"Farris, do you have a plan?"

"Yes, just trust me. Just this once, please."

"Okay," Nicole said. "Just this once. I'll believe you."

Once Nicole turned to alert the others, Farris patted his waist, feeling for the concealed knife there. Of course he had a plan.

Morrigan came here to kill the Lady, but she'll fail. I'll do it first.

Farris ran from the burning camp, making his way to the stone structure. As soon as he was out of sight of the others, he let the forced smile leave his lips. Anxiety turned to rage in his chest, and he tightened the grip on his dagger with each step.

We risked so much to protect Her, he thought, descending the stairway two steps at time. *And this is how She repays us?*

He emerged into the empty outpost and sprinted across the open floor. Once he reached the crooked stairway leading down into the shrine, he slowed his pace, hoping to surprise the Lady.

Oh, but She's probably seen this happen already! Even as rage thundered through his body, tears continued to stream down his cheeks.

"Meadhbh!" he roared as he approached the altar. He held his dagger before him in a trembling hand. "I need to speak with you!"

The Lady manifested before him, Her glowing body lighting the dark temple. She stood on bent knees, as if ready to spring forward at moment's notice.

"Farris Silvertongue," She said. "I did not expect to see you here."

"Oh, that's a fucking surprise," he rasped between sobs. "Did you see what happened up there? Buried alive, the lot of them. She killed them all!"

"I respect their sacrifice, but I fear it may be in vain."

"You're right about that," said Farris. "I'll strike you down right now and make sure it was!"

The Lady's stance straightened. "Farris, please, listen to me. You have the sceptic mind of a Simian, but the bleeding heart of a Man. Your emotional side is clouding your logic once more. Surely you can see that you stand no chance to kill me with mere steel. And the Godslayer will be here any moment. You will not last a second if she sees you."

Farris paused for a moment, and slowly let the dagger fall to his side.

"I... I just don't know anymore," he whispered. "Is this really it?"

The Lady stepped towards Farris and rested a warm hand on his cheek. Her dark blue eyes stared deep into his own, and for a moment, the despair in his body vanished.

"We have one more chance," She whispered. "But my own fate is already sealed. If you are to stand a chance against the Godslayer, you must do this one thing."

"Anything," said Farris, his trembling lips barely able to form the words. "Please."

"Leave here," she said. "Leave me to my doom and find Firemaster Fionn out in the battlefield. He'll know what to do next."

Farris shook his head. "The ground swallowed them all. He's dead. He's dead with the rest of them."

"No," said the Lady. "He survived. This, I know. He—" She cut herself off. "The Godslayer is here. Go, now. Find him, whatever the cost!"

Farris turned to see the figure of Morrigan slowly descending the crooked stairs. Without making a sound, he darted across the shrine to hide behind a bent column at the foot of the stairway. Although his body shook with anguish, he focused on calming his breath, and becoming as silent as the stone that surrounded them.

"Meadhbh," came Morrigan's voice. "Your own light forsakes you."

"My light has forsaken us all," replied Meadhbh. "But this was destined long before Creation."

Morrigan appeared at the bottom of the stairwell, her feathered wings moving gracefully with each step.

"I have seen the Beginning and the End," said Morrigan, "But it was only a glimpse. I want you to show me more."

"You have seen far more than the Lord intends," said Meadhbh. "And He will not fall so easily."

"Yes," said Morrigan, raising a hand before her. "Not as easily as you."

Morrigan threw her hands forward, and fire streamed from her fingers. Meadhbh recoiled, and the light surrounding Her light grew in intensity, absorbing Morrigan's flames with its brilliance. For a time, it held, but the Lady's face showed the strain of effort, changing from the perpetual regal look it always held.

Morrígan's assault continued, and with each passing second, the Lady exhibited further mortal emotions: Anguish and agony. Grief and despair. And then defeat, with eyes closed, and head bowed.

As the flames consumed Her, She screamed. To hear a god cry with pain was as unnatural as a darkened sun or a dried ocean.

Under the cover of that terrible sound, Farris slipped from his hiding place and tore up the crooked stairs, not daring to look back as he did. Fortunately, Morrígan had not noticed him, for by the time Farris reached the top of the stairwell, the Lady's cries were muted. And the pulsating blue light that once shone through the temple was no more.

CHAPTER 9:
THE GREY PLAGUE

Argyll the Silverback woke with a stir. His mouth was dry, his mind was foggy, but after a few orientating moments, he realised he was in a bed in one of the clinics of the Triad's hospital wing.

The Godslayer... King Diarmuid... What happened?

Only now did he see he was not alone. Ruairí Ó Críodáin sat beside his bed. His eyes were closed, with his fingers clasped around one another.

"If you're praying that I wake up, you can stop now," said Argyll.

The Human jumped. "He's awake!" he cried, turning his head towards the clinic's door. He was almost giddy with the news.

"Get them to bring me something to eat too," added Argyll. "And why can't I feel my legs?"

Ruairí's expression went dark. He went to speak, but the words failed him.

The door to the clinic burst open, and three healers rushed in to attend to Argyll. After taking some measurements pertaining to his heartbeat and his breathing, one of them, a Human male with a neatly trimmed grey beard, placed a hand on Argyll's shoulder.

"I'm afraid there has been significant damage done to your lower spine. We've done all we can but...."

No, thought Argyll. A pang of terror ripped through his body at the realisation that he had no feeling from the waist down. He tried to move his toes, his feet, then his legs, but none complied, as if he was trying to move limbs he never possessed. The healer was still speaking, but the words seemed drift through Argyll's mind, only some being comprehended at a time. Every so often, some words the healer said landed, "...unlikely to walk again," and "maybe... with lots of intensive work," or "... a very slim chance."

Argyll pressed his hand against his head.

No. I am their rock. I cannot falter.

"Spare me the details," he barked at the healer. "If I cannot walk, then fetch me a chair set upon wheels."

He turned towards Ruairi. "And we have much to discuss. Tell me what became of the horde."

The healers quickly withdrew to do as they were asked, which often happened when Argyll used that tone. Ruairi was trembling, only ever so slightly, and there was a slight quiver in his voice when he spoke.

"After Morrígan and you... fought," began Ruairí, "She vanished, and the horde fell without her. Afterwards, the army of the Triad took flight to Dromán, where Lady Meadhbh resides. The plan was to defend her, in case Morrígan came to kill her too."

Argyll had many questions. *How much time has passed since I fell? Which ships did they take? Were the Church involved? Did Fionn go with them?*

They would get to those eventually, he reckoned, but one thought brought a smile to his lips.

"The Lady Meadhbh?" Argyll asked. "But I thought you didn't believe in the Trinity beyond Lord Seletoth."

"I did," said Ruairí. "But I spoke to Pyromaster Fionn before he flew out. And...." Ruairí flinched. His gaze broke from Argyll and went straight to the floor.

"These times have challenged us all in many ways," said Argyll. "We can assume there is worse yet to come."

Damn my eyes. Had I not been such a fool atop Sin, I could have been awake these past few days. And I could have ensured Fionn remained in the city.

"There's something else," said Ruairí. He stood up, and slowly walked to the window. He pulled back the thin veil of a curtain that hung before it, revealing the view to Argyll.

No!

He would have dashed to the window if he could. The familiar skyline of the Dustworks and the Basilica to the south were all visible and intact, but the scene was wholly alien now.

A thick blanket of snow covered the city, more drifting down in thick flakes, buffeted by rough winds. Ice filled the streets, with large mounds of snow piled up either side. Whereas only the peaks of the Steel Mountains would see snow at the height of winter, to see the same snowfall cover the land like this was an abomination.

"It just started yesterday," said Ruairí. "The Rustlake and Móráin Sea are frozen over. I've heard rumours that the Eternal Sea is turned to ice too, but that would be—"

"Expected," said Argyll. "Expected under the direst of circumstances. It means the Lady Meadhbh has been killed."

"Excuse me?" said Ruairi. "We've had no communication from the army stationed at Dromán. Are... are you saying—"

"I'm saying not to expect any from them," Argyll cut in. There was so much to plan, so much to prepare in so little time, he was loath to spend the time they had explaining all he knew to Ruairí.

But he'll need to be in the know for when the time comes.

"The Church has had very tight control over all of our airships for as long as we could fly," Argyll started. "But over the past few years, we have manged to sneak some vessels over the Móráin Sea to explore the lands to the east."

Ruairí's raised his eyebrows. "Lands outside of Alabach? But what about the Grey Plague?"

"I'm getting there," snapped Argyll.

Skies above and below, there's so much he doesn't know, he thought. *I invite him into the inner circle of the Movement, and he presumes to think there's no more secrets kept from him.*

"We found lands to the east and to the south of Alabach," Argyll started. "Some as close as a hundred miles away. But they were not inhabitable. An eternal winter grips them, with sheets of ice and plains of snow spreading out for as far as we could fly.

"My whole life, I had doubted the account of the Grey Plague as the Church had put it. If the Firstborn were fleeing some sort of blight, or an illness, then why risk bringing it to their so-called Promised Land? I've seen these lands of ice and snow with my own eyes, and once I did, I understood." He pointed to the window. "This. This is the Grey Plague. If ice has ravaged the rest of the world, then there was just one source preventing it from doing the same to Alabach. The answer lies within your sect's scriptures."

"'Against our enemies, He is our sword,'" muttered Ruairí. "'Against the plague, He is our shield....'"

"Not quite. The Church has a verse just like this, but with minor changes. Referring to the Trinity, an old version of a similar creed reads it 'Against our enemies, They are our sword. Against the *blight*, They are our shield.' This was before the Church conceived the lie that God Grey Plague was a disease from which the Firstborn fled. For here it is referred to as the more ambiguous term 'blight.'"

Ruairí shook his head. "So, if they—He, was our shield against this, does this mean the Godslayer killed Him?"

"It is a possibility. Either that or His power is weakened, which could be the case if the Lady has fallen." On seeing Ruairí's scowl, he added, "According to the Church, of course."

The door to the clinic opened. Two healers came in, pushing a large leather chair atop a set of tiny wheels appended to the bottom of its feet. The healers pushed it using two handles protruding from the back.

Argyll looked at the chair, then back up to the healers.

"Is this all you have?" he said. One of the healers nodded meekly.

This won't do at all, thought Argyll. *It's far too heavy. It requires another person to push it. The centre of gravity is too high. Skies above, the frame is made from timber!*

"Bring me a pen and parchment," he said, extending his hand. "Then leave us in peace."

One healer pushed the chair beside Argyll, who regarded it with disgust. The other healer handed him a roll of empty parchment and a Simian-made inkpen. Then both vanished from the room.

Argyll began scrawling widely on the page, in silence.

"You were saying," said Ruairí. He craned his head to see what Argyll was drawing, but the Simian leaned back, keeping the contents of the page out of sight.

Conceal what you know. Let them see you as weak. Let them underestimate you.

"Yes," said Argyll. "The gods are no longer a concern of mine. Nor should they be on of yours. If Morrigan has indeed transcended to godhood, either by killing Meadhbh or Seletoth or both, then there's no use trying to stop her."

Ruairí started. "But we must do something! Are we supposed to just wait until she returns?"

"Of course not," said Argyll. He quickly flicked one piece of parchment behind the other and continued with his work. "You said the Triad took ships to Dromán. Did they take them all?"

"What?" said Ruairí. He seemed confused.

Please keep up, lad, thought Argyll. *You're slowing us all down.*

"Oh...." said Ruairí, eyes closed in thought. "*The Dreadnought, Sinfall,* and *Thunder* are still docked in Sin. Farris convinced the Church to hand over focus-crystals for the engines of the rest of the ships, but they denied him those needed to fly the three larger vessels."

"Of course," said Argyll. "And if Farris couldn't convince the Church to hand them over, I doubt anyone would."

Ruairí frowned. "But what does this have to do with Morrigan?"

"We are leaving Alabach. Between the three ships, we can take most of the city's population with us comfortably. Perhaps all of it with a squeeze."

Ruairí's mouth was ajar. He stroked his chin. "But you said the lands outside of Alabach were uninhabitable."

"Only to the south and to the east. But we'll travel west."

"West? Over the Eternal Sea?"

"No sea can be eternal," said Argyll. "Our best astronomers theorise that the world is set upon a globe. And the lands east of those to the east of us can be reached by travelling west. They discuss this only in secret, of course. Lest they anger the Church.

"This globe, they say, is over twenty thousand miles in circumference. In comparison, the distance from Elís Point to Gorán is around three hundred and fifty miles. Our supposed Promised Land of the Church is a mere speck upon the vastness of the earth."

"So... how far is the Eternal Sea, then?"

"That much we do not know," said Argyll. "But properly fuelled and properly fitted, the long-distance ships can sail for some two thousand miles without needing to land. Given the largest ocean we observed to the east was in the region of six hundred miles, we should have more than enough to span the Eternal Sea, even if it's three times as wide."

Ruairí clasped his hands together. "Many Humans, even the Sons, would consider this talk blasphemy. But with the threat of Morrígan, and the Grey Plague upon our lands now, I don't see us having much of a choice."

Argyll didn't respond and started sorting and folding the pieces of parchment he had been drawing on. When he was done, the pages formed a tight rectangle, with the text and drawings inside concealed within.

"Take this to Red Ezra's workshop in the Stone Ward," said Argyll, handing the pages to Ruairí. "They are for his eyes only. Confirm that he can follow the instructions without issue, then report back to me."

"Of course." Ruairí pocketed the parchment. "I'll get to it right away."

Shame there's no seal, thought Argyll. In truth, it was no real worry. Ruairí had demonstrated his loyalty to Argyll many times in the past. He certainly was one who could be trusted.

But his god shall always come first, Argyll reminded himself. *If the situation arose, he'd choose his faith over my life.*

Ruairí threw on an overcoat and left the clinic with a curt nod.

Argyll sighed as the door closed. Then he rested his eyes.

Once he was alone, and he was sure he was alone, Argyll the Silverback wept.

CHAPTER 10:
THE BLOOD OF GOD

If there was any light left in this world, today it has gone out. For the Lady Meadhbh is dead. Slain by the Godslayer Morrigan.

Gods, ink upon paper shall never do justice to the devastation she wrought today, wielding the elements as if they served only her. The earth, I fear, is no longer our own as long as she walks upon it.

I would have joined the dead, crushed by the darkness of the pit, had it not been for Farris.

Farris Silvertongue. The traitor and turncloak, prevented me from riding out to join the cavalry charge. He saw the trap for what it was, and for that, the thrice-damned bastard saved me.

Once the chaos died down, we started the unsurmountable task of counting the dead. Though Morrigan had seen so many of them already buried, there were few bodies left for us to give back to the land.

She destroyed all of our ships, killing some forty-odd members of their crews: those that stayed aboard to prepare for a return journey that would never come.

Most of our camp is destroyed, though it'll do for tonight, given we have so few left to shelter. Tomorrow, we march to the Academy in Dromán, where we'll take refuge as we consider our next steps.

But what those could be, I can only guess.

Farris claimed to have been there when the Lady died at the hand of the Godslayer. He said Her last words were that Firemaster Fionn was alive, despite being among those who fell to their deaths deep in the earth.

I had tried to make him see reason, but he refused. He took a handful of fools, Chief Engineer Nicole and Lady Carríga, among them, and raided the sapper's tent for shovels and entrenching tools. They wish to dig the young Pyromancer out from the mass grave.

I should not make light of it. The minds of men are broken easily in war. And this has been no normal war. I curse the others though, for enabling the Simian's delusion.

Though as I write this, deep into the night, they have yet to return.

Could it be that Farris is right? He saw Morrigan's trap for what it was before anyone else did. And he did save my life.

It is growing cold. Colder than I ever could have imagined it be. My body craves rest, but I don't think I can sleep knowing they're out there in the dark, digging for a man surely dead.

Dearest Journal, what should I do?

Journal of Padraig Tuathil, 15th Day under the Moon of Nes, AC404

Nessa wiped sleep from her eyes as she straightened her stance. Although she had been pulled from bed mere minutes ago, she was now wide awake with excitement rising in her chest. However, the same couldn't be said for the other four girls, standing on either side of her, each of whom seemed to be struggling against sleep.

Don't they know who it is this time? thought Nessa, suppressing a smile as Madam Mac Cába marched up and down the line, fixing and fussing over each of the girls' appearance in turn.

The tiny brothel nested in the corner of Barrow's Way had always been more glamorous than its competing businesses—something that certainly wouldn't be inferred by its exterior. The hallway where Nessa stood was circular, with silk curtains draping over every inch of stone wall. Heavily scented perfumes covered the typical stench of Barrow's Way, though Nessa had grown used to both odours over the past two years. The secluded and elusive nature of Madam Mac Cába's establishment attracted all sorts of wealthy lords and merchants visiting the capital, though none quite as noble or high-born as tonight's patron.

"Now, remember your manners," said Madam Mac Cába as she fidgeted with Etain Ní Mháille's hair. Not that it ever needed tending to. Etain's hair was always beautifully straight; something Nessa could never quite figure out.

No matter, she thought, fixing her skirts. *She won't be smiling so much when he picks me.*

"And don't speak until he speaks to you," continued Madam Mac Cába. "Some ladies of the court spend half their childhood learning how to act in front of a—"

The brothel's front door swung open, and a chilling breeze ran into the chamber. From outside strode three figures, two Simians in thick armour, and a young man with his hood up. Nessa's heartbeat accelerated wildly as the man stepped inside, for even before he lowered his hood, she knew exactly who it was.

King Diarmuid, Third of His Name, Nineteenth Incarnate, stood before the line of women. Unlike most men Nessa had serviced here, Diarmuid's face was perfectly clean-shaven. Once his radiant blue eyes met Nessa's and his slender lips formed a wry smile, it was clear the other girls didn't stand a chance.

"Your Grace," said Madam Mac Cába, curtsying deeply. "You honour us with your presence. It is said that your coronation was a sight unlike anything the kingdom has seen before. We pray that the same shall be said of your reign."

"Thank you for your kind words," said the young king, his gaze not leaving Nessa's. For that moment, she could have sworn the two were alone in that crowded room. "I hope all of our prayers are answered."

"Of course, Your Grace," said Madam Mac Cába. She gestured to the other women. "These are my most experienced girls. Though it is customary for our clients to pick just one, given the circumstance we can—"

"That won't be necessary," cut in Diarmuid. He strode towards Nessa, promptly taking one of her hands in his. Her hands would have been trembling, Nessa was sure, if the king's grasp wasn't so strong.

She looked up at those blue eyes, framed by radiant golden locks. What felt like a thousand eternities passed before the king spoke again.

"What is your name?" he said, another smile escaping his lips.

Nessa struggled to find the answer but smiled back instead. Either the king knew her name already or no longer cared to hear it, for the next thing Nessa knew, he was leading her away from the other girls.

He picked me, Nessa realised as they crossed the hall. *Of all the women in Cruachan, he picked me!*

***

Fionn gasped for breath when he returned to consciousness. Enveloped in darkness, the only thing he could make out from his surroundings was the fact he was surrounded by others. Many others. His body lay in a crooked position, with his legs bent painfully backwards. All around, low groans came from amidst a mass of twisting limbs.

What happened? Fionn asked, but Sir Bearach did not respond. The mage shut his eyes and tried to recall what had transpired earlier.

Morrigan, and the army. We fought and—

Terror struck his body.

The earth. The earth opened and devoured us all.

Before panic could set in, however, some more memories came back to Fionn. A woman named Nessa held hands with a much younger King Diarmuid. Fionn strained to recall what else happened.

Just another dream, Fionn thought, turning his attention back to the problem at hand. But before he opened his eyes, a blue light blurred his vision. The same blue light he had seen back in Meadhbh's temple.

Then everything went dark once more

***

"Well?" said the girl. "Do you know what it'll be?"

Cillian the White sighed deeply. He removed his hand from the girl's enlarged belly.

She really thinks it matters, he thought. *They all think it does.*

"It'll be a boy," said Cillian, straightening his healer's robes.

"A prince?" cried the girl, her voice growing shrill with joy. "I'm going to have a little prince?"

"Yes," said Cillian, trying hard not to roll his eyes. "You are due in another four moons."

At this, she shrieked in joy again, as if she would even live half that long. "Oh, I can't wait until Etain finds out I'll be having the king's son!"

"Of course," muttered Cillian, turning away. He slowly strode across the clinic to his study. Taking a seat at the table, he picked up a quill and inked it. "Before you leave, remind me. What was your name again?"

"Nessa," said the girl. "I never knew my parents, so I don't have any other name than—"

"That'll be all, Nessa," cut in Cillian. "Please, close the door on your way out."

The girl practically skipped from the clinic, humming a jolly tune as she went. Fool. She really had no idea. In any other circumstance, a healer would recommend medicines and schedule follow-up appointments to ensure a safe pregnancy.

"Shame," muttered Cillian. He set the quill to the page and began scribbling.

Nessa, he wrote. *Slender, with dark curly hair. Due in the first week of the Moon of Dana. Located in Madam Mac Cába's establishment on Barrow's Way.*

He folded up the note without signing it. There was no need to elaborate more than that. The Wraiths never needed much information to get the job done.

***

Fionn's eyes flashed open once more.

"What's going on?" he muttered. It seemed much time had passed since he last woke. The writhing and moans around him had stopped, and the darkness that engulfed him had somehow grown even deeper.

He had seen the girl Nessa again, but this time, through the eyes of a healer named Cillian. Fionn strained to recall the details of the dream, or the vision, or whatever it was, when everything around him went dark once more.

A blue light shone.

***

Bronach Mac Cába burst into the girls' chambers. Fortunately, Nessa herself was the only one sleeping there tonight.

"Wake up," Bronach said, pulling the bedclothes off the girl. "You haven't much time."

Nessa looked up at Bronach with weary eyes.

"Madam Mac Cába, what's going on?"

Gods above and below, thought Bronach, striding across the room to fetch an overcoat and boots for the poor girl. *She really has no idea.*

"You need to leave," Bronach said. "There are men coming who want to hurt you. And hurt your baby."

"No!" cried Nessa. "Not my prince! I won't let them hurt him!"

"Good," said Bronach, throwing the overcoat over Nessa. *I won't let them take another one of my girls.*

"Listen to me," Bronach whispered. "There is a caravan leaving the city in an hour. I've spoken to the merchant, and he'll take you far away. Once you leave the capital, you'll be on your own. But safer than you are now."

Nessa nodded and stood.

A knock thundered through the building.

"Go!" rasped Bronach. "Through the window. The caravan will be at the North Wall. Go!"

Nessa scrambled over the empty beds towards the open window. Without looking back, she darted out, leaving Bronach alone.

She waited there, for a moment, silently praying that Nessa would somehow leave the city, and somehow find a safe place far from the reach of the Church.

The door to the private chambers creaked open behind her, but Bronach did not turn around.

"You're too late," she said over her shoulder. "She's long gone. You'll have to kill me twice before I tell you anything."

"That can be arranged," croaked a wicked voice. A hand reached out for Bronach's shoulder, pressing down hard and forcing her to turn. "The Lord is capable of far more than you can imagine."

The last thing Bronach saw was the Wraith's hooded figure, heavy dark robes revealing nothing but a twisted smile.

***

"Bronach... Nessa...." mused Fionn as he woke again. "Who are they?"

But before he could finish that thought, the pulsating blue light engulfed him once more.

***

On weary legs, Nessa stumbled across the road of a strange city. She had travelled through so many towns and slept in so many odd places she had long since lost count. The sky above roared with thunder as more rain pelted down upon her, but Nessa's stride did not slow.

I've come so far, she thought, a hand placed over a stomach almost as heavy as herself. *I'll keep you safe, little prince.*

Although the names of the places where she had travelled were lost to her, Nessa never stopped keeping track of the moon's turn. If the sky was not covered in thick storm-clouds, the Moon of Dana would be shining down on her.

It's almost time, she thought as she crossed a street so thick with rainwater it could have been mistaken as a river.

She stopped short once she saw what stood waiting for her across the way. The tall, slender figure stepped forward in silence, raising a single hand towards her.

"No!" Nessa cried. "You will not hurt him! He's mine. He's the king's. Your king's!"

"The child belongs to nobody but the Lord," said the Wraith, hissing each word through his teeth. "And the Lord has been looking for you for quite some time."

"My prince will be born soon," sobbed Nessa, taking a step towards the ghostly figure. "He'll grow to be a great leader, and he'll hang your kind from their toes!"

"No," muttered the Wraith. He reached into his cloak. "The bastard will never be born. He'll perish in a gutter along with his whore mother."

Before Nessa could react, the Wraith pulled a crossbow from under his robe. With a smooth manoeuvre, he fired a bolt that struck Nessa in the chest. She fell forward and landed with a splash in the rainwater.

No, she tried to say, but blood already filled her lungs. *Not my baby. Not my little prince.*

***

Alone and afraid, the young mage lay in his coffin made of flesh.

"I'll die here," thought Fionn, struggling to move. But once he shifted his body, he found he had more room than before. Although nothing but bloodied flesh surrounded him, something quickly became apparent. This was not the pit in the fields of Dromán.

This is from my old dream, Fionn realised. *Not the chasm Morrígan created, but this.*

He pushed at the walls, kicking with his feet. Indeed, the walls were not made from the bodies of the dead, but of flesh from something else.

He twisted where he lay and kicked again.

I will not die here, he thought. He punched and clawed against the walls over and over, not quite sure what he was hoping to achieve. Suddenly, a glimmer of light fell upon his body. He paid little mind to what the light illuminated, but instead kicked again and again. A small hole had opened somewhere below, letting more light enter the bloody chamber.

For what felt like the first time in his life, Fionn inhaled in a mouthful of air.

I'm almost out, he thought, kicking again and again, until there was a cool breeze upon his face.

***

Bláithín the White held her tongue as Brother Niall and Brother Dillon struggled to find the words to explain what had happened.

"We were walking out at night when we found her, dead in the streets, s-sir," stammered Niall. "We brought her back, and our healers said she had been gone for three days."

Arch-Mage Ferdia looked down expectantly at the two Brothers, then he turned to Bláithín. She nodded curtly, as if to confirm the brother's words, but nothing else.

It would be easier if I could just tell him straight, she thought.

"No, Niall," cut in Dillon. "You're leaving out the most important part. Arch-Mage, sir, the reason why we're bringing this to your attention so late at night is because the woman was with child."

"This I already know," said the Arch-Mage. "If there's more to tell, spit it out."

Spit it out, echoed Bláithín to herself, her white robes still covered in blood after all that had happened. Surely the Arch-Mage was expecting a far more gruesome account than Dillon and Niall were providing.

"The child," whispered Niall. "The child was...."

The brother's voice trailed off again. Never in her twelve years in service to the Academy of Dromán had Bláithín seen such overt cowardice.

Why is it that learned men experienced in the grisliest aspects of healing and medicine balk at the mere mention of the female reproductive system?

"Tell me," said the Arch-Mage. He leaned forward. "What happened?"

To hell with both of them.

"The child was already born," said Bláithín, stepping forward. The two Brothers looked back at her blankly, and the Arch-Mage's brow quivered with anger. Of course, she was breaking all sorts of rules of etiquette by speaking out of turn, but the way things were going, it would take these two fools all night to describe what happened. And she had many other patients to attend to.

"The child was already born," she repeated. "When they were both brought here, I pronounced the mother dead by three days, caused by a crossbow bolt to the lung. But the child's cord was still intact. It seemed he had been outside the womb for just a few hours when we found him."

"Impossible," said the Arch-Mage. "An unborn child cannot survive so long independent of its mother."

"But this one did," said Bláithín, hoping the others would catch on. They did not, so she continued. "For three days, the child lay awake in its mother's womb, before managing to force its own way out."

"Ridiculous!" The Arch-mage jumped to his feet. "What you say flies in the face of all we know about Human anatomy. How can this be?"

Bláithín gritted her teeth. *Fools. Must I spell it out to them?*

"By all rights, the foetus was never meant to survive the trauma of his mother's death," she said slowly, as if speaking to children. Once it was clear that the three understood this much, she went on. "But this child did not die. He did not die... when... he was... *supposed* to."

At last, a wave of understanding moved over the Arch-Mage's face.

"No..." he said. "Divine Penetrance. The Lord's gift."

"Exactly," said Bláithín, aware that neither of the two Brothers had reached the same conclusion as the Arch-Mage yet. "The child is alive and well in the clinic. The morticians are dealing with his mother's remains. What we are to do with the child is up to you, sir."

The Arch-mage paused, deep in concentration. He stroked his narrow grey beard, as if hoping those old hairs would hold the answer.

"Nobody else can know," he said finally. "The Wraiths of Seletoth have killed many to ensure no king can ever father a bastard. Right now, I fear for the child's safety, and indeed our own, if anyone else was to learn the truth."

"Understood," said Bláithín. "The Academy has taken in orphans before. It would not be unusual if we were to raise this one as our own."

"Yes," said the Arch-Mage. "It will be done. Now, return to your posts, everyone, and erase this meeting from your memories."

"Of course," thought Bláithín, as she turned to leave. She would be happy to forget this terrible night.

For the sake of this child, she hoped the others would forget too.

***

Something changed in the air around him, and Fionn's eyes blinked open. He strained to see, but all he could make out was light, dim lights of fires, from torches, perhaps.

"He's breathing!" cried a man's voice, laced with sobbing tears. This was a voice Fionn could remember, but from where? Not from the vision where he was Nessa, nor Bronach, nor Bláithín, but from before, when he was just Fionn. The accent he could place, from the Kingsland, possibly Cruachan. And when it spoke again, Fionn found that he could indeed put a name to it.

"Farris, I don't know how you do it," he said. "But you've proven me a fool twice in one day."

"I told you, the Lady showed me," said another voice. Simian, for sure. "She said he'd know what to do next."

"We'll let's hope he does," said the first voice. "For the sake of us all."

CHAPTER 11:
INCARNATE

The most disturbing case of madness at the hands of a Seeing comes from an account written by Garvan Hawkeye, Simian astronomer from Penance in AC376. Whereas once he spent his days mapping and charting the movements of the heavenly bodies for the sake of navigation, Garvan suddenly turned his attention to something less practical: what he called the 'voids of space' that lie between the stars. His clear and accurate accounts lost most of their scientific rigour. Sometime later, Garvan was found dead in his laboratory, which had become a dwelling of festering decay over the course of weeks of studying in solitude. Dehydration was pronounced to be the cause of his death, though his workspace had been well-stocked with food and water. Most troubling was what he had apparently spent his last days of life creating; a huge mural of stars and constellations that filled a once blank wall at the back of his laboratory. Although the representation of the firmament here was as accurate as any, a thick line of blood meandered through the stars, annotated with nonsensical characters of no known language.

Except from The Progress of Truth, a collection of accounts regarding the so-called Seeings of Seletoth, put together by an unknown author.

***

"No!" cried Fionn. He awoke with a jolt, like he had so many times before. This time, he no longer lay in darkness, among a mass of dead limbs, but in a bed. A bed of many blankets and quilts in a bright room. The aches in his body were gone, and fear had somehow left as well.

"Fionn! You're alive!"

The mage looked up to see Farris standing by the bed, next to Nicole, Aislinn Carríga, and Padraig Tuathil. All wore many layers of furs and coats. Farris rubbed his hands and held them to his face. Despite the warmth of his bed, Fionn felt a chill in the air.

We made it? said a familiar voice inside Fionn's head. With each word Sir Bearach uttered, some of Fionn's old strength return. *What happened?*

"Yes," said Fionn aloud. "What happened?"

"It was all Farris," said Nicole, beaming with pride. "After Morrígan decimated our forces, the Lady Meadhbh told Farris to find you. Once Morrígan was gone, he urged us all to return to the battlefield and start digging. The other survivors helped, and we gave the dead a proper burial. But you...."

"You were still alive," said Farris. "Unconscious but breathing. The camp's healers had no idea how you didn't die."

"Well," Fionn said, the contents of his dreams beginning to come together in his memory. "I think I have a vague idea why. But it'll take a lot of explaining."

Farris stepped forward. "Time, we don't have, but if you know something we don't, then you best start talking."

Fionn sighed. "I had a vision. I was multiple people and saw through their eyes. One of them was a woman. She was a whore who slept with King Diarmuid and bore his child."

"This is something that has happened many times before," said Farris. "The Crown was always quick to send the Wraiths out to deal with any potential royal bastards."

"But not this time," said Fionn. He closed his eyes tightly. "She came to Dromán, and... left the child with the Brothers here."

He paused for a moment, looking to Nicole, then to Aislinn, then to Farris. "It was me," Fionn whispered. "The Brothers of the Academy raised me to be a mage, never telling me who I really was."

The room fell to silence. Aislinn continued to stare at the ground, head bowed, while Nicole seemed to struggle to find the right words.

"Where did these visions come from?" she said.

"Between each one, all I saw was blue light. Like from back at the Temple of the Lady."

"Yes," said Farris. "I too have seen visions from Her, and they also came with blue light."

"And where is the Lady now?" asked Fionn.

"Morrígan killed her," said Nicole, barely a whisper. "The Godslayer claimed the Lady's power as her own, just as predicted."

"Yes," said Farris. "And the Lady also knew you would survive. She knew you would not die... because you cannot."

"No," said Fionn. "You mean Divine Penetrance? It can't be."

Nicole placed a hand on Fionn's shoulder. "You were out there for two full days before we found you. Nobody else made it."

"But I can't be... I can't be *immortal?*"

It's true, lad, said Sir Bearach. *Think about it.*

As if the memory was fresh, Fionn recalled the troll that came from the Glenn, tearing his arm from his socket. Even the healer who tended to his wounds had said it. *'It's a miracle you're still alive.'*

"But we've more pressing matters," Farris said. "The Lady said you would know what do to next."

Fionn shrugged. "Even if I am the son of King Diarmuid, She was wrong on that other matter. I've no idea."

Farris swore abruptly. "Look outside, lad!" he roared. "Our army is a tenth of what we came here with, and those that survived are barely capable of marching. And then there's the snow. We need answers now more than ever!"

"Snow?" said Fionn, leaning forward. He craned his neck to look out the window. Indeed, the snow covered the spires and towers of the Academy, like mountain peaks in winter.

But far more unsettling than this was the sea, Móráin Sea, now nothing more than a huge sheet of ice extending out to the horizon.

"No," muttered the mage. "We seldom see anything more than hail out here, this time of year. Did Morrígan do this?"

"We don't know," said Nicole, rubbing the back of her neck. "We don't know anything right now. Did Meadhbh give you any clue, anything at all, about how we are supposed to proceed?"

Slowly, Fionn sat upright. He flexed his over-sized hand, grimacing with each movement.

"She told me nothing more," he said. "Her visions just showed me that the king is my father, and that means I can't be killed."

Fionn's eyes went wide. "That's it. We failed to protect Meadhbh from Morrígan and lost so may lives in the process. We're in no position to protect Seletoth from the same fate... but perhaps I can. Perhaps I can protect Him. By myself."

"No, lad," said Padraig. "To climb Mount Selyth alone is suicide!"

Farris scoffed. "Skies above, Tuathil, haven't you been listening?"

"Farris is right," said Fionn, smiling despite it all. "I'd have to make the journey alone. Morrígan needs to be stopped, but we can't risk any more lives in doing so."

"But how do you mean to protect Seletoth?" asked Nicole. "Surely you can't fight Morrígan by yourself."

Fionn flexed the fingers in his oversized arm. "I know… but it's the only hope we've got."

That's right, said Bearach. *And you won't be alone, as long as I'm here.*

***

The grounds of the Academy of Dromán had once been meticulously well-kept, with neatly trimmed lawns and hedges surrounding the old castle. Facing Móráin Sea, the walls of the easternmost wing formed a wide circle. Within this, neat winding paths of stone spiralled through the lawns, serving no purpose other than aesthetics. Though once a serene escape from studies for the students of the Academy, now many of the stones lay upturned, with the wildflowers along the perimeter dying in this new, frightening frost.

Farris stepped through the courtyard, the frozen grass crackling with each step. He wore a heavy rabbit-fur cloak procured from the Academy's stores. Winter-wear had become a sought-after commodity since the host settled in the Academy, and although the cloak fitted Farris terribly, and the fur of a dozen or so rabbits scratched irritably against his own, he was fortunate to have some protection from the frost.

Most of what the survivors of the outpost could take with them was scattered about here, sacks of grain, barrels of drinking water among them. Nicole had led an expedition back to the camp to see what they could recover. They salvaged many weapons and armour, and some tents to store them, which were presently being set up in the centre of the courtyard. The Reapers, unfortunately, were not recovered. Although designed to withstand any attempt to be manipulated by Human magic, Nicole had found them crushed under rocks pulled from the ground.

We can be fortunate that they weren't being piloted at the time, thought Farris. Logically, he knew this was where his focus should be, on those that were still alive, on the number of people he had managed to save. But no matter how much he tried, his mind drifted elsewhere.

The fires that burned through the sky. The ground that swallowed up the Triad's army. The family in Point Grey, fighting for their home....

As he walked, one footstep made a crack more audible than the others, and Farris paused. Beneath his heavy boot lay the broken stem of a rose, its thorns glistening with frost.

He stooped down to pick up the flower. Through heavy fur gloves, he barely felt it between his fingers.

Where have all the flowers gone?

"Farris," came a voice from across the courtyard. He turned to see Nicole, having returned from another expedition to the outpost. Farris had been asked to join these excursions, of course. He was no stranger to riding with the light cavalry, and for a time before, he had even enjoyed it. But now, he always managed to find an excuse, either the quartermaster needed help with supplies, or the medics needed help with the injured. These he aided, for a time, but these past three days, he just wanted to be alone.

"How's our patient?" she asked, dismounting from the great beast. The elk put its head to the ground, searching through the frosty stone for something to graze on.

"He's good," said Farris. "He's out of bed since the morning now and doesn't show any sign he'll be back in it any time soon."

"He truly is his father's son," said Nicole. Something about her words just felt... warm in Farris's ears. Not so long ago, he seemed the only Simian who believed in the king's Divine Penetrance. Now, to hear someone as learned and respected as Nicole making such an off-handed comment that supported its existence made Farris's heart soar.

"Well, he's been in the library for the past six hours straight," said Farris. "That much, he must have gotten from his mother."

Nicole laughed, and suddenly Farris deeply regretted not joining her on the skirmish.

"Has he mentioned," Nicole's voice dropped to a whisper. "Him wanting to go to Mount Selyth and all?"

Farris shook his head.

Nicole stole a quick glance at the other scouts behind her; they tended to their mounts. "We checked the outpost's interior, this time. The Lady's Tomb was destroyed, the ceiling collapsed on itself. But the railway tunnel is still intact."

Farris laughed. "You're saying your father had a better understanding of structural engineering than the gods?"

Nicole smiled, leaning in. "What I'm saying is we can go home, Farris. Rather than trek through the ice and the snow, we can travel through the tunnel all the way back to Penance in a fraction of the time. We're spreading the word now and preparing everything we need to leave in the morning."

"Home?" said Farris. "But we can't. Morrigan is—"

"You heard Fionn. Morrigan is no longer a problem we can resolve," said Nicole. "The Lady is dead. This war is lost."

"But... Meadhbh said that Morrigan will destroy Seletoth and put an end to the Age of Life."

"I know," said Nicole. She closed her eyes. "And it pains me to admit that now, we're at her mercy. If we try and stop her, she'll just kill us sooner."

Farris took as step back. "So, you don't want to even try?"

"I know this is hard to hear," said Nicole. "But we just found out that Fionn cannot be killed. If he wants to climb Seletoth's mountain, why would we risk our lives going with him." She gestured to the rest of the camp. "These people have experienced so much pain, Farris. They want to see their families one last time before the world falls apart."

She took Farris's hand into her own. "We should join them. This war is no longer one we can win. It may not even be one anyone can win."

Farris considered her words for a time. For how long, he was unsure, for with his hand in hers, the world around them seemed to stop.

Can we just give up like this? He had never admitted defeat like this before. Known it, he had, many times before. But to concede a victory, no matter how slim, just wasn't something Farris Silvertongue did.

Things are different now, he thought, looking into Nicole's deep, shining eyes. *If I had given up sooner, maybe the family in Point Grey would still be alive. Maybe the soldiers of the Triad could have died in their lover's arms, rather than buried under a battlefield by a mad god.*

"And what about Fionn?" said Farris. "Do you think he's prepared to make the journey alone?"

"You'll have to ask him," said Nicole. Tears were in her eyes now.

Farris nodded and reluctantly turned away.

It's his fight now. And skies above, he better be ready for it.

***

Through a meandering labyrinth of shelves and bookcases, Fionn wandered, a Pyromancer's torch clenched in his hand. Although the fire between his fingers burned brightly, mist still escaped his mouth with each breath.

The brothers would skin me if they saw me with an open flame here, he thought, scanning the hundreds of leather-bound spines presenting themselves along the shelves.

Do you still not know what you're looking for? asked Sir Bearach. If Fionn didn't know any better, he could have sworn the knight spoke through chattering teeth in the cold.

I already found it, replied Fionn, reaching up to take a particularly large tome from a high shelf. Although the library's skylights were thickly crusted with snow, enough light shone down upon the book's cover to reveal the title: *The Progress of Truth.*

Fionn sat where he stood in the middle of the aisle and pulled open the cover. Inside, chaotic scribblings filled the pages, with only the occasional printed text in margins being legible.

I spent a lot of time here when I was younger, Fionn said, licking a finger as he leafed through the pages. *I've read every book here at least once, even if I didn't understand most of them.* Once he reached the centre page, he stopped. A messy cloud of wild scrawls covered the centre between two pages, with circular shapes like eyes dotted around the outside. In the margin, a footnote read, 'Replicated from the logbook of the Simian astronomer Garvan Hawkeye.'

But even though I never understood this book, I always came back to it. Just to look at the pictures.

What's it about? asked Sir Bearach

People, replied Fionn. *Humans and Simians who claimed to have had Seeings from Seletoth. Garvan Hawkeye was the first Simian who claimed to have had contact with the Lord. An atheist and a scientist too, right beforehand.*

Fionn continued through the book. Its author had spent many pages and paragraphs interpreting each of the wild ramblings of those who had had contact with Seletoth. And at the centre of each conjecture was a reference to the Truth.

Is the Truth about me? wondered Fionn, flicking past a stirring illustration of a green valley flooding with blood. *That I'm the last heir of Seletoth?*

Perhaps not, said Sir Bearach. *Didn't the Lady say that the Church was established hundreds of years ago to hide it? Making the Truth far older than you.*

Fionn frowned. They knew far too little so far. If anyone would know, it would be Him. The Lord.

My... ancestor?

"Fionn?" came a voice from down the aisle. "Are you alone?"

"No—I mean... yes," said Fionn, standing to face Farris. The Simian had done a spectacular job of making himself unheard, although his frame was almost too large to weave through all those shelved books.

Wasn't he a thief before? asked Sir Bearach.

"What brings you here?" asked Fionn instead, shaking his head to drown out the knight's words. "Shouldn't you be with the others?"

"I should," said Farris. "The soldiers are making their preparations to return to Penance, but many are reluctant to leave. To leave this quest unfinished, after so many have died, isn't sitting well with many of them."

"I don't blame them. We all left Penance thinking we'd end this, but it looks like we've only made things worse."

"And you... are you still planning on going on this trek to Mount Selyth?"

"You came to convince me not to go?" Fionn smirked. "You can't claim it's too dangerous for me."

"I suppose I can't. Tell me, how does it feel, to be a living god?"

"If you came here to mock me, you can leave," said Fionn, slamming the book closed.

"No," said Farris. "I'm serious. I mean, did you ever, suspect it? Before being buried alive and surviving and all that. Did you ever feel... special?"

Fionn paused for a moment. "No. I felt different from the other students in the Academy, sure, but that was mainly because I had a different upbringing to them. I assumed I was so adept with magic because I grew up here, surrounded by books and scrolls detailing the arcane arts. And as for narrowly avoiding death so often, I just assumed that I was lucky."

"Most do," said Farris. "I once knew a Simian who thought he was lucky. Turned out that he—"

"Was there anything else?" asked Fionn, opening the book once more.

"The others are worried about you." Farris's voice was sterner now. "Anyone else would collapse under the weight of what's been thrust upon your back. You need to speak to the rest of the camp. And tell them that you have everything under control."

"Under control?" said Fionn. "How can you say that everything's under control after all that's happened?"

"I never said you would tell them the truth," replied Farris. "Let me tell you something about leadership. Once a group, any kind of group, has a leader at its head, the burden of responsibility is lifted from the many, and rests with the one. Plackart played this role well. In truth, he knew little of the ways of magic or the nature of our enemy, though he was a good leader regardless. But with him gone, the responsibility he held has spread throughout the camp. And unlike other burdens, when responsibility is shared too thin it festers into helplessness. Right now, there's all sorts of rumours spreading about what happened to Meadhbh. And what happened to you. The soldiers need to know, Fionn. They need to know that there's some hope yet of overcoming all this."

"You really think there's hope? After all that's happened?"

"Of course," said Farris. He stood a little taller on saying this. "When King Diarmuid first met the Lady, She said we were all doomed to our destinies. But when She saw us, and we were still alive, She said there was hope. Even though She knew well that Morrígan would strike Her down, the Lady still believed not all was lost. She said that you would survive, which you did—and that you'd know what to do next, which you do. When we all start the march back to Penance, it'll make everyone happier knowing that at least someone knows what must be done. And the responsibility of this war will be left with you and your journey to Mount Selyth, leaving everyone else free to return to their homes."

"I don't know, Farris," said Fionn. "I know only as much as you do with all this. Me travelling to Mount Selyth is nothing more than... a lucky guess. I don't think I can pretend it's anything more than that."

The Simian raised a finger and smiled. "Ah, you have a lot to learn about lying, lad. Never let others know how much you know, and always let on that you know much more than that. People will be happy to fill in the gaps themselves. Even if you think it'll make no difference, and we'll all die horrible deaths at the hands of some psychotic demi-god, what harm would it be to tell the others that everything will be okay until then?"

"I don't know. It just feels... wrong to say that."

"It wouldn't be *wrong*. It'd just be *incorrect*." Farris smiled. "I'll give you some time to think on it." He turned to leave. In the waning light of the frosty dusk outside, Farris's figure disappeared into the shadows.

Maybe he has a point, said Sir Bearach. *Is there any harm in lying to those that shouldn't know the truth?*

Perhaps, thought Fionn. *He could have a point. What harm is there in lying, if there's a greater good to come from it?*

*****

Throughout the rest of the day, news spread that the young Pyromaster was planning on addressing the camp. Although the soldiers of the Triad and the Churchguard were all stationed throughout the old castle, the message had no problem reaching every inch of the Academy grounds. Known to some as Fionn, to others as simply the Last Battlemage, this young man suddenly filled the role of a leader of sorts for an army desperately in need of one. And there were other rumours too—that he had been buried for two days in the pit that opened beneath the battlefield and lived to tell the tale.

By nightfall, dozens of men and women filled the Academy courtyard. Farris stood to the front, and constantly turned back to gauge who else was there. The Carriga woman stood behind Farris. Despite all that had happened, her steel-plate still shone. Even though the last day of everyone's lives lay just around the corner, she had taken the time to clean her armour. Farris wasn't quite sure how to take this.

Next to her was Padraig Tuathil. He avoided Farris's gaze, standing straight and tall.

I saved his life many times over, realised Farris. *The least he could do is thank me.*

"What do you think he'll say," whispered Nicole, over Farris's shoulder. "Did you talk to him?"

"We'll see," said Farris, eyeing Fionn as the young lad paced up and down ahead of them. "Soon enough, I hope."

Abruptly, the mage stopped. He turned to the crowd and narrowed his eyes. His lips moved silently, but what words they formed, Farris could only guess.

"My name is Fionn," he announced. All went still on hearing this. "I never had a second name. I was brought up in this very castle as an orphan, training to be a mage while never knowing where I came from."

He paused, and locked eyes with Farris.

"But now I know," Fionn continued. He looked up at the crowd. "Now I know that King Diarmuid, Third and Nineteenth, was my father."

A ripple of excitement tore through the army, but the mage didn't give them a chance to consider the implication of this revelation themselves.

"The blood of Seletoth runs through my veins, as does His holy power. Power that Morrigan seeks. Power that drove her to taking everything away from us. The Lady Meadhbh showed me this truth before She died, and She showed me what we must do next to win this war. I must travel to Mount Selyth alone and protect the Lord Himself."

Gasps sprang up throughout Fionn's audience, and some of the joy and excitement vanished from the atmosphere.

"Madness," muttered one voice. "There's nothing but death there."

"And what are we do to?" shouted another voice. "Can we go home?"

In response to this question, all went silent.

"Yes," said Fionn. He paused, and his eyes met Farris's. "This is a journey for me to make, alone. I will not endanger any more lives. For this is my fight, and no one else's."

An excited murmur resounded through the courtyard. Farris felt something warm grab his hand. He turned to see

Nicole, beaming back at him. Farris smiled back, wrapping his fingers tightly between hers.

It's over. We can go home. To be together while Fionn makes one last attempt to put an end to all this.

"You will not travel alone!" cried a voice. Padraig Tuathil stepped forward. He unsheathed his sword, fell to one knee, and raised the blade up towards the mage.

"I failed to protect your father, but I will not let you down. I put my life from the late king's hands into yours. You will not make the journey west alone. I pledge my life to yours, King Fionn the First, Twentieth Incarnate of Seletoth."

The crowd stood in shocked silence. Fionn too, didn't seem to know how to respond, his eyes wide, his mouth wide with shock.

Padraig fucking Tuathil! That spineless coward? What does he seek to gain from this?

"King Fionn, First and Twentieth!" came another voice. Lady Aislinn Carriga stepped forward. She too unsheathed her sword and lay it before Fionn. "The Godslayer destroyed all that is dear to me. I have no home left to return to. My Liege, this sword is yours as long as I'm alive to wield it."

"Don't they understand?" whispered Farris. "He *wants* to go alone. Do they think Divine Penetrance will protect them too?"

"Fools," replied Nicole. "Their allegiance to their dead king has blinded them. If they want to throw their lives away, let them."

Farris couldn't help but agree. If they wanted to trek across this desolate land, they were welcome to. It was none of Farris's business.

No. It is my fault. I manipulated him into instilling confidence in the others. I didn't expect him to instil enough to make them want to go with him.

Both Aislinn and the Padraig had seen the true extent of Morrigan's power first-hand. They were not naive to what lay ahead of them. But they were naive in their own, Human way.

Honour. An absurd Human notion of doing something foolish in the name of something that doesn't exist. Farris had seen honour claim the lives of many men, from those who threw away their lives on the battlefield for a king that didn't care, to those who chose imprisonment over denouncing an allegiance. Sure, Farris had always been loyal to the Silverback. But he happily denounced his name many times while working for the Crown. Some Humans would have a great deal of trouble doing the same.

But is this the same? Is it honour that drives Padraig and Aislinn to their knees? Or something else?

Farris closed his eyes. *Perhaps they just want to fight. Perhaps they just don't want to give up so easily.*

He turned to look at Nicole. As if sensing something was amiss, she squeezed his hand tighter. Farris's chest was suddenly hollow. His breathing turned short.

Everything that I could have wanted is home in Penance. We could live out the rest of our lives together, without fear. Without pain. We could finally be... happy.

Farris let go of Nicole's hand. And stepped forward.

But what joy can there be, in a life lived in hiding? At the mercy of someone to come and take it away?

For once, Farris did not have to choose between what was right, and what must be done. Here, there was one option that satisfied both.

"I'll come too," he said, loud so all could hear him. "I'll see you safely to Mount Selyth, King Fionn, even if it kills me."

Fionn nodded in response, still clearly in shock. Aislinn turned to face Farris, sorrow and dread upon her features. Padraig turned too, though his expression gave away little of his emotions.

But Farris dared not turn back to see Nicole's reaction.

***

That night, Farris lay in bed. The struggle to sleep was a battle all too familiar. Often before an important day, he would spend many hours awake, worrying about it. Then upon realising that the night was growing deeper with him still awake, he would start worrying about not getting enough sleep instead, which would deter him from sleeping all the more.

This night, he was on the cusp of this transition, slowly growing frustrated with his lack of slumber.

It might be my last night in a comfortable bed, he realised. This, of course, caused his heartbeat to increase, pulling him even further from sleep.

Before retiring for the night, he, Fionn, Padraig, and Aislinn had briefly discussed the journey they were to embark on. It would take four days, all going well. They would travel north at first light in the morning, reaching Hunter's Den by nightfall. From here, they'd cross the Godspine, which Padraig reckoned would take most of a day, allowing them to rest at Ardh Sidhe. From here, they'd head south across the Midlands, to Rosca Umhir. This would leave them with one more night's rest before spending another day climbing Mount Selyth.

He hadn't spoken to Nicole, who had been helping the rest of the army with their preparations to return home. Her journey would be far more straightforward, fortunately. Some estimated they would all be home in Penance by overmorrow.

Farris turned in his bed. The Academy had housed a thousand or so students in the past, and about a hundred teachers, mentors, and staff. There had been plenty of dormitory rooms for the students to sleep in, and a handful of private bedrooms for the staff. Upon arriving, Farris had taken the initiative to claim one of the latter for himself, before anyone else could. This one belonged to someone called Brother Dillon the White. Both a healer of the Academy and a druid of the church, Farris reckoned, based on the name. Other than this, Dillon seemed a rather plain, simple fellow, with very few of his own furnishings or personal items. Beside the door was a large stack of parchments, detailing the ailments and illnesses of his patients. These made for some rather droll reading material.

Farris sat upright. Perhaps reading through some medical histories of dead Humans was just what Farris needed to fall asleep. He lit an oil lamp beside his bed and walked across the room.

He approached the writing desk just as a loud knock thundered upon the door.

As he opened it, he knew well who would be standing on the other side.

"Good evening, Farris," said Nicole. "Sorry to disturb you. May I come in?"

"Sure," Farris said, so excited to see her he struggled to get the words out.

She stepped through the threshold, and Farris closed the door, gently. Once it clicked shut, she whipped around to face him.

"What the *fuck* is wrong with you?" she hissed. "After all we talked about, after all you promised me, you just turn around and throw your life away, for Diarmuid's bastard son?"

She was visibly shaking now. Farris raised his hands in submission, with the words 'calm down' upon his lips. He opted for another strategy, however.

"He's just a young lad, Nicole. He's frightened of all of this, just as much as we are."

"How does that concern us? How does this concern you?"

"It doesn't," said Farris, "But it's the right thing to do, Nicole. We can't let him go alone."

"You're right about that. But he's not travelling alone now, is he? Padraig and Aislinn already volunteered to go."

"And I had to, too." Farris sighed. "I don't know why. I... I can't explain it."

"By Sin's Stones, Farris, you better try."

"This... this is bigger than me. Bigger than us. I fought alongside Argyll for so long, for a cause I truly believed in. And I still believe in that fight. But this one is even bigger, Nicole. You have to understand."

She snorted. "Oh, I understand very well. You've spent too much time living among Humans. Their warped sense of duty, honour, whatever they want to call it, has rubbed off on you."

"Now that's not very fair. I've no love for the Crown."

Nicole gestured towards the door. "You just announced your allegiance to the Crown, in front of everyone! You're choosing to put your life on the line for the immortal bastard of the man you conspired to murder!"

"Don't say that."

"The world we knew is gone, Farris. Who cares who you may or may not have poisoned in the old world?"

"Not that," said Farris. "You call Fionn a bastard, as if it's an insult. But Simians don't marry, so doesn't that make us all bastards too?"

"No." Nicole folded her arms. "It's a Human term, you know that. They'd see his birth as a symbol of Diarmuid's lust."

"Perhaps they would have," said Farris. "But tonight, they saw him as something else. A chance to end all of this. If there's a chance, even a tiny one, that we can defeat Morrigan, I'll take it. I'll swear allegiance to any king, Arch-Canon, or god if it means we end this war."

"And what if there's no chance," said Nicole. "Would you still fight then?"

"Yes," said Farris.

"Then you are a fool, Farris Silvertongue. I have nothing more to say to you."

She went to leave. Before she could, Farris said, "Garth. Garth would have done the same."

Nicole turned. Her brow was narrowed. She bared her fangs. "Don't you *dare* put words into the mouth of the dead. You have no way of knowing what he would have done."

"I do," whispered Farris. "He did as much back in Saltworks. He sacrificed himself to let us escape."

Nicole didn't respond to this. Knowing he had hit a nerve, Farris pressed on.

"Do you remember what his last words were. He told me to protect the king, no matter the cost. In his last moments, he knew what really mattered the most. I failed him. But now... now I have a chance to make up for it."

"Then go," Nicole whispered, still facing away. "And you better get some rest first."

As she left, Farris closed the door and returned to bed. But he did not heed Nicole's advice. Instead, he lay awake staring at the ceiling for hours into the night, until the sun's light filled the room.

CHAPTER 12:
HUNTER'S DEN

Today, I went against all my own self-interests and agreed to travel to Mount Selyth with Firemaster Fionn. No, King Fionn, First of His Name, and Twentieth Incarnate of Seletoth. I failed to save his father when the Silverback opened his throat. Furthermore, I betrayed him in my duties as captain of the City Guard, letting myself become seduced by corruption.

Everything I did then, I did for Aideen and our unborn child. But I never should have put my own love for her above my duty to the king. If not for my failures there, we perhaps would have had Farris in chains instead of an agent of the Crown.

But the Simian continues to surprise me. He too agreed to travel to Mount Selyth with us, despite him having little love for the memory of King Diarmuid. If he plans to betray Fionn, he'll find his blood upon my sword.

No, it is unfair of me to make such conjecture. Farris led the charge to dig up the dead, and despite our protests at the time, we *did find Fionn, alive and breathing, when all reason dictates he should have died with the rest of those who were engulfed by the earth.*

Furthermore, if not for Farris Turncloak, I would have been buried there too.

Journal of Padraig Tuathil, 20th Day under the Moon of Nes, AC404

***

Hundreds of soldiers flooded the Academy Courtyard the following morning, making their final preparations for the journey home. Amidst cries of commands from their lieutenants, Humans and Simians worked in sorting the remaining arms and armour, separating those they'd leave behind from those worth taking. Others rolled barrels of provisions across the courtyard and loaded them onto wooden carriages. Even the horses and elk tied up by the ruined castle gates seemed to share the same resigned relief that lay upon the soldiers, as thick as the snow that fell upon them.

Fionn shivered as he pulled his cloak tighter across his chest. Most of his own preparations had already been made, for he had very little to bring.

You'll need armour, said Sir Bearach. *Just because you can't die, doesn't mean you can't be rendered incapacity by a punctured lung.*

The knight had a point, but Fionn preferred to see those more suspectable to death protected from it before he was. Across the courtyard, Padraig, Aislinn, and Farris tended to their mounts: horses for the Humans and an elk for the Simian.

"Your Grace," said Padraig, approaching. "We are almost finished our preparations for the long journey ahead."

"Good," said Fionn. "But please. My blood may be blue, but I am no king. With no crown nor coronation, I deserve not titles or honours. Just call me Fionn."

"Yes, my... Fionn."

They prepared their mounts, and ensured their sacks and satchels were well-fastened and full. Fionn was no stranger to riding, but he had never made a journey this long. He looked to the others. Aislinn, he knew, had ran half the length of Alabach to escape the horde, but had she made a journey like this before? Padraig certainly held an air of authority in the planning and preparation of their route, but perhaps this was just a symptom of the type of leadership Farris had described back in the library.

As for Farris himself, Fionn could not figure him out. So strange, that he too was the Simian named Chester he had travelled across the Glenn with. Even then, he had seemed so comfortable with everything that was happening. Perhaps there was more Fionn could learn from him in that regard.

"Firemaster Fionn," came a voice. He turned to see a Simian, mounted upon an elk. They came pulling a cart filled with weapons and armour, both of which were made from blue-tinted steel. The Simian also wore such armour, with thick slabs of plate and a large, cube-shaped helm over their head, with only a thin slit across the front to see through.

This she removed, revealing herself to be Nicole.

"These here are weapons and armour made from Simian steel," she said. "The Godslayer will be unable to bend and twist this steel, but they won't stop the ground from opening up beneath you."

The others thanked her and dismounted to pick through the contents of the cart.

"Farris," said Nicole, rather curtly. "There is also a full set of armour in there that should fit you well."

"Oh, thanks," said Farris, examining one of the firearms up close. "That is... very kind of you."

What is with those two, said Sir Bearach. *Aren't they lovers?*

Fionn ignored the words of the dead knight, waiting until the others had taken what they needed before finding himself a chest-plate that fitted well enough beneath his cloak. It was clear these were all designed with Simian bodies in mind, giving the Humans few options.

"And you," said Padraig. "Are you not a little overdressed for your journey back to Penance?"

"No," said Nicole. She looked to Fionn. "Firemaster, I wish to join you on your journey to Mount Selyth."

"Oh," said Fionn. He was on good terms with the Simian, but surely that wasn't enough to compel her to come on this terrible journey. If she had another motive, Fionn knew nothing of it. Fionn looked at Farris, but he seemed even more confused than the rest of them.

"Your company is most welcome," Fionn said. She donned her helm once more, and once the rest were ready, they made their way towards the Academy's gate with the rest.

***

The army of the Triad all left together, some mounted, many on foot, marching through the icy path of the Hazelwood. All around them, the forest's trees were heavy with sheets of snow. Together, the great host followed the path westwards, which eventually rose to a hill, and came to a fork: one path to the north, another to the south.

The bulk of the host took the path south towards Dromán, where they'd soon come to the great clearing surrounding the outpost, and the railway tunnel that lay beneath. On the other hand, Farris, Nicole, Padraig, Aislinn, and Fionn took the north road, deeper into the Hazelwood. Many of the others stopped their own march to see them off, but there was no fanfare. No celebration. Just scared faces watching the five individuals break away from the host, in silence, until their path took a sharp turn westwards, out of sight. Then they were alone.

From there, they travelled on without speaking much to one another, the only audible sound being the snow-encrusted stones that crunched beneath them. Fionn felt his lips beginning to crack and freeze, cold air passing over them with each breath.

"Hunter's Den awaits us at the end of the day," said Padraig, as if sensing Fionn's discomfort. "It's an odd settlement, starting off as an inn to house hunters of the Hazelwood. Hunting is thirsty work, so the inn built a great tavern to satiate them. But the inn and tavern were remote, deep inside a thick forest, so housing was built for the staff to live in. Since living out there required other services and commodities, it slowly grew into a town."

"Peculiar," said Fionn. Despite its proximity to the Academy, Fionn knew little about it and the surrounding areas. He had only travelled to Dromán's marketplace a handful of times in his youth. The furthest he travelled was to Cruachan, where he boarded *The Glory of Penance*. Before everything changed.

"A shame," cut in Aislinn, riding on the opposite side of Padraig. "Such work went into building that town, only to fall to the horde."

"Do you think nobody survived?" said Fionn.

"No," said Farris, riding ahead. He glanced over his shoulder. "We found Point Grey in ruins. With no survivors. With the horde only growing in size since that was taken, we can assume the same for everywhere else."

This did make sense, though Fionn wished it weren't true.

Snow began to fall as they ventured deeper into the Hazelwood. The great conifers swayed dramatically in the winds that beat against their branches. Fionn, Aislinn, and Padraig struggled to brace against the coming storm, raising a forearm of their heads to keep their eyes clear. Farris and Nicole rode on with little hassle, it seemed, with their thick Simian-made helms keeping the snow off their faces.

Sometime later, they rested at a river. The mounts grazed on what sparse vegetation was available to them. Unfortunately, the river's water was frozen solid, depriving them a chance to refill their flasks. That was until Padraig had the idea to crack the ice with the flat side of his longsword. After three heavy strikes, cracks formed upon the surface, revealing flowing water underneath. With much cause for celebration, the travellers refilled their waterskins, before allowing their mounts a chance to drink from it.

With little time to give for resting, they set off again. The path continued to carry them northwards. As they went, Fionn noticed that here and there, just off the path, some smaller brushes and trees were bent and broken.

Perhaps the horde came this way, suggested Sir Bearach. *They would certainly struggle to stay on this path.*

Fionn nodded, caring not that the others might see this as odd. If one of Morrígan's early goals was to take the Academy, and claim the power of all the mages within, it would make sense that she came this way.

He considered Aislinn. She had come to Penance fleeing from the horde at Rosca Umhír. If the horde left Roseán, then travelling east to take Point Grey and Ongar before heading south towards the Academy and Dromán, then when did they come across Rosca Umhír before marching on

Cruachan? The only explanation was that they crossed the Godspine at one point, perhaps after taking the Academy.

She wanted to be sure, Fionn realised. *She wanted her horde to be as large as possible before laying siege upon Cruachan.*

And if that was her plan, this only left one possibility.

Everyone south of the Glenn is dead. His imagination strained to consider the number of lives this would entail.

Thousands upon thousands upon thousands.

A truly uncountable number, and to think that behind each increment, there was an entire life. An entire person, with their own likes and dislikes, their own hopes and fears. Their own plans for the future, for their later years, for their children, all snuffed out like a candle in a storm.

And to what end? What does she even want?

The Lady had said Morrigan would see a glimpse of the Truth, and it would drive her to madness. But what set her on this path in the first place? Surely it must have been more than just a lust for power?

What does it matter, said Sir Bearach. *Can't we just defeat her without understanding her motive.*

That is true, said Fionn. *But if we do, how do we prevent something like this from happening again?*

The knight had no response to this. Fionn understood. To think that something as horrible as this was not only unstoppable, but *repeatable* even if they did... it was an unsettling thought.

***

This certainly wasn't built for comfort, thought Farris, squinting through the thin slit of his helm. It frustrated him how he had to move his entire head to see what was to his left and to his right. But perhaps the discomfort was worth it. Between this armour, the pair of daggers held at his waist, and the short sword across the small of his back, he felt almost as invincible as he would have been had he too been born from King Diarmuid's loins.

He threw a glance towards Nicole, still wondering why she came. Perhaps she had listened to what he had said the previous night. Or perhaps she was making some sort of strange point in coming. Either way, he felt partially responsible for her presence.

No. If she didn't want to come, she wouldn't have come. She's made that much clear before.

Soon, a settlement became visible through the trees of the Hazelwood. There was one building, circular in shape, with walls of thick, timber logs and a heavily thatched roof. Snow lay in a delicate layer atop the building, like the icing of a cake.

Other structures came into view as they approached. Their architecture was similar, built in an almost-perfect circle around the first.

As they entered the settlement, Farris called out, "Hello! Is there anyone here?"

Though a quick scan of the settlement's skyline told Farris that it was indeed uninhabited, as with the temperature being what it was, surely there would be a fire burning somewhere nearby if not.

They dismounted their horses in front of the main building, which held the letters *Hunter's Den* above the door. It was unusual, for an inn to claim the title of an entire settlement. True enough to what Padraig had said earlier, this place was certainly built with hunters in mind, as stables with ample space were available to house their mounts.

Evening was starting to set in. It had crept up on the party over these past few hours. Without being able to follow the path of the sun behind the blanket of thick, grey clouds overhead, Farris found it hard to keep track of the passage of time.

"Does anyone want a drink?" said Farris, approaching the front door of the inn. "I doubt the horde would have taken the ale here with them."

He pushed open the double doors of the inn, revealing the most splendid of sights. He stood before a huge, circular chamber. Long, wooden tables curved with the shape of the room, with cushioned chairs on the inside, and cushioned stools on the outside. In the centre, several taller tables stood, high stools reaching up to meet them.

But one thing caught Farris's attention more than all this. Against the far wall was a bar of black slate. Behind it, shelves held ceramic and glass bottles of various shapes and sizes, each with paper labels.

"They've thainol!" called Farris, as the others came in. "I didn't think we'd find any this far from Penance or Cruachan."

The others walked through the tavern with wonder. Hunting trophies of stags, boars and beadhbhs hung on the wall, some stuffed and mounted, others bearing only their bones.

"I could do with a drink," said Padraig. "Given all that's happened."

"Are you sure that's a good idea?" said Aislinn. "We have many miles to travel in the morning."

"And we'll travel them all the same," he replied. "If anything, it'll help us sleep through this blasted cold." He looked to Fionn, then towards an empty fireplace against another wall of the tavern. "Firemaster, your talents are required."

Fionn smiled, and quickly went to work. Well, it wasn't what one could exactly call 'work,' since he set the hearth ablaze in a matter of seconds. Farris perused the bottles of thainol, pulling down one that was equal parts rare and expensive. Better to enjoy it here, he reckoned, than let it go to waste.

Padraig held a cup under one of the beer taps, but nothing was produced upon turning it on. He frowned and tried again.

"The line might need tending to," said Farris. "They often keep barrels in the basement, but I'm not well versed in how the pumps work."

He poured a second glass of thainol and passed it to Padraig. "Maybe this will do instead."

Padraig considered the glass for a moment. "The last time I was offered thainol, the horde was laying siege on the Grey Keep. It's not a memory I'd like to recall."

Farris pushed the glass closer. "Then see this as an opportunity to associate the taste with the end of the world instead."

Padraig smiled and took the glass in his hands.

"If you say so," he said. "But I'll drink this one slowly."

The rest gathered around the fire. Nicole and Aislinn had found their way into the pantry and brought out salted meats and fish to cook over the fire, which they had with roasted broccoli and turnips. Padraig had found a sack of potatoes, a bag of onions, along with cured sausages, bacon, and carrots, from which he made a strange, watery stew seasoned with parsley. It was a dish of the people of Cruachan, he claimed, though Farris found it rather tasteless. It tasted a lot better with bread, claimed Padraig, upon seeing the meagre reception his dish was getting. Which was a shame, for the bread was all they lacked, it being the only food that had spoiled in the pantry.

After they ate, Fionn offered to clean the dishes, to which Padraig asked, "And for whom are we cleaning them for?"

which was met with laughter, even from Farris. Sure, Farris hated the man to his very bones, but he was happy to cast those thoughts aside, at least for the time being.

Farris opened a bottle of thainol and offered it to the rest of the party. Nicole and Padraig both accepted it, presumably since neither were a stranger to the taste. This prompted Aislinn and Fionn to try too.

"This isn't the first time Farris offered me this stuff," said Fionn. "Do you remember, Farris? Back in the Glenn, when you were known as Chester?"

Farris smiled. "I do. You told me about how Pyromancy works. Then I showed you a beggar's flame."

"Beggar's flame?" said Aislinn. "What's that?"

"I'll show you," said Farris. He drank from his glass, downing most of its contents, then tossed the rest into the fire. Sure enough, the crackling red flames abruptly turned a bright blue, burning silently in the hearth.

"Blue fire," said Aislinn. "Just like... the Reapers."

"That's right," said Farris. "In fact, it was my conversation with Fionn that inspired that aspect of the Reapers' design."

"What?" said Nicole. "Didn't you show me how to make those flames back in the hanger?"

Farris's heart pounded. It was the first time she had spoken to him since they had left.

"True," said Farris. "But I never would have thought to show you that if it wasn't for you telling me about what mages can and cannot manipulate. I never would have realised beggar's flames fall into the latter, if Fionn hadn't tried to manipulate them back in the Glenn."

A silence hung over the party as Farris said this. Eventually, Fionn spoke.

"Nicole, did your Reapers play a big role in fighting back the horde?"

Nicole nodded. "The Saltgate eventually fell to undead trolls, but they were held off for time by the brave pilots of the Reapers." She went to speak more, but her voice cracked. Farris knew why, so broke in.

"The horde was defeated because Argyll killed Diarmuid," he said. "And this gave Morrigan what she had come for. But more, indeed, many more, may have been killed by the horde if not for Nicole's Reapers. From what we know about Morrigan, she would have killed everyone in Penance to get to Diarmuid."

A lull fell over the group. The fire within the hearth turned from blue back to its natural colour, crackling away upon its coals. From both Nicole and Fionn's expression, Farris reckoned both were having the same realisation: things would be much worse if not for them.

If not for us. He took a deep drink, then poured another glass. Padraig held out his own empty one too, which Farris happily filled.

"What do you mean?" asked Padraig, taking a short sip. "When you say, 'from what you know about Morrigan?' to what do you refer?"

Farris threw his gaze to the floor, and a quick wave of fear passed over him. Something from the tone of Padraig's question shook Farris, as if he was abruptly caught out in a lie. After a few bated breaths, his panic passed, for there was no lie he was caught in, no secret exposed.

"I can answer that," cut in Fionn, before Farris could fully collect himself. "Though it is a long story."

Padraig leaned forward. Nicole cocked her head, glancing at Farris. From these reactions alone, it seemed Fionn had little choice to tell the tale, lengthy may it be.

"Over a year ago now," he began. "I travelled aboard a ship named *The Glory of Penance*, from Cruachan to Penance. The ship crashed into the Glenn, and Farris, myself, and some other survivors were set upon by hungry beadhbhs. We escaped them, and—"

"My brother!" cut in Aislinn. "He was aboard that ship! Sir Bearach Carríga of Rosca Umhír. Did you see him?"

Fionn had started with the air of an eager storyteller, but this interjection had the most peculiar effect on him. He did not respond to Aislinn, but murmured unheard words through quivering lips. His head shook slightly back and forward, and he shuffled as he sat.

Caught out on a lie? wondered Farris. It didn't seem so. This seemed somehow... worse. Fionn placed a hand on the side of his neck, rubbing and squeezing at his skin. This was often an attempt to comfort oneself: a common response to stress. Farris watched on as he did this, his oversized hand almost large enough to cover his entire neck.

Of course, realised Farris. *That is the arm of the knight we travelled with. He announced as much to the Council of the Triad.* He glanced at Aislinn. *And she was not there. She does not know.*

Farris closed his eyes to try and recollect the other details of the journey. *They travelled together. Yes, those two and Slaine the White. Did they know each other prior?*

And there were the connections Farris had made back in Penance: Fionn claiming the procedure of attaching the knight's arm to his body also gave him the power of the Bearach's soul, empowering his own magic as a result. This magic, Necromancy, being the very same that Morrígan used to grow her strength. It was this revelation that had driven Farris to rescue King Diarmuid and Padraig from Cruachan.

Well, the latter was unintentional.

So many memories and connections surfaced at the front of Farris's mind that for a moment he struggled to recall what had even prompted them to do so. He looked back towards Aislinn.

Yes, he thought. *She had asked a simple question of Fionn.*

If Fionn's delayed response was caused by a storm similar to what presently raged in Farris's mind, perhaps the lad just needed some help in the telling.

"He was, my lady," said Farris, keeping his tone formal. "But Sir Bearach died a hero's death. On our journey from the Glenn, our party was ambushed by a mountain troll. We fled for our lives, towards a village at first, but Sir Bearach steered us away, into the fields of the Clifflands. The beast caught up and knocked me aside. Our path had unfortunately crossed with that of a family of villagers, tending to their crops, even before the sun had risen. But Sir Bearach was a knight true to vows and put the lives of the innocent and the weak before his own. He died, along with many others of our party, but he saved the lives of myself, Fionn, and a young girl from the village."

A silence hung after he finished. Aislinn's eyes were closed.

"You are wrong about one thing," said Fionn, his gaze locked on the floor. "The young girl neither weak nor innocent. For she was Morrígan."

Padraig swore under his breath upon hearing this, then drank deeply from his glass. Aislinn bowed her head, and Nicole's expression gave away no emotion nor reaction.

"I met her," said Fionn. "Briefly, before I left Roseán. The girl had just lost her mother, and questioned me endlessly on the purpose of our journey. I have no doubt she blamed me for her death. And the next time I saw her, she was marching on Penance, leading an undead horde."

"And now she's a god," said Farris. "She's killed two of the Trinity already, what hope do we have to stop her from taking the power of the third?"

"I don't know," said Fionn. "It is said that the Wraiths of Seletoth serve Him directly. Perhaps they too are aware of the threat Morrígan poses to Him."

Farris scoffed. "You're not seriously saying we're going all this way to *help* the Wraiths, after everything they've done?"

Fionn sighed deeply. "I don't know. We need all the help we can get, but I didn't want to risk the lives of more soldiers in getting it. If these Wraiths have already given their lives to serve the Lord, why not allow them to continue doing so, for an even greater good?"

"Let's hope the Lord Himself has a better answer than that," said Padraig with a yawn. "Otherwise, we'll just end up repeating what happened out in Dromán."

This brought a deep lull to the group, which continued for a time as the fire died down.

"It is time we rested," said Aislinn, getting to her feet. "We may as well make use of the inn-quality bedding on this journey while we can."

Fionn yawned too, as if in agreement. He bade the others good night, and made his way to the stairway, behind Aislinn. Nicole then stood but left without saying a word.

Farris stretched, then stood to follow, but Padraig stopped him.

"Farris," he said solemnly. "I just wanted to... thank you, for all you have done. You stopping the charge of my battalion at Dromán marked the third time you saved my life. Even after you rescued me from Cruachan, I still wished you dead.

A feeling I had assumed was mutual, but when the horde came to Penance, and then when Morrígan came to Dromán, you proved otherwise."

Farris nodded. In truth, he had only sought to keep Diarmuid alive those first two times. But the third....

"You are welcome," said Farris. "I had no intention of going on this journey. With the Lady dead, I saw my role in all this come to an end. To follow Fionn into death, when he himself cannot die, seemed redundant. Illogical, even. But when you pledged your sword to Fionn, despite all that had happened, it made me reconsider. Perhaps me saving you in Dromán was illogical. But I can't claim to have had a logical mind that day. Skies above, when the army was swallowed by the ground, I went down to kill Meadhbh myself."

Padraig guffawed. "You what?"

Farris laughed meekly. "I was just angry. Angry at everything. I picked up a dagger and went down to kill her."

Padraig raised both of his hands and roared with laughter that echoed through the inn. "Farris, what were you thinking?"

"I wasn't thinking at all. To tell you the truth, we Simians have always held logic to a higher esteem than any other influence on a decision. But when I saw you and Aislinn bend your knees to Fionn, I thought, perhaps logic does not need to guide us so much. And now that I consider it further, I cannot claim logic guided me exclusively throughout my life."

Padraig nodded. "Sometimes we need to know there's a purpose greater than our own to live by. A life lived under the Will of Seletoth, guided by the Light of the Lady, and so on and so forth, can be fulfilling in ways the non-religious can never understand."

"Perhaps," said Farris, taking to his feet. "And maybe I'm only beginning to understand now." He bowed his head to Padraig before turning to leave, following the same stairs the others had taken upstairs.

But unfortunately, there's not many gods left these days.

Chapter 13:
The White Rose

Ten years after we landed, our settlements across the south grew in populace and size. Unfortunately, any attempt to press our borders northwards were met with hard resistance from the natives. At the time, if we had engaged in open-field combat against them, we would have won an easy victory, with their primitive weapons no match for our magic. But it seemed that they were always aware of this, only choosing only to fight us when the advantage was on their side, through ambushes and short skirmishes.

But ten years in, some progress was made. Some natives had learned our language, very quickly, I might add, and began to treat with us. These ones seemed to know it was only a matter of time before the land was ours, and provided valuable information regarding the movements of those plotting against us.

So once more, we set out northwards, with some natives on our side, and our own numbers stronger than before. This time, we knew, we would find Seletoth.

The Truth, by King Móráin I, AC55

***

Argyll's chair rattled with each cobblestone they went. Ruairi cursed the lack of paved basalt roads in the Dustworks of Penance. Seemingly, Argyll had ordered a new chair—a design of his own of some sort, though it would likely still need Ruairi to push him around.

We'll get what we need soon, he reminded himself. *The Simians will get their freedom, and we will get our knowledge, and all shall see the face of God.*

The night was growing late, with the streets occupied only by revellers on their way home, and those with more sinister motives that still lingered in the streets.

And there's no motives more sinister than our own, thought Ruairi, taking a turn from the main road into a darkened alley. This had even more cobblestones, from which came even more rattling. It was illuminated by several dimmed oil lamps, attached to the stone walls that stood tall either side.

"You're sure he'll be here?" asked Ruairi.

"Yes," said Argyll, stern and still facing ahead. "He risked far more than this the night the horde came."

It was a strange thing, to speak to someone before you, without expecting them to turn around to speak back. Ruairi found he had to strain his ears to listen to Argyll more than before, for the Simian's strong voice was difficult to hear when projected in the wrong direction.

They passed a group of youths, loitering beneath the window of a tavern. They stopped what they were doing, abruptly turning to look at Ruairí and Argyll as they passed. Argyll turned to stare back at them; something the Simian often did to fill the hearts of others with fear. Despite his condition, it had the same effect now as it always had.

Just bored children, thought Ruairí, shaking his head. *Nothing to be concerned about.*

Eventually, they came to their destination: the back door into *The White Rose*, a regular meeting place for Argyll, and those who served him. The front of the tavern was closed, of course, given the time of night, but as Ruairí knocked on the back door, it opened slightly at first, then fully when the proprietor saw who was there.

"He's here alright," the landlady said, ushering both in. She was a robust Simian, toughened by dealing both with the clients of her establishment and the associates of the Silverback. Bruna the Beauty, she had been called once, but never to her face. As Argyll had once put it, she had been loyal to all of his causes, from the days of the Guild of Thieves to the more recent plans to dismantle the Church and the Crown.

"Madame Bruna," said Ruairí with a nod. "I hope business is going well."

"It would be going better if I didn't have to close early!" she snapped. "Your man is inside. Far side of the bar."

Ruairí nodded and pushed Argyll through the empty tavern. It had a low ceiling, held up with thick stone columns draped in red curtains. The floor was made from concrete, and smooth to move over, much to Ruairí's relief. Wooden tables with low, iron cushioned stools lined the left-hand wall, with a long bar of marbled stone to the right.

There, sitting on a table adjacent to the bolted-shut front door, was a lone Simian, cradling a glass of thainol.

"Edward of Engine Alley," said Argyll. "Or Ned the Liberator, as you are more recently known."

"I am called both," said the Simian. "You require no introduction."

"But perhaps you need a better one." Argyll rested his hands on the table and turned to look up at Ruairí. "Do you know what Ned the Liberator did the night the horde came?"

"I do not," said Ruairí, adding an air of amusement. Of course, he did, but this was part of the act. The more time he spent with the Simians, the better he got at playing their games of deception.

"The Basilica has both men and Simians in their ranks," began Argyll. "Due to the needs of the local population here in the Dustworks, Simians make up the majority of their numbers. Regardless of their own beliefs, these Simians are loyal to the Arch-Canon, the Trinity, and the Church."

"Traitors," rasped Ruairí. "Traitors the lot of them."

"Not quite," said Argyll, turning back to face Ned. "They only serve the Church because the Basilica's presence in the city leaves them lacking so much. It is such a disgusting thing the Church has done. First, they tax the poor to pave their own walls with gold. Then, they hire the same poor to defend those same walls. Humiliating."

"You do not have the full picture," said Ned. "But by and large, this is true."

"Yes," said Argyll. "But you chose to defy the Church when a real threat emerged. You chose to release those imprisoned in the Basilica, rallying your fellow Churchguards together to defend the Dustworks, not the Church, from the undead."

"It was not my idea. A prisoner helped me understand what I needed to do. He deserves as much praise as I do."

Argyll looked back at Ruairí. There was a strange glint in the Simian's eyes, as if he shared a secret Ruairí should know too. But Ruairí didn't. He had heard of Ned the Liberator but wasn't aware of who was actually imprisoned in the Basilica. Argyll had imprisoned Farris when the king arrived, though that was just to appease the Church.

No.... Argyll now smiled openly at him. *Farris? Farris actually* convinced *his captors to set him free?* Of course, Ruairí had come across Farris at the Dustgate that night. He hadn't quite questioned why Farris had been accompanied by so many Churchguards.

The mastery that Simian has over subterfuge knows no end.

But Farris was likely dead now, along with the rest of those who tried to defend the Lady.

"This may be true," said Argyll, turning back to Ned. "But this prisoner would not have gone far without your co-operation."

Ned snorted. "I did what I did to protect my family. Because of that prisoner, they are still alive. As am I."

"And still in the job, if my information is correct."

"True. The Church chose not to dismiss those who abandoned their posts that night, considering it an extraordinary circumstance."

"And the others..." said Argyll, leaning in towards Ned. He lowered his voice. "How have they received our message?"

"They received it well. Their faith in the Church has been shattered given all that has happened. Rumours have spread that an evacuation of this land is planned, should she who brought the horde choose to return."

"Correct, and only with your help, Ned the Liberator, can this be achieved. We have three long distance ships ready, but the Church still holds the means for us to fly."

"Blue focus-crystals. This much I am aware of. The vaults of the Church are filled with many treasures and secrets, along with many crystals storing Human magics. Even with snow filling the sky, and with the Eternal Sea itself frozen, the Church hoards crystals capable of supplying us with heat to see us through this strange winter."

Argyll nodded. "Speak with your fellow Simian Churchguards, and you will be free to plunder all the riches of the Basilica."

"That will be trivial," said Ned, frowning. "But what about the Humans?"

"They will not come to our side easily. I understand Simians in the Churchguard outnumber Humans two to one."

Ned folded his arms. "You're saying there'll be violence?"

"Violence in our favour. After the riot at the Basilica last year, the battlemages in the Church's ranks were sent to Dromán, so you'll face no magic."

Behind them, Ruairí shook his head. Argyll's plans often involved a very high rate of success, with little room for error or variance. Even with the Simians of the Churchguard on his side, there was still a chance things could go awry.

Perhaps there is something I can do to help....

"Either way," said Argyll. "We appreciate you coming to meet us tonight. Dead drops and secret messages can only communicate so much."

Ned looked puzzled. "Is that all?"

Argyll nodded, as did Ruairí.

The Simian Churchguard slowly stood, then left without saying any more. Ruairí slipped into seat where Ned had sat, now facing Argyll. When the back door opened and slammed shut, he spoke.

"He seems confident. We were concerned that the goals and the needs of the Simian Churchguards wouldn't align with our own. But are you concerned about fighting off the Humans in their ranks?"

"No," said Argyll, with a slight pause. "Between the Simians in their ranks, and the Sons within ours, the odds favour us strongly. How many Sons are still in the city?"

"Some four hundred," said Ruairí. "Though the fervour of our faith has grown significantly since Diarmuid died, so that number is ever-increasing."

"And why would that be?"

Ruairí paused. This was a rather strange question for the Simian to ask. Likely one that he already had the answer to. Ruairí took a breath, then answered, slowly, choosing his words carefully.

"Because the king's death shows that the power of the Trinity is not as the Church claims. If Diarmuid is not a god, then how did you kill him?"

Argyll learned forward. Something akin to a sneer laced his lips. "Because... he has an *heir*."

No! Ruairí's mind reeled. He cursed himself. So many times, he had felt he was one step ahead of Argyll, holding on to one piece of knowledge outside of the reaches of the Silverback's network, but so many times, without fail, the upper hand was quickly lost.

"A... what?" was all Ruairí could manage. To stall for time. To hope Argyll would elaborate.

"An *heir*," repeated the Simian. "Farris, in his work with in Cruachan, proved to me that Divine Penetrance is true. If the king was to bear a son, the power of immortality would pass on to him."

Ruairí shook his head. *But Argyll had denied this for so long, dismissing Farris's work as sloppy and biased. Could that alone have convinced him? Does he know about the boy?*

"No," said Ruairí, trying not to let his own trail of thought be shown. "The Church has denied this power for generations."

"The Church denies many things. When Morrigan claimed the soul of Diarmuid, she became a god. If he was a mere man, this would not have happened."

Blasphemy! thought Ruairí; a thought almost reflexive. *There is only one God. And Seletoth is His Holy Name.*

Argyll pressed on. "But Diarmuid died when I slew him. With a simple dagger, no more. Therefore, there must have been some power within him for Morrigan to take, even if he did not possess Divine Penetrance."

Ruairí leaned forward. "What are you saying?"

"Firemaster Fionn," said Argyll. He leaned back in his chair. "The illegitimate son of our late king. It has been a very well-kept secret for his whole life, and I made sure to keep him close at hand, in case the need every arose. If we were to challenge the authority of the Crown, and if they did not capitulate as we planned, then I was to present Fionn and his Divine Penetrance to the world and hold the kingdom ransom until the needs of Old Simia were met."

Ruairí wanted to cry out loud, to violently display his disdain for the things that lad's mere existence drove him to do.

I tried to kill him, muttered a voice from deep within. Ruairí quickly began to pray, to drown that voice out, but it spoke truths far greater than those within the verses and passages of his faith. *I laced his glass with poison, so see if what the Earthmaster claimed was true.*

Ruairí closed his eyes tightly. Earthmaster Seán had been a Son, devout as any, but kept his faith a close secret. For someone so brash and so loud, the Earthmaster kept many secrets. But when he came to Ruairí with knowledge that Fionn might be an heir of King Diarmuid, based on some very faint whispers in the Academy of Dromán, Ruairí had to act. For the lad's life represented something both incredibly important to the Church, and something incredibly profane to his own faith. If he really was immortal, then the entire gospel of the Sons was in question.

So Ruairí had to find out. An act he took no pride in. An act that left only two options: to kill an innocent young man, or to prove his entire faith a falsehood.

And since Fionn had not died to the lethal dose, the latter and worse of the two outcomes was realised.

Ruairí realised that Argyll was studying him severely now. Indeed, all attempts Ruairí had previously made to mask his true intentions were attempted no more, for those feelings were too strong to be restrained in the Simian's game of subterfuge. His motives too plain to hide.

"This may come to a surprise you," continued Argyll. "But you must not let any challenge to your faith shake your allegiance to your cause. The population of Penance could very well rely on us these coming days."

Ruairí nodded, remaining silent.

"Furthermore, you would do well not to forget what our cause has done for the Sons so far. The riot at the Basilica, the information we spread in its wake. With our goal shifted now, is your allegiance still firmly with us?"

"Of course," said Ruairí.

"And what of this voyage? Do you still wish to leave this land, promised by your god?"

"Yes," said Ruairí, perhaps a little too quickly.

This wasn't the full picture, however. That much he would show Argyll later.

"And do your followers wish to leave too?"

Ruairí closed his eyes. A shudder ran through his body.

Lord Seletoth, I seek forgiveness. For I shall find your Truths and read them. Lord Seletoth, I seek courage. For I shall find Arch-Canon Cathbhadh and slay him. This I promise. In your most Blessed and Holy name, I–

"End your prayer and answer me!" barked Argyll. Ruairí jumped with fright.

"Yes," he said. "We follow your orders to the letter."

"Then take me home." Argyll, gestured to his chair. "We have much to do tomorrow."

Ruairí stood and prepared Argyll's chair for the return journey.

Seletoth hear me. Soon we shall destroy the Church and the false gods they hold. And if your grace is good, and your love for us is true, we shall succeed.

CHAPTER 14:
GOD'S SPINE

After a long journey north, we have found respite in Hunter's Den. The inn is abandoned, as expected, but we found plenty of food and drink to see us off to bed. But I doubt I'll rest much tonight.

As I retired, Farris confided in me that it was my pledge to Fionn that drove him to the decision to join us. Furthermore, as I prepared for sleep, Aislinn Carríga came to my chambers to speak to me. We stayed up for some hours, reminiscing of the times before the horde, before Morrigan. She too commended me on my loyalty to Diarmuid. She was preparing to join the others on their journey to Penance but changed her mind upon seeing me agree to go with Fionn.

Gods, this is a large responsibility to bear. The Lady Meadhbh had told us that it if not for Farris, we would all be dead. Now, as I write this, I realise that if it were not for me, Fionn would likely be taking this journey alone.

If the Tapestry of Fate dictates that we are all to fail, I can only hope we have strayed very far from its threads.

Journal of Padraig Tuathil, 21ˢᵗ Day under the Moon of Nes, AC404

Fionn found himself standing in a chapel. He did not recall how he got there, but already he was walking, slowly down the aisle. Ahead of him was an altar, with a stained-glass window behind it. It depicted the popular image of the birth of King Móráin to the Lady Meadhbh and the Lord Seletoth. The Lady appeared just as Fionn had seen her in Dromán, though instead of the blue light, here, She wore a cloak of red and green. Seletoth stood beside Her, dressed the same, but with a stern scowl upon His thickly bearded face. Between them was an infant, golden in colour, clutching an axe and a shield.

"If our ancestors claimed this land from the Simians using magic," came a voice, "what use were an axe and a shield?"

Fionn turned abruptly to see a young girl, sitting in one of the aisles, alone. She wore a simple brown tunic, with wooden pins holding her black hair in a braid.

"Morrígan?" said Fionn, walking towards her. "Is that you?"

She seemed so fragile and harmless. Just a child.

"Mother," sobbed Morrígan. "Why did you have to go? Why couldn't it have been someone else?"

Fionn sat beside the girl. "It's okay," he said. "I'm sure she—"

Just as he said this, the doors of the chapel burst open. There stood Morrígan, the real Morrígan, who had led the horde and slew the gods. She moved down the aisle, her black wings gliding gently over the wooden pews. She passed Fionn and the child, as if unaware of their presence. Instead, her gaze was locked ahead. Fionn looked towards the altar, to see that the stained-glass window had been replaced with a pair of doors. Giant, stone doors, thick and heavy upon their hinges. An intricate design of spirals filled the borders, stretching inwards to form the shape of a single eye that stared outwards. The crack between the two doors overlapped with its pupil, but as Morrigan approached, it began to open, and a bright light spilled forth.

Beside Fionn, the child leapt out of her seat into the centre of the aisle.

"No!" she cried. "Don't go in! Look not upon His face!"

But the winged Morrigan did not listen, and instead pressed onward. The light was blinding now, and it filled the rest of the chapel. The child-Morrigan dropped to her knees as the light spilled over her.

"No!" she cried, once more, her voice cracking into a shriek. "Don't!" As the light consumed her, she crumbled into dust, and disappeared into its golden rays.

***

"Don't!" cried Fionn, waking with a start. His heart pounded as he tried to recognise his surroundings. He was in the neat and tidy room of Hunter's Den. He closed his eyes.

A dream. Just a dream but it seemed so....

Different? suggested Sir Bearach. *I saw it too. I've seen your dreams before, lad, and they are usually formless and abstract, only producing an occasional recognisable scene. But this. This was different....*

I am no stranger to strange dreams, replied Fionn, thinking of the vision the Lady had shown him, of Nessa. Of his birth. *Was this from Her too?*

He looked out a nearby window. It was morning, that much was clear, but its hour was less so. The snow continued to fall upon the settlement of Hunter's Den, gently smothering the landscape.

He made his way downstairs, where Padraig was preparing a breakfast, of sorts. He fried sausages and bacon on a pan, and boiled eggs in water, without their shells.

"Still no bread," he said, as Fionn sat with the others. Nicole sat beside Farris, but neither seemed to acknowledge Fionn. Aislinn sat on the opposite side, drinking deeply from a thick mug of broth.

"That's okay," said Fionn. "We should take as much as we can from here. We won't have much comfort as we cross the Godspine."

"Don't you worry about that," Padraig said, running to the table with a pan of fried tomato slices. He forked one onto each plate. "I travelled through here before, and the road from Hunter's Den to Ardh Sidhe is an easy one to follow."

He sat down before his own plate and took a bite from a strip of bacon. He gestured towards Aislinn. "And when the road emerges, we see your namesake lake first, and gods above and below, it is a wonderful sight to behold."

"We went there once," said Aislinn with a smile. "Bearach and I were kids, we tried to swim the length of it, and almost drowned." She turned to look westwards, through a window on the far side of the bar, frosted fingers grasping at the edges of its glass. "It's probably frozen over now."

Fionn looked inwards, focusing his attention on Bearach, but the old knight said nothing. Fionn had asked him many times now to communicate with Aislinn. But given how adamant Bearach had been the last time Fionn asked, he thought it better to not ask any more.

A *shame*, he thought, not expecting a response.

Still, he was disappointed when none came.

After breakfast, they gathered their things. Nicole busied herself altering some old potato sacks with some leather straps she found while raiding the cloakroom. It seemed many people had left here in such a hurry when the undead came, they never thought to put their coats on. When Fionn stepped outside into the frigid air, Aislinn had fastened additional sacks onto the elk mounts, which Farris promptly filled with food from the pantry.

"It's a wonder they can carry all this," said Fionn, considering the mass of both Simians, dressed head to foot in thick armour.

"They can handle more with less," Nicole said, pulling a square helm over her head, covering her entire face. "They're made of far stronger stuff than your horses," she added, in a muffled voice.

Padraig and Aislinn came out behind them. Both were smiling in a very specific way that Fionn hadn't seen in a very long time. He looked at them, expectantly, ready to hear a shared joke, but Padraig's face immediately went straight as he tended to his horse.

As they left the settlement, a cold wind blew in from the north. The path that took them from Hunter's Den was similar to the one that took them to it. For a time, they moved ahead at an accelerated pace, with hooves crunching into the snow. The forest was strangely silent here, with no sign of life bar the frozen brushes and trees that slowly passed as they went. Padraig led the way, confident as he was that he could follow the paths through the Godspine and out into the Midlands. Aislinn rode beside him, with Farris and Nicole lingering behind. Abruptly, Fionn felt very lonely, the only one taking the centre space of their advancing column.

Eventually, they came to a crossroads. Or at least Padraig identified it as such. To Fionn's eyes, the path they were on continued northwards only.

"Here," said Padraig, pointing towards the ground where a lone, wooden stake stood. "This marks the junction in our route. This westward path will take us through the mountains."

"This path?" asked Farris, riding up to take a closer look. "Looks more like a game trail than a path."

"No matter what you call it," said Padraig. "We are to take it westwards until we reach Ardh Sidhe."

Fionn considered the path himself. Indeed, the freshly fallen snow obscured the ground beneath, but there certainly was a parting of the grass adjacent to the stake, and it wound through the trees until it disappeared into distant hills obscured by mist to the west.

"The stake," said Nicole, nodding towards it. "Was it a sign of some sort before?"

"Yes," said Padraig.

Fionn narrowed his eyes, then looked to the two Simians. They too didn't seem happy with Padraig's response, but what other choice did they have?

Why not continue down the main path? asked Sir Bearach. *It may cost us more time to circle around the mountains, but it's better than being lost.*

No, replied Fionn. *Every hour we spend dithering and deciding what to do next is an hour Morrigan steps ahead of us. We need to reach Mount Selyth before she does.*

I don't know, Fionn, replied the knight. *If she wants to get there before we do, she surely would have done so with ease already.*

Fionn didn't reply. He hadn't considered that until now. And considering it now didn't bring him much joy.

He urged his mount towards the captain. "Have you taken this path before, Padraig?"

"I have," he replied. "Though I admit it was a long time ago. Without the snowfall, it would be clear that this stake once marked a significant junction in this road. This much, I am sure of."

There was no strong objection to this, or perhaps none could think of any. Nonetheless, the company reluctantly steered their mounts westwards, and stepped off the main road. They trudged slowly through this new path. Fionn often had to stoop his head low to avoid being brushed by snow-covered branches as he went. To his relief, there certainly was a path of some sort beneath the hooves of his horse, even if he couldn't see it under the snow and the ice.

Soon, the trees grew thinner, and the path sloped upwards. The grassy ground surrounding them slowly rose above to give way to steep, rocky foothills. The snowfall gradually grew thicker too, until Fionn had to squint through the sleet to see through it.

All conversation among the party stopped now, as their focused remained only on the path ahead of them. Padraig led the way still, though it was only now that Fionn realised how much they had truly staked in the man's confidence.

They went on like this for some time; a time that felt to Fionn far longer than the few hours that elapsed. The path continued to slope upwards, until it began to wind around tall peaks of mountains. Fionn did not take in much of the scenery as he went, keeping his jaw clenched firmly shut, and his eyes focused only on the road before him. The cold fangs of the howling wind bit into his face, constantly, with each step. A time to rest was warranted, but Fionn dared not suggest one, for the faster they made it through these wretched hills, the better.

At times, Padraig would pause and survey the area, then direct the company to move forward again. Given the conditions in which they presently travelled, Fionn felt he was in no position to question the captain's navigation skills. On the other hand, over the screeches of the billowing winds, Fionn heard the Simians behind him. One of them, or perhaps both, was expressing concern with Padraig's ability.

Still, Fionn dared not say a word.

Onwards they went for some hours, until Fionn reckoned they had gone well past noon. He periodically looked upwards, hoping to gauge the time of day. With the sky so overcast, it was difficult to distinguish between afternoon and dusk.

We still have some time until sunset, right?

That much is true, said Sir Bearach, *but despite how long we've been travelling, I fear we are still far from seeing the other side of these mountains.*

Fionn couldn't help but agree. From his memory, the Godspine was thinnest at the point west of Hunters Den. This trek through the mountains really should not take more than half a day. As Padraig had put it before, the plan was to reach Ardh Sidhe by nightfall.

But if they were still within the Godspine at this time, perhaps three hours from nightfall by Fionn's reckoning, then what chance did they have to cross the Midlands and the banks of Lough Aislinn at within that time too?

But Fionn kept his hesitations and his questions to himself. After the night in Hunter's Den, spirits were high, so he didn't feel the need to cause a ruckus for no reason.

As the hours when on, and darkness slowly descended upon the mountain path, Fionn felt the need to renege on this position. But just as he was about to speak up, Sir Bearach spoke first.

Have we been travelling south?

I don't think so, replied Fionn. *The path is still taking us westwards, no?*

I believe you are mistaken. This road has been sinister its steering. We were travelling westwards initially. But the path took a gradual, southern bend that gained more and more influence these past hours.

No! Fionn looked ahead through the thick snow. Padraig and Aislinn were still riding ahead of them, with the captain looking this way and that. Fionn sighed and moved forward, dreading the discourse that was to come.

Fortunately, Farris bound past on elkback and caught Padraig before Fionn could.

"Shouldn't we have reached the Midlands by now?" the Simian asked curtly, as if it was more a statement than a question.

"We should have," replied Padraig, "but our progress has been slower than it ought to have been. We should press on until we reach the other side."

"No, we should not. If we press on any further, we'll be pressing into the night. Should any of our mounts take a fall in the dark, we'll all be travelling on foot. We should find a place to camp while there's light to find one."

Padraig turned to look at Aislinn, who exchanged a confused glance with him. He gave Farris a similar look.

"But we don't have any gear for camping. We planned only to rest in settlements like Ardh Sidhe or Hunter's Den."

"And we did not plan on getting lost," said Farris. "But for our own survival, we now must improvise."

Padraig scoffed. "We are not lost. We're just behind on time. If we continue on, we'll—"

"South!" cut in Fionn. "The path is taking us south."

Both the Human and the Simian gave Fionn a curious look.

"How do you know this?" said Padraig. "Intuition? Or have you a ship's compass under your cloak?"

"The path has curved southwards," he said. "It was gradual, so we didn't notice without the setting sun to confirm our orientation. I think we really are lost."

"If this is true, then we have no choice but to rest," said Farris. "We should find shelter from this storm and start a fire if we can."

"I suggest we reconsider," said Padraig.

"You have lost your right to reconsider!" roared Farris. "We have lost our way, Captain Tuathil, and you may very well have led us to our death!"

"There's no need for that," cut in Aislinn. "Things may not be that dire. If we work together, perhaps we can find—"

"A better guide? I think a dowsing rod will serve a better guide than this buffoon."

Padraig scoffed, but he didn't have much more of a follow-up. Fionn reckoned the captain was well and truly lost.

"We must consider the worst possibility," said Fionn. "There is a distinct chance that we are far from where we expect to be, and we may not find our way out of the mountains until the morning. Furthermore, if this storm gets worse, or the terrain grows less welcoming than it is now, we will surely perish in this cold."

"We?" said Farris. "The only ones to perish here will be..." He trailed off. "Never mind. Well said, Firemaster."

Padraig moved his mount towards Fionn. "What would you have us do? Camp here, in the middle of the road, in the middle of a storm?"

"No," said Fionn. "Half a mile back, the road took us through high rising cliffs. There may be cover there, or even a cave, if we're lucky."

"I have considered myself lucky before," said Farris. "Maybe fortune will favour us more under a new guide."

He threw a glance to Padraig, who after a long pause, gave a reluctant nod. With that, the party turned, and tracked back towards where they had come.

At first, Fionn had regretted speaking up so assertively, but even during the few minutes it took them to return to find shelter, the storm grew harsher. Sure enough, when they came back to the area he had spoken of, somewhere behind him Farris remarked that this was indeed well suited for a camp.

It's his grudge with the captain, remarked Sir Bearach. *Farris sees this as getting another one over Padraig.*

Why would that even matter? replied Fionn. *Making it through the night now is all that does.*

Together, they dismounted, and surveyed the area for a place to settle. Without any camping equipment or supplies, their night's sleep was sure to be a harsh one. Farris found a spot in the bend of the road, where the high mountains sheltered the space from the roaring winds on three sides. All were about to agree to rest here, until Padraig shouted out, claiming to have found a cave.

"It's just here!" he cried over the wind, beckoning the others to follow him. As they did, the black mouth of an open cave emerged from around a bend.

"Not much of a cave," remarked Farris. Indeed, when Fionn was close enough to look inside, it was no more than ten feet deep, sloping gently downwards.

"And have you found anything better?" snapped Padraig. "As the Firemaster says, we may not have a better time than now to find a place to rest."

"This may be our best option," said Nicole, stepping inside. "We should take all the furs and clothes we have and pile them on top of us."

"I can work on a fire," said Fionn, stepping in.

"A fire?" said Farris. "In such an enclosed space, shouldn't we be concerned about inhaling smoke?"

"Not with me here," said Fionn. "I can direct the heat of the flames inwards, and the plumes of the smoke outwards."

With that, they set to work on the meagre camp. Padraig and Nicole unpacked and lay whatever materials they had available on the floor of the cave. Farris tied up the mounts up, expressing concern that the horses might struggle in the cold. Fionn searched for firewood, but no dry kindling could be found.

I'll have to fashion a fire without fuel, he thought, walking back to the cave.

Is that a problem? asked Bearach. *I thought you didn't need fuel.*

That is correct. Although he didn't directly express it to Sir Bearach, this would mean he would need to stay awake to keep the fire going and ensuring the party weren't engulfed in smoke. Without better cover than this, the fire would need to burn throughout the night to ensure the safety of the group. Fionn tried not to let this bother him. After all, he had already been through worse than a night without sleep.

As the darkness of the evening settled in, the winds of the storm rose to a mighty pitch, seemingly threatening to blow the mountains themselves away. Thick snow pelted the ground, with more blots of white visible in the air than the black space that separated them.

Fortunately, at this point, the company had all settled in the cave. Padraig and Nicole lay side by side, both in their armour. On either side of them was Farris and Aislinn. Fionn had suggested they all sleep as close to one another as possible, and fortunately none had protested. Fionn sat at the foot of them. He breathed slowly, staring out into the storm. Focusing on the cold air against his skin, he made an estimate of the temperature of the room. Once he was confident in his assertion, he went to work.

He clicked to together the flint rings on his right hand and deftly pushed the power of his soul into the spark that emerged. With a *whoosh*, the spark turned into a flame, which Fionn cradled into his hands. He quickly estimated the temperature of the flame, and using Rionach's Theorems of Heat Exchange, he calculated the rate of heat loss and heat transfer throughout the chamber. Once he had this worked out, he pushed upon the flame, slowly increasing its temperature.

Moving into more advanced aspects of Pyromancy, he took both hands, and pulled at either side of the flame. He was careful not to do so too quickly, otherwise the denominators of Rionach's Fourth Theorem would be larger than their numerators, and this would cause the output to be less than one, which of course would not create a rational product from Rionach's Sixth Theorem, which would come later.

Although slightly out of practice, Fionn managed to strike the balance well, pulling the flames apart with both hands and stretching it like warm dough. Rionach's Theorems allowed for the manipulation of fire well beyond what would be possible without magic, though any miscalculation would case the flame to extinguish. Or worse.

Slowly, Fionn stretched the flames around him, forming them into a ball of orange, pulsating sludge. He pushed upon his soul once more, extending the mass to surround the perimeter of the caves. This, fortunately, Fionn had been able to measure to a decent level of accuracy before he began. Once the flames filled the walls, Fionn ignited the flame of his soul once more, and the walls came alight.

"Amazing," said Farris, looking up to Fionn. Nicole, Aislinn, and Padraig didn't add to this, each just started up at the fires with awe. Farris reached out to the flames. "They're hot," he said. "But they do not burn."

"They only burn what I want them to burn," said Fionn. "Now we better sleep while we can."

The others didn't need any further convincing, Fionn lay down, but he had no intention of sleeping. His focus remained firmly on the flames that surrounded them.

Sleep lad, said Sir Bearach. *You'll need it for the journey tomorrow.*

I can't, replied Fionn. *I need to keep the fire lit, or we'll freeze.*

I think I can help there, said the knight. *I lent my soul to help your magic before. Perhaps I can do the same now.*

Fionn hadn't considered this, but he welcomed the possibility. *Don't you need to sleep?* he asked.

Of course not! I don't have a body that needs rest. When you sleep, I just lie in wait until you wake.

And the flames, said Fionn. *Do you know how to manipulate them?*

I don't think I need to. Out in the Goldgate, I just added my soul to the magic you had already conjured. With the hard work already done, I believe all I need to do is switch the fuel source from yours to mine.

Fionn frowned. This much he hadn't tried before, at least not intentionally. The first time he did, he was being attacked by Firemaster Conleth. The last time was when the horde was upon him.

Let us try, then, said Fionn. *I'll start counting, and I'll stop adding to the flames on three. Once I do, see if you can take over. If you do not do so by the time I reach five, I'll take them back again.*

Of course, said Bearach. *I'm ready.*

Fionn closed his eyes. *Alright. One. Two. Three!*

Fionn ceased his Pyromancy, and the flames all around them shook, their tongues flailing overhead.

Four....

Panicking, Fionn reached back out to the flames again, but before he did, the shaking stopped.

Five, said Sir Bearach. *I have them now, lad. You should get some sleep.*

Fionn scanned the walls. Indeed, the flames around them were just as stable as they had been when he had their control. Perhaps Sir Bearach could maintain them throughout the night. Perhaps he really did need some sleep.

But what if....

But before Fionn could finish that thought, he drifted into a deep slumber.

CHAPTER 15:
SCARLET ROBES

ATTENTION ALL CITIZENS OF PENANCE:

On the 23rd day under the moon of Nes, a fleet of airships shall leave Sin. Boarding will begin at noon, with a plan to depart before nightfall. The journey shall take us over the Eternal Sea, to a new land free of the horrors we have witnessed these past few weeks.

All are welcome. Those attempting to bring excessive belongings aboard will be refused passage, for we must ensure room for all who wish to come, Human and Simian alike.

Pamphlet distributed throughout Penance on the 21st day Under the Moon of Nes.

***

A silvery, cold dusk had fallen over the Stoneworks of Penance as Ruairí wheeled Argyll's chair through its wide streets. The Stoneworks was one of the more expensive parts of the city to live, and as a result it was mainly Humans who lived here. Naturally, Argyll's reach wasn't as strong here as he would have liked it to be. It was on Ruairí's account they came, though, so Argyll had no choice but to come too.

The sooner my new chair is ready, the better, thought Argyll. Red Ezra had said that it would be ready for him first thing in the morning, but he could scarcely wait any longer. The new chair represented freedom, and independence, and not needing to be wheeled around by a man he could only half trust.

Though the chair wasn't the only thing Argyll longed for. Looking down at his useless legs, he couldn't help but wonder how much easier all the work these few days held could have been if only he could still walk.

Tears welled up in his eyes, which he quickly cast aside. Fortunately, with Ruairí spending so much time looking at the back of his head, the times Argyll's emotions betrayed him were not shared with the Human.

I must be their rock, Argyll reminded himself. *I must not falter.*

"Where are we going, anyway?" he barked. More often than not, being blunt and abrasive did wonders to hide how he really felt; something he found himself doing more and more these days.

"To a sermon," said Ruairí, taking them off the main road to a narrow alley that ran between widely spaced-out bungalows.

"Presumably, there's more to it than that. And I've sat through enough of them already."

"This one will be different." Ruairí stopped before a back door to what looked like a tavern. Empty barrels lay stacked next to it, with empty glass bottles boxed and ready for collection.

Ruairí unlocked the door and pushed Argyll through, with some effort. They crossed a kitchen packed with cooking utensils, hanging from the walls and ceiling like weapons in an armoury. Ruairí wheeled Argyll through, out into a wide tavern space.

With windows shuttered, and the front door barred, the place was barren and bare. The two made their way across this, to a staircase that descended into darkness below. And from this darkness, a low voice echoed.

Argyll turned to look up at Ruairí. "I assume we're going down?"

When Ruairí nodded, Argyll sighed. It wasn't the first time they had to descend a staircase together, but it was a never a simple task. Ruairí took to them backwards and slowly, pulling Argyll down, one careful *thud* after another.

Fortunately, there's no one to see this, thought Argyll. *The mighty Silverback, defeated by a simple staircase.*

When they reached the bottom, Ruairí took a moment to catch his breath, leaving Argyll to wait in silence as he panted. When he caught it, he took to the chair once more, and pushed Argyll through a long corridor. Muffled voices at the end of it were growing clearer now.

"We open our hearts to Seletoth," muttered one low monotone.

"May He fill them with love," was the response, distorted from the many voices who said it.

Ruairí and Argyll entered wide chamber with a tall ceiling, void of furnishing, packed with many people. Humans, all of them, maybe a hundred, all eyes closed in prayer, facing one man who wore a heavy pendant across a white shirt.

"We open our eyes to Seletoth," he said.

"May He show them His Truths," came the refrain.

Argyll turned to look up to Ruairí, as the prayers droned on. "This really is different to the others," he whispered. "No pomp or spectacle. Why so much secrecy?"

"We open our minds to Seletoth," said the priest.

"May He fill them with wisdom," said the rest.

Ruairí didn't answer but left Argyll alone and moved through the crowd.

Argyll sighed. *And now I've no choice but to sit through the rest of it.*

The priest, upon seeing Ruairí, paused and extended a hand to him.

"Brother Ruairí," he said. "We are truly blessed to have you in our presence."

Argyll leaned forward. *This is new.*

Ruairí stood beside the priest, bowing gently to him, then turned towards the congregation.

"Sons of Seletoth," he said, using the flat tone reserved only for sermons. "Against all odds, you survived the night of the horde, and here you stand in defiance against those that would have seen you perish. These are frightening times, for the plague that the Firstborn fled has reached our lands, and there are rumours that our Lord is dead."

Concern rippled through the crowd. Near Argyll, one man shook his head, looking to his neighbour with a brow lowered in concern.

Ruairí raised both hands up, and the murmurs stopped. "But I have come to tell you that the Lord still lives. For last night, He granted me another Seeing. And He has told us what we must do during this trying time."

With this, he made direct eye-contact with Argyll, and more whispers resounded through the chamber.

"The Simians of the Triad are planning on leaving this land. We must do what we can to help them. But the Lord demands that we are to stay."

No! Argyll gripped the sides of his chair. *What is he doing?*

"For this land was promised to us from Him," continued Ruairí, "And for as long as He lives, we must remain. For this is the word of Seletoth."

"Blessed be His holy name," responded everyone else. Everyone other than Argyll.

He's up to something. There's something he's not telling me.

"Thank you, brother Ruairí," said the priest. "For you have provided us the gospel Truth, from His lips to yours.

And now, for a sermon from the writings of Brother Caolán of Dromán, who's Seeing of Seletoth in the year 350 AC has given us a glimpse into the heart of the Lord, and the love He shares for us all."

As the priest continued, Ruairí made his way back through the crowd, where Argyll greeted him with a curt "What do you think you're doing?"

"I can explain," said Ruairí, turning Argyll's chair around and exiting the chamber. They took the same narrow hallway that had brought them there.

"Then explain," said Argyll. "But you will answer my own questions directly, and you will speak plainly. First, is it true that you had a Seeing last night?"

"Yes," said Ruairí. "I would not lie to my people."

"But do you do realise that you could? That all you would need only to preface any claim with 'Seletoth told me,' for them to believe you?"

"Even if that is true, it is certainly not the case."

"And do you realise that..." Argyll trailed off as they passed the staircase which had brought them down to this place. "Where are you taking me?"

"I have one more thing to show you," said Ruairí. "Something that will make you understand."

"No!" roared Argyll. "You will stop what you are doing and explain yourself."

Ruairí halted, as both faced a wooden door at the end of the corridor. "What I wanted to show you is just beyond this," he said. "If you could just allow me to explain."

"You have condemned them all to death. Don't you see? You have taken their faith and you have turned it against them. You've ensured they'll perish in this dead land because *you*, not Seletoth, told them to."

"No," said Ruairí, stepping around Argyll to face him. "I have saved them." He pushed open the door. "I have saved them from you."

The door opened to reveal a small room. A cloakroom, fitted with poles across the ceilings, where rows of cloaks hung like shadowy figures.

As Argyll's eyes adjusted to the darkness of the room, he saw that these were not just cloaks, but robes. Bright, scarlet robes he had seen many times on the streets of Penance.

"The red robes of the Churchguard," he whispered. "Who...." He looked to Ruairí. "Those in the congregation. There's Human Churchguards among them?"

"No," said Ruairí, smiling. "All of them are Churchguards."

The rage within Argyll faded somewhat, and he nodded with reluctant admiration.

"You see," said Ruairí, upon seeing this. "Your plan pitched Simian Churchguards and Sons of Seletoth against the Humans of the Churchguard. But I've already merged the latter two groups into one. Now, there'll be no need for violence when we take to the Basilica tomorrow."

"True," said Argyll. "But there must be more." He leered at Ruairí now, looking for any sign of weakness. "Was this all this just to save the lives of those you were willing to kill before?"

"Not quite," said Ruairí. "There is something more that I require from the Basilica. A book."

Argyll raised an eyebrow. "Is that all?"

"It's called *The Truth*, written by King Móráin the First himself. It's a first-hand account of the journey the Firstborn took across the ancient lands to the east, to find Alabach, led by the wisdom of Seletoth."

"And why is this of so much interest to you?"

"Our scriptures are riddled with holes, with each Son getting only a glimpse of the Truth through their Seeings. Our sect works hard to piece together this disassociated knowledge, but each fragment is so small. Sons who witness too much of the Truth are usually in no state afterwards to retell what they saw."

"They lose their minds," said Argyll, recalling Fionn's account of his encounter with Firemaster Conleth.

"Most Seeings come upon those who are not ready for such a revelation. But if the Truth was in our hands, we could study it, decipher it, and know the face of God."

Argyll considered this for a moment. They were planning on plundering the Church's stash of focus-crystals already, perhaps they could take this book at the same time. "This will be well protected, I assume," he asked.

"Yes, hidden in the deepest of the Church's vaults. But with the full contingent of the Churchguard on our side, plundering them will be easy."

Argyll raised an eyebrow. "I know of these vaults. Aren't they only accessible by the Arch-Canon himself?"

Ruairí hesitated, frowning slightly, as if caught in a lie. "That... is accurate. Our information from the inside says that there is a door in the third-floor basement, accessible only to those wearing the Arch-Canon's sigil ring."

"Which he won't hand over easily, I assume."

"Yes."

"So, you wish to kill him?"

"Yes."

Argyll sighed. *This option does spare many more lives than one.* Though something else bothered him.

"Why must you all stay?" said Argyll. "It sounds like we have everything in place to take the focus-crystals and this book from the Basilica with minimal bloodshed. Why doom your followers to stay in this dying land when all is said and done?"

"Because the Lord has willed it."

"And if He's wrong?"

"The Lord's word is not to be questioned."

"Even in the hypothetical?"

Ruairí paused. "If there is a possibility that the Lord is wrong, then He is no god worth worshipping."

Argyll gave up, silently gesturing Ruairí to bring him home.

Sounds to me like there is no god worth worshipping. They stopped abruptly as they approached the dark staircase. With a grunt of effort, Ruairí pulled the chair backwards, raising the front wheels into the air, and Argyll braced himself for an uncomfortable ascent.

Though if Seletoth could give me my legs back, I'd be the most devout Son there ever was.

Chapter 16:
The Silverback's Reach

With the help of our native guides, we made significant progress northwards over the following months, fighting our way through traps and ambushes lain by those who opposed our landing. We razed numerous settlements to the ground, a decision that was not easy to make. Still, all dissent must be routed out, and with fewer places to call home, these Simians, as they name themselves, will have no choice but to capitulate.

As we forged northwards, the call of Seletoth grew stronger. We were getting close to Him, this much I was sure of.

We were met with a significant setback as we reached the northern mountains of this land. The natives had occupied and fortified important paths bypassing the mountains, halting our progress. We could have attacked them head-on with a high chance of success but would have taken significant losses as a result.

One of my generals found another way through the mountains, via a valley uncharted by the locals. Our Simian informants strongly objected, naming this valley a cursed, desolate place, but refused to *tell us why. This was peculiar behaviour, for I had not known the natives to hold any of their land holy or sacred. So, against the advice of their counsel, I led my men through that valley.*

A valley we would later name the Glenn.

The Truth, by King Móráin I, AC55

***

Fionn walked eastwards, his back to the morning sun, leaving the village of Roseán behind. However, the young mage paid little mind to where we walked. Eyes closed, his attention was turned inwards, towards a chorus of voices that rang out in his mind.

Halfwit! You left me for dead!

Alone and dead!

No light, no light! No lighter than the Holy Hell!

The Holy Hell would be a paradise compared to this fate.

Pain! Pain! Pain! Pain!

Fionn opened his eyes and saw that he had strayed from his path. He stood alone in an empty forest of decaying browns and blacks.

The young mage looked around, trying to find his way back to the path, when a whirring sound sang through the trees. A crossbow bolt struck his chest, bringing with it a sharp, searing pain. With a wheeze, Fionn fell to the ground.

"Oisín, you fool!" called a rough voice from the trees. Gasping for air, Fionn's vision blurred. He heard heavy footsteps along the ground.

"I didn't have a choice!" called another voice. "He was coming towards my hiding spot. And look at his cloak. He's a mage!"

Fionn couldn't tell how many there were, as two, perhaps three crouched down beside him. Fighting against his falling lids, Fionn closed his eyes.

"A mage, eh?" said the first voice. "Maybe he'll fetch himself a ransom, if we play our cards right."

"Not likely," said a third voice. "Oisín may be a fool, but you can't fault his aim. That there is a lethal shot, right through the lung."

"Ah shit," said the second voice. "It was meant to be a warning. I didn't mean to kill him!"

"You didn't," said the first voice, sterner than the others. "He's still breathing."

***

"Do we really need to go through this much effort?"

"The gaffer is scared shitless of him. Says he's a demon."

"A demon? Come on now, he's just a lad! A mage, as Oisín put it, right?"

"No. Mages die just like any other men. This one survived a pierced lung. Then the gaffer tied him up, put a spear through his heart, and a blade across his throat. Each time he just passes out and wakes a lil while later."

Slowly, Fionn opened his eyes. Every bone in his body ached, agony tearing through his body with each breath. His thoughts struggled to form anything coherent, and for now, he had no idea where he was or how he ended up there.

He was on a boat, rocking across a still sea, surrounded by darkness. The vessel bore no lights, illuminated only by the waning moon overhead. Two figures stood on the deck. With backs turned to him, they spoke in hushed tones. Fionn noticed now he was bound to a stool, his hands tied behind his back, his mouth gagged with a cloth. At his feet, thick chains coiled around his ankles where a heavy iron sphere fastened them together.

What's going on? thought Fionn. Another voice in his head cried out in pain, but Fionn did not understand its source.

"If it were up to me, we'd just bury him," said one of the figures. "But the gaffer said it wouldn't be enough. He said that there were stories from long ago, of the dead rising from their graves at the hands of a group of evil druids. He reckons the same is happening here."

"He won't be rising out of this grave, that much is for sure," said the second. He turned to look at Fionn. "Hush now, he's awake. Let's get it over with."

Fionn attempted to cry out but nothing but a low gurgle escaped his dried lips. Before he could figure out was happening, he found himself being pulled, then carried, then pushed over the side of the boat.

With a heavy splash, he fell into the freezing water and sank into the darkness below.

***

Time passed. How much, Fionn did not know. He sat at the bottom of the sea, the weight of the chains pulling him down against the ocean floor. All he could do was stare up into the faint light of the sky and watch as day became night became day became night.

Until one day, the light grew brighter. Brighter and brighter that before, until it threatened to blind him. He closed his eyes tight, hearing only the sound of rushing water all around him.

"Fionn," came a voice. It was the first time he had heard anything for some time. "Fionn the Red."

Fionn opened his eyes, and he saw a woman. A woman dressed in dark clothes with giant, black feathered wings spread out from each shoulder. She hung in the air. Fionn still lay on the ocean floor, but the ocean itself was parted around him, with sea rushing like waterfalls either side.

Did she do this? thought Fionn. The woman was strangely familiar, but Fionn could recall little from the life that came before this. "Come, Fionn," she said, reaching out a hand. "Lord Seletoth is waiting for us."

***

Fionn woke with a yelp, grabbing at his throat. His heart raced. When he realised where he was, in the cave in the Godspine with Farris, Padraig, Aislinn, and Nicole, his breathing returned to a natural pace, and he started to relax.

Was that a dream? he thought. Again, it seemed far too realistic, far too *intentional,* for want of a better word, to be a dream.

He was walking from Roseán, he recalled. After Yarlaith had healed him. Then he was ambushed.

Something about that was vaguely familiar to Fionn. Like he heard of something like that happening before.

Of course, he realised. *The Lady said that was fated to happen, but it did not come to pass.* He recalled her words. *"Fionn the Red. Set upon by bandits on the way from Roseán to Point Grey."*

He pressed his hand against his head, trying to recall more details.

They saw I could not be killed, so they buried me at sea....

And then Morrígan had found him. He closed his eyes tightly, trying to recall what she had said.,

Seletoth is waiting for us? That doesn't make any sense. Sir Bearach what do you think?

But there was no response. The dead knight would never pass up the chance to make a quick comment about Fionn's dreams, so why was he holding his tongue on this occasion?

Sir Bearach? said Fionn, standing up. *Sir Bearach? Where are you?* The familiar source of magic, the remnants of Sir Bearach's soul that had always been so close to Fionn... was gone.

"No," said Fionn out loud. He sprang up to examine the walls of the chamber.

"What's the matter, Firemaster?" said Padraig, yawning. "It looks like your magic has saved us yet again. And the storm seems to have passed."

"I don't care," snapped Fionn, pressing is hands against the stone. It was still warm to touch.

"It must have burned all night," he whispered. "Bearach...."

"What did you say?" asked Aislinn, gathering her things from the floor.

"Nothing," muttered Fionn. "Just... just a dream."

The others went to work repacking their belongings. Farris went off to fetch the mounts. All five had made it through the night in good health.

But Fionn's thoughts remained on the knight.

Was it too much for him? To keep the fire going so long? Did it... burn him out?

Usually, if a mage was to overspend themselves, they would just require ample rest to restore their energy. For this reason, in marching armies, it was important for the battlemages to have better conditions to sleep in than the rest of the soldiers.

Perhaps that was where his mind was, thought Fionn. *Thinking my rest was more important than his.*

He cursed himself. Sir Bearach had already given his life to protect a family from a mountain troll. And now he had given his soul just so Fionn could get a good night's sleep.

In a daze, Fionn ate with the others. They broke their fast with food pilfered from Hunter's Den, though Fionn couldn't taste anything.

They set off, back over the path Padraig had led them, and then beyond, deeper into the mountains. Although snow covered the trail, they progressed with ease, and a much faster pace than before.

After some hours, when the sun stood high in a clear, frigid sky, the path took a sharp turn south, sloping downwards aggressively. Upon seeing this, the party broke out into a fast trot, which they maintained for an excited half hour, until the trees westwards grew thin, and the wide, flat Midlands came into view.

After all the narrow roads and tight passages they had come through, this was truly a welcome sight. To the west lay the city of Rosca Umhír, with the fortress of Keep Carríga roaring over its walls. To the south, a tiny fishing village hugged the southern coast. And far to the north lay the city of Ardh Sidhe, with many tall towers and spires blurred in the distant mist.

Though these sights all paled in comparison to what lay further west, beyond Rosca Umhír: a mighty mountain that dwarfed all that surrounded it. It stood alone, in the middle of the flatlands, like a wart upon smooth skin.

The company all paused as this came into view. Padraig whooped in delight.

"I told you!" he said. "I told you we were on the right track!"

"I believe you are still mistaken," said Nicole. She pointed northwards. "We're far from our destination, now closer to the River Tine than Ardh Sidhe. Your path, Captain Tuathil, has taken us far further south than you had intended."

The smile faded from Padraig's face. "Perhaps we took the wrong path through the mountains. It would certainly explain the delay."

"You're admitting your wrongdoing?" asked Farris. "Well done, Captain Tuathil. That takes significant strength."

"I'll heed your words, Farris, and ignore your tone," said Padraig. "Our final destination is due west ahead of us, though too far to make in one day's travel. This road looks like it'll take us to Rosca Umhír, though it'll be past nightfall when we reach there. Does anyone object to walking in the dark?"

"We're not likely to run into any trouble," said Nicole. "Unless any highway men survived the horde."

"Though unlikely," said Padraig. "Any who managed to would certainly be a force to be reckoned with."

The others laughed at this, but Fionn didn't join in. He couldn't help but recall his dream. What had the Lady said, that Farris had indirectly saved Fionn from this fate?

He threw Farris a quick glance. Unlike the others, the Simian was not laughing.

***

So easy for them to laugh, thought Farris, urging his mount to move. *But others have survived the horde.*

He put a hand to the halberd attached beside his saddle. If it came to it, he wouldn't hesitate to defend himself, or the party. Perhaps striking down an attacker would be easier to do than stealing food from an impoverished family.

I cannot blame myself, he thought, keeping his eyes focused Rosca Umhír, far ahead. *I must not blame myself.*

Onwards they went, down into the hills of the Godspine. The path took them through a snow-laden forest, which was every bit as still and silent as the Hazelwood. Then it brought them into the wide prairies of the Midlands, taking them through its gentle slopes. Late in the afternoon, they took a quick break, feeding themselves and their mounts for a hard ride into the night.

By the time night came, they were riding with great speed towards Rosca Umhír. Farris couldn't help but glance behind him every now and then, ensuring they were not being followed, but the road behind them was every bit as desolate as it had been when it was the road ahead of them.

Soon, they came towards the gates of Rosca Umhír. Although Farris had expected them to be unguarded, he did not expect to them to be in the state he found them.

The gatehouse lay in ruin, nothing more than a mass of red rubble piled up before a huge gap in the city walls. Beyond that, many buildings were destroyed: burned frames of blackened wood either side a cobblestone path littered with debris.

"The horde attacked in full force," said Aislinn, her voice cracking into a whisper.

Of course, thought Farris. *She was here when it came. She rode out to meet him, when her lord father was content with locking himself away in his keep.* He couldn't help but admire her bravery. However foolish it was.

But does bravery even come in other forms?

They walked slowly though the ruined city. The place was certainly in a worse state than Point Grey. Considering this, Farris wondered how Cruachan was faring. Though he didn't consider it for much longer.

"We should find a place to stay," said Fionn. "Perhaps the keep is in a better condition than the buildings here."

"I'm sure it is," said Aislinn. "And with a heavy heart, I can only hope the horde found a way in and left a way for us to follow."

"If not, I'm sure Farris here can break and enter for us!"

Farris, however, wasn't paying them any notice. His attention was fixated on a cobblestone path extending eastwards near a row of hedges, away from the main road on which they stood. A path they likely would have passed with little mind, Farris noticed now that some stones here were cracked. Cracked in a manner far more intentional than the rest of the ruined city. Elsewhere, cobblestones were broken and upturned and scattered, but here, they were in place and fractured only slightly. These cracked stones formed the shape of two circles: one within the other. Farris squinted down the path, and indeed, his initial suspicion was proven correct when he saw that beneath these concentric circles were more cracked stones made a sharp V shape.

"Cant," said Farris. He stopped and dismounted.

"You... can't?" asked Padraig.

"Thieves' cant," replied Farris, before rushing towards the shape on the ground. The two lines forming a V pointed towards a stone building, with walls that still stood, but it bore no roof, having likely been once thatched before the horde's fires burned it away.

Above its door frame was the same symbol, scratched into its surface and barely visible.

Without hesitation, Farris pushed through the remnants of a small wooden gate upon a low stone wall and bolted into the building.

The interior was a mess, blackened with burns and void of anything of use. Farris ran through the rooms, searching every wall for more markings, but found none. Behind him, Nicole stepped into the building.

"Farris, what's going on?"

"Thieves' cant," he repeated, gesturing to the symbol on the cracked stones. "A code, devised by the Guild. We mark buildings for burgling, warning or informing other thieves of what's inside: valuables, guards, dogs, mages, children, focus-crystals, traps, friends of the Guild, enemies of the Guild… we have a specific symbol for each.”

“Is this what you mean?” asked Padraig from outside. “This symbol over the path?”

“Yes, and there's one over the door too,” said Farris. “That one indicates a cache is here, waiting to be picked up. But it was never picked up, otherwise the glyph would be crossed out.”

“And why does it matter?” said Padraig. “What use is gold to us right now?”

Farris ignored the captain and went out through the back door of the house. He came into a small stone alley, facing another row of burnt-out houses. Stepping backwards, Farris examined all the walls, looking for another glyph, until he spotted a scratching on the ground. Barely visible beneath the flame-scarred stone, was another symbol. This one had an image similar to the first, but instead of a V underneath the concentric circles, this one bore an X.

“Here,” said Farris, crouching. “It's under the stone. But we'll need a specific tool to open it.”

Fionn appeared by his side. “If its ordinary stone, I can help.” The mage rolled up his sleeves. “But I was never very good at Geomancy, so it might take some time.”

Farris stepped aside to let the mage get to work. Either Fionn was a liar, or underestimated his own skill, as he made quick work of the task. The symbol was actually etched upon a stone slab, made to blend perfectly in with the rest of the ground. With seemingly little effort, Fionn lifted this stone slab upwards, then cast it aside, leaving a square hole. Farris quickly reached inside.

He felt something at the bottom, like a heavy box. Taking more time than Fionn had opening the hole, Farris pulled the object out. It proved to be a wooden chest, bound shut with iron straps. He placed it on the ground.

"It's locked," he said, then turned again to Fionn. "Can you open it? If not, I may be able to pick the lock, though for that I'll need—"

Before Farris could finish, Fionn waved an arm over the box, and the iron straps pierced the wood. With another quick gesture, the wood shattered, revealing the contents inside.

Firearms. The chest contained a dozen firearms. With wooden handles and brass spouts., they were each small enough to be held on one hand. Farris passed one to Nicole, who examined it closely.

"These are mine, alright. Argyll had me manufacture more than I can count, but I always assumed they remained in Penance, though. I wonder how they made it all the way out here?"

"There were Simians here," said Aislinn. "Most lived in peace, but there were a group that called themselves the Knights of the Wood and claimed responsibility for a great deal of crime in the city."

"I've never heard of them," said Farris. "But the Silverback often said that he had allies throughout the kingdom."

Nicole threw Farris a glance, with narrowed eyes. Farris considered her warning for a moment, then went on anyway.

"The Silverback was planning to attack the Seachtú," he said, presenting a firearm to the rest of the party. "It's possible that he had allies armed and ready here, ready to attack Keep Carríga at the same time he was planning on striking Point Grey."

"The bastard!" cried Padraig. "So, the rumours were true this whole time." He leered at Farris, who ignored him.

"A co-ordinated attack?" cut in Fionn. "It would have forced the Crown to either spread its resources out thin to defend everywhere at once or prioritise one Seachtú over another."

"Essentially handing whichever one lay undefended right into Argyll's hands," said Nicole.

"The Silverback's reach surely knew no end," said Farris, carefully eying an irate Padraig. "He'd often balance so many plans and schemes at once, I never knew how he'd keep up with them all." He reached into the chest. Among the firearms, was a small white satchel. He picked it up and rattled it. It gave off the sound of many tiny metal objects inside.

"Ammunition," said Nicole. "We may find use for these. Take what you can. firearms. In the morning, I can show you all how to fire them."

"That is a kind offer," said Padraig. "But I'm much more comfortable with my sword, and what use would we have for these with the Firemaster at our side?"

Farris didn't pay the others much mind, instead reaching into the chest for the last object inside. He pulled out what at first looked like a rock, but on examining it, he saw that, although made from stone, its surface was perfectly smooth. It felt like a ball used in some sort of sport, but it seemed too heavy for any practical use. He tossed it from one hand into another, gauging its weight.

"Farris, no!" cried Nicole, stepping forward. She snatched the ball from his hand. "Where did you find this?"

"Inside," said Farris, nodding towards the chest. "With the others. What is it?"

Nicole held the ball in her hands, cradling it against her chest.

"A... weapon I developed, perhaps a year ago. I only made a few protypes, and I thought Argyll had them all destroyed."

"A weapon?" asked Padraig. "A weapon for what?"

"It's an explosive," said Nicole. "Though more potent than anything ever conceived before. Inside is an array of compartments, filled with chemicals set to react with one another once they come into contact. This reaction takes the form of an explosion big enough to crack a mountain in half."

The group fell silent. After a pause, Fionn spoke first.

"And why would Argyll have them destroyed?"

Nicole sighed. "I wish I could say that it was because I found their design inhumane. All it would take a single smuggler to plant one of these in a castle's foundations to destroy the whole structure. But Argyll expressed another concern. With the surrounding material being simple stone, a Geomancer could crack it from afar in a fight, rendering it useless in magic warfare."

"It makes sense then," said Aislinn, "to bring it to Rosca Umhir. Keep Carríga had the reputation of an impenetrable fortress. If one of these things can destroy a castle, what better one to destroy than this?"

Nicole pulled off her pack and placed the stone object gently inside. "Help yourselves to the firearms, but I'll keep this one safe."

They then made their way to Keep Carríga, a steady stream of destruction leading them to the castle's moat. The drawbridge was lowered, its wood cracked and splintered along the way.

"Why is the bridge lowered?" asked Padraig. "Didn't you say your father had barricaded himself inside the keep?"

"He did," said Aislinn, slowly. "It was lowered for me to ride out against the horde, but it was promptly raised again."

"Perhaps your actions gave your father a change of heart," said Farris. "Maybe more followed your heroic example and rode out too."

Farris had no way of knowing, of course, but he reckoned it was what Aislinn needed to hear right now. But she gave no response either way and led them across bridge.

When they entered the keep, a great hall met them. Huge stone pillars held up a vaulted ceiling painted with an array of greens and browns, mimicking a forest canopy. On the wall of the far end of the hall hung a huge tapestry, depicting an army of green and red figures of green and red wielding spears. A banner flew over their heads, with a blue swan upon a black field, its majestic wings spread outwards.

"My father commissioned that," said Aislinn. "It is meant to show how our family fought with Móráin the First in his conquest, even though House Carríga wasn't even established back then."

They left their mounts there in the hall, figuring the animals could do with some better shelter than the previous night. From there, Aislinn directed them to the keep's living quarters, with Fionn and his Pyromancer's torch leading the way. The mage also ignited torches in their sconces as they went. As with Hunter's Den, the vast surplus of living space now meant each could have their own room. Farris found his in the keep's eastern wing, looking out over the vast darkness of the Midlands.

He made no delay in preparing for sleep. The room was equipped with a thickly curtained four-poster bed with heavy, down bedding. His muscles sighed with relief as he lay down. For a few blissful moments, he closed his eyes, letting his body relax and rest... until he realised that he had forgotten to dampen the room's torch. Reluctantly, he dragged himself out of bed. But as he did, there was a gentle knock on the door.

"Yes?" said Farris, his heart racing. "Come in."

Nicole stepped through the door, slowly, avoiding Farris's eyes.

"Your room is very nice," she said. Her demeanour seemed far different from the last time she paid Farris a late-night visit, but he dared not speculate as to why.

"And isn't yours?" he said. "They should have given you the countess's quarters."

"Mine's dark and cold," she said. "And not as large."

"You can stay here, if you want." Farris barely realised the words as they escaped his lips.

Nicole smiled. "You haven't changed one bit." She brushed passed him towards the bed and climbed in.

What's gotten into her? thought Farris. *Doesn't she hate me?*

Farris extinguished the torch, then sat on the edge of the bed.

"Do you still feel the same as you did before?" he said. "About this journey?"

"You need to sleep, Farris. We're climbing a mountain tomorrow, remember?"

He sighed and lay down next to her, pulling the covers over both of them. He lay on his back at first, staring into the darkness, until Nicole shimmied towards him. She took his arm and put it over her shoulder, forcing him to face her. She pressed her back against his chest.

"No," she whispered. "I'm glad you decided to go. And even gladder that I joined too."

"What changed your mind?"

"You did." She caressed his arm, making each hair stand on end. "I meant why I said, the night before we left. That the immortal... lad doesn't need protecting." She paused and took a deep breath. "I wanted to protect *you*. I wanted to convince you not to come. And when I saw there was no changing that stubborn mind of yours, I knew what I had to do."

"You didn't have to do anything."

"No, you were the one with the choice. Not me. And each day, it's looking more and more like you made the right one. I don't know how you do it. In Hunter's Den, Aislinn told me about your plan back in Penance. How you refused to choose between starving an army or starving civilians, and went to Point Grey to make sure none had to. You've always been one to see right through a problem to find a solution no one else could. It's admirable."

A breath caught in Farris's throat. "It wasn't admirable."

"Of course, it was! All that food would have gone to waste there, while the people of Penance would have gone hungry."

"There was a... family." Farris's voice cracked. "A... a family. In...."

Nicole's delicate stroking of Farris's arm came to an abrupt halt. "No...."

"F-farmers," spluttered Farris. Tears came streaming forth, and he could not hold them back. "There were children, and we —"

"Shhh," hushed Nicole. She grasped Farris's arm. "You had no choice."

"*They* had no choice. We ordered them from... from their home. And one...."

Nicole pressed Farris's arm against her lips. The warmth of her breath soothed the fear that raged through his body. "It's okay," she said. "It's okay now."

Farris closed his eyes tight, so tight that blurred colours formed in his vision. But those blurs took the shape of the young lad in the rafters. The one who tried to defend his family. The one Farris had killed.

Like a fever, a trembling anxiety took hold of his chest. He was openly sobbing now, in front of another person, but his fear was so great now he no longer cared who saw him. So many memories surfaced in that moment. The other starving Simians growing up in the Dustworks. Fistfights and scraps that got out of hand between rival gangs. The traitors of the Thieves Guild he killed in Penance. The lies he told King Diarmuid. Chester the Lucky floating down the canal. *The Glory of Penance* crashing out of the sky. The beadhbhs of the Glenn that preyed on the survivors of the wreck. The troll in the Clifflands. The horde in Penance. Morrigan opening the ground at Dromán to swallow the army of the Triad. All Farris wanted to do was close his eyes, so he would not have to see these memories again, but his eyes were already shut tight, and there was no escape. Only a voice, a soothing voice telling him that everything was going to be okay, over and over again, quelled the storm. As he focused on her voice, and the touch of her hand on his arm, Farris's heartbeat slowed, and his breaths grew longer and full. His mind turned its attention away from those terrible memories to the Simian lying next to him, hushing him, soothing him, like a mother would a child. Something Farris had never felt before.

As if realising her effect, Nicole went quiet, and the two lay there in silence. His breathing matched hers, both chests rising and falling together. Farris's mind relaxed now, idle thoughts winding through it. All of his attention remained fixed firmly on his heartbeat, beating loud, yet slow, and tranquil. In the silence, he could even hear Nicole's heart beating too, sharing the same rhythm as his own.

Some time passed, and Farris found sleep setting in. But just as he was about to give in fully to slumber, Nicole whispered something. Three words Farris had never heard whispered before. Three words surely no sane Simian had ever said. Farris's eyes remained closed as she said whatever she said, for he was sure she had misspoken. Or maybe he had misheard. Perhaps she had been asleep and spoke in the way that nonsense mutterings sometimes escape the lips of those deep in dreams. He considered saying something. He considered waking her up. For a maddening second, he considered saying those same three words back to her. But he could not bring himself to, for they were Human words for Human hearts. How foolish it would be, he thought, if he had misheard, or she had misspoken, and he was to say them back?

Hadn't she scolded him before for acting too much like a Human? Surely it was more likely, Farris reckoned, that she had not said those words, and that he had just wanted to hear them so badly he imagined it.

Part of him pondered on the small chance he had heard her correctly, and she really did mean it, which would allow him to say those words back to her and really mean it too.

But the odds of that, he reasoned, were so infinitesimal that he may as well not even consider it a possibility at all.

No, it was far easier for Farris to pretend he was asleep and say nothing. This he did, and continued to do so, for the rest of the night.

CHAPTER 17:
AS IT WAS WRITTEN

After a terrible journey through the Godspine, we have arrived in Rosca Umhir. This place is a welcome most warm, compared to what we came through to get here.

As we arrived, Lady Carríga said–

Journal of Padraig Tuathil, 22nd Day under the Moon of Nes, AC404

***

Fionn found himself in an unfamiliar place. He looked out a tall tower, over a dark and still landscape. The breeze from outside brushed cold upon his cheeks.

Where am I? he thought, moving towards the window, which opened over the roof of an adjacent tower, its peak was lower than the one he stood in.

He looked outside.

There, sitting on the edge of the roof of the lower tower, was Morrigan. She turned to look at Fionn, then gave a knowing, malicious grin.

***

Abruptly, Fionn awoke. Beads of sweat ran down his brow, and heat pulsed through his body like he had a fever. He glanced around the room, confirming that he was indeed back in his bed chambers in Keep Carríga.

What was that dream? Where was I?

You were looking out from the Northern Tower, lad!

Fionn gasped. *Sir Bearach! You're back! I thought you were dead!*

It doesn't matter what I was, she's there. The tower from your dream is here in Keep Carríga. Go, lad! Go!

Without hesitation, Fionn obeyed the dead knight. He leapt out of bed and threw a cloak on over his underclothes without fastening its strings.

He ran out into the empty hallway, stepping from cold, damp stone to a dusty carpet that ran through the centre of the floor.

Fionn realised that he had no idea where to go.

Left! roared sir Bearach. *Past the study!*

Doing as he was told, Fionn bolted across the hall, lighting a Pyromancer's torch to illuminate the way. He paid little mind to the portraits and coats of arms that rushed past.

Door here, to the right!

Fionn stopped in his tracks and pushed through an old wooden door. It revealed itself to be partway up a spiral, stone staircase.

Which way should I—

Up, you fool!

Fionn tore up the stairs. With the excitement of waking up so abruptly now fading, he was becoming aware of how uncomfortably cold his bare feet were.

He reached the top of the tower. It seemed quite different than the one from his dream, as this one had a black and green tapestry hung on the far end of the large, circular room, and its windows were shuttered closed.

Apparently sensing Fionn's apprehension, Sir Bearach yelled, *Out across the battlements, lad, go!*

Taking a deep breath, Fionn pushed through a reinforced wooden door, and ran out into the freezing night.

Me and Ash used to hide up here, said Bearach, as Fionn crossed the castle walls. Up ahead, two towers stood, one slightly taller than the other. *Whenever we had chores that we didn't want to do or lessons we didn't want to learn.*

Barely listening, Fionn increased the heat of his flame and held it close to his chest. Through gritted teeth, he grimaced as the cold air entered his lungs.

He welcomed the relative warmth of the Northern Tower as he entered and sprinted up its steps. As he approached the top, he recognised his surroundings, focusing on a window that opened into the darkness, over the slated roof of the smaller tower.

Even before he reached it, Fionn saw there was a figure sitting outside.

He readied a fist of fire. After all that she had done, from Penance to Dromán, from her hometown to the capital of Alabach, Morrígan would finally pay.

Fionn ran to the window, ready to launch a ball of fire at the figure, until it turned, revealing herself to be indeed Morrígan. She spread her great black wings outwards, a stark contrast to her pale, expressionless face.

"Lower your weapon," she said, her voice cold and even. "We both know that neither of us can die, so fighting would be pointless."

Fionn paused but did not quell his flame.

She's lying! roared Sir Bearach. *Kill her now and end it all!*

"As I'm sure you know," she said, "I can destroy this tower, and the land beneath it faster than you can click your fingers. You may also be wondering why I haven't done so already."

Considering this, Fionn slowly let the fire in his hands go out.

What are you doing? said Sir Bearach.

If she wants to, she could bury us, replied Fionn. *Best not to give her a reason to. Not yet, at least.*

"What do you want?" he said aloud.

"Many things, Fionn the Red. But for now, only to talk."

Fionn paused for a moment, considering her strange request, given all that had happened. He was well aware of how warring generals would often parlay on the eve of a great battle. Even King Móráin the First did this with the Simians when he landed in Alabach. It was an honour to be upheld no matter how both sides hated one another. Maybe she would uphold the same here?

Don't be daft, lad! cried Sir Bearach. *She opened up the earth itself to swallow an entire army, you included! Where is the honour in that? Incinerate her where she stands!*

But we have so many questions, said Fionn, attempting to convince the knight. However, the mage's mind was already made up.

"Fine," he said. He sat on the windowsill and let his legs dangle off the ledge, facing Morrígan, who stood on the roof of the lower tower. "What do you wish to talk about?"

Morrígan smirked. "I am seeking your help."

Bearach guffawed loudly. Fionn almost wanted to do the same. "Why in the Holy Hell would I ever, *ever*, want to help you?"

"Because, Fionn the Red," said Morrígan, shuffling and unfurling her wings, "both of us have been lied to."

"You will need speak more plainly than that. And you keep using my old title. I'm a Firemaster now."

"No. According to the Tapestry of Fate, you never made it to Penance, and you never killed Conleth to earn the title of Firemaster."

Fionn balled his hands into a fist. For her to speak so casually about what happened to Conleth, all he wanted to do was kill her there and then.

No lad! said Sir Bearach. *Let her speak first.*

What happened to incinerating her where she stands?

Do that afterwards!

"Sure," said Fionn, relaxing his fingers. "The Lady Meadhbh said I was meant to die on the way to Penance."

"She lied," said Morrigan. "Or at least, She did not tell the full truth. Fate dictated that you were to set upon by bandits, but they did not kill you. They tried, but your Divine Gift frightened them, and they sank you to the bottom of Heretic's Bay."

"The dream," said Fionn. "I saw...."

"I showed you," said Morrigan. "I showed you what the Tapestry dictates should have happened. In reality, Farris the Simian killed those bandits on his own journey to Penance. A journey that was never meant to happen. For instead of dying at the Clifflands, as he was meant to, he spread seeds of chaos throughout the threads of fate."

"And you were meant to find me," said Fionn. "You opened up the ocean and found me on its floor."

"This is what concerned me," said Morrigan. "The power of Meadhbh allows me to see Tapestry as it was originally written, but I lack her centuries of wisdom to fully interpret the meaning. That is why I need your help."

Fionn nodded slowly.

"As it was written," Morrigan began, "you were buried in Heretic Bay, and I came to find you. But I do not understand why I would do that."

"Was it not to claim my power too?" said Fionn. "As you did with Diarmuid and Meadhbh? As you seek to do with Seletoth?"

"That is what I assumed," said Morrigan. "As it was written, I killed Diarmuid in Cruachan, Meadhbh in Dromán, then Seletoth atop Mount Selyth. These, I was destined to do in quick succession, urged by a lust to become like the gods themselves.

"But when I slew Meadhbh and saw the Tapestry of Fate for myself, I stopped to study it. For it was written that I would never reach Penance, which I already had, and that I would kill King Diarmuid in Cruachan, which I never did. Upon searching for an answer, I saw the actions of Farris the Simian, like a scorch-mark through its threads, unravelling them wherever he went. Other Simians bore similar marks upon, though none as large as his.

"And as I examined them, I saw what was meant to become of you, which then brings me to how I was meant to find you on the bottom of Heretic's Bay."

"Why is that so important?" said Fionn. "You said so yourself, you want to steal the powers of the gods. Surely this would include me too?"

"That is logical," said Morrigan. "But the words I was meant to say upon finding you were not. As it was written, I said, 'Come, Fionn, Lord Seletoth is waiting for us.'"

Fionn stared back. He recalled that she said those words in his dream; the dream she had apparently shown him, but still, he didn't follow.

Morrigan sighed. "Consider this," she said, adapting the air of a teacher. "My words imply the Seletoth was still alive at this point, as it was written, and that I had spoken to Him. Furthermore, they also imply that He knew you were alive, and wanted both of us to come to Him."

"Sure," said Fionn. "So, this means you were fated to find Him, speak to Him, then come to find me afterwards?"

"Correct. But whenever I try to look at that part of the Tapestry, where I speak to Him, the threads become unclear, and something in my mind seems to... unravel. All I know is that when I was meant to walk through that great iron door atop Mount Selyth, something terrible happened. And I was no longer myself afterwards."

"I see," said Fionn. "Then why do you seek my help?"

"Because you already have some of Seletoth's power. Perhaps whatever was meant to happen to me up there will not happen to you."

"The dream in the church," said Fionn. "With you as a child, and you as you are today, waking down the aisle and through that door. Was that your work too?"

"Yes," said Morrigan. "Though I cannot interpret the details, I know that I must not confront Seletoth Himself, despite what the Tapestry says should have happened."

Fionn's brain struggled to keep up with this. "What do you want from me, then?"

"You are already on the way to confront Seletoth. I need you do continue your quest, confront Seletoth, and kill Him."

Fionn gasped, echoed by Sir Bearach.

"Are you serious?" said Fionn. "Why would I do such a thing? Seletoth is our last chance at... at defeating you!"

"When you learn of His lies," said Morrigan, "perhaps you will understand. If you do this, and acquire His power, we can both wipe away the life He created here and start anew, as two gods."

"No!" said Fionn. "Nobody else is going to die. I'll fight you with every fibre of my soul if it stops you."

"Those created by Seletoth are lives with no value. Together we can create life with *real* meaning. With *real* purpose."

Having heard enough, Fionn readied a ball of fire in his hands. With his other hand, he held the side of the window, reeling back to hurl the flame at Morrigan. She reacted quickly, throwing herself off the roof into the darkness below. With his heart pounding in his chest, Fionn raced to the edge, scanning the darkness for a sign for where she went.

Then, far to the north, he saw a dark shape dart away through the sky. As he looked on, a soft voice spoke in his ears:

"Find Him, learn the Truth, then kill Him. If you change your mind, you will know where to find me."

CHAPTER 18:
AT MOUNT SELYTH'S PEAK

We struggled at first in our journey through the Glenn. The wildlife stalked us and hunted us with the ferocity of no animal I have ever seen before. One of my men, a naturalist in his spare time, noted that this was likely a result of the vegetation that grew there, for every plant, every leaf, every blade of grass was imbedded with poison. As to why the plants had grown this way, he had no answer.

This desolate place did not obey the laws of nature as we knew it. Even with that sickly presence thick in the air, we ventured on, for Seletoth's voice called to us.

And I knew He was close.

The Truth, by King Móráin I, AC55

***

The next morning, the party made their preparations for the final day's journey. Mount Selyth was six hours' ride south, through hills thickly wooded with snow-laden conifers. Despite the expected ease of this route, they still prepared as if it was to be a lengthy expedition. Padraig and Aislinn donned the colours of their respective houses, as if riding out to a great battle. Fionn wore his bright red cloak, fastened thickly against the cold to come, with layers of furs packed against his chest underneath. Both Farris and Nicole wore their thick, Simian armour, the former not acknowledging the latter as he did.

I opened up far too much last night, Farris told himself. *Best to forget about it and focus on the journey.*

They left Rosca Umhír far more armed than they had when they arrived. From the Silverback's cache, Farris wore a holster around his hips with two firearms strapped within. Nicole bore the same, with a leather satchel over one shoulder, containing ammunition, and among other things, her round, explosive stone.

With each step he took, Farris could have sworn the frozen countryside grew quieter and quieter until a silence heavier than the hills themselves bore down upon them.

The road wound through frosty hedgerows and hills towards the great mountain. Like an abscess upon the land's surface, swollen rocks rose over one another, forming a bloated mass of icy stone.

Farris rode next to Fionn, both having travelled in silence for most of the day. Eventually, Farris spoke.

"So, what are you gonna ask Him?" he asked.

Fionn didn't respond but stared blankly ahead. Sure that he had heard, Farris went to ask again, but before he did, Fionn responded.

"Why?"

"Well, I thought it was worthwhile—" Farris cut himself off. He realised Fionn's response was literal. Of course, no question other than *Why?* would be worth asking.

But could there even be an answer worth hearing.

Abruptly, the path turned towards the towering stone; walls of ice and rock higher than Farris could see. Despite his layers of chainmail and plate, a breeze more chilling than any before pierced his chest, causing the fur on the back of his neck to stand on end. Hastily, he pulled on his helm, cringing under the steel's chill.

Through limited vision, Farris turned his attention to the road ahead, daring not to speak any further. Many said that none who climbed this mountain ever returned, but no one ever elaborated on why this was the case.

Higher and higher they went, the path becoming tougher to traverse with each step. Padraig had suggested that they tie up their mounts much earlier in their hike, but only when they reached an icy slope as steep as a wall, and Fionn made the same suggestion, did the others listen.

Farris took to the wall first, firmly planting two climbing spikes an arm's reach overhead. Despite the weight of his armour, he pulled himself up with little effort, stabbing into the ice with each thrust. Aside from the cold, Farris had climbed walls in far worse conditions back in Penance.

With a thick hempen rope dangling from his waist, Farris reached the top of the incline after a few short minutes. Once he reached the summit, he planted the rope into the ground and signalled for the rest to climb up. Fionn struggled the most out of the other four, due to his mutilated fingers, but made it up in good time with help from them.

"Which way now?" asked Nicole.

Without saying a word, Fionn started on down one path, and the others followed. Farris couldn't help but wonder what was going on inside that mage's head. It seemed as if he was getting some sort of information from an unseen source, like guidance from a god.

I hope he knows what he's doing, either way.

Onwards they went, walking on weary feet. Breathing came harder to Farris the higher they went, his damp breath bringing drips of warm water to the inside of his helm. He shuddered to think what it must smell like.

"Stop," rasped Fionn abruptly. The mage halted the others with a half-raised arm. "There's something up ahead."

Squinting through his visor, Farris saw that this indeed was true. The path carried on forward, meandering through icy rocks like a river. At what would have been its bank, an old wooden structure stood.

"A guardhouse," whispered Padraig. "I fear we may be —"

A hissing shot rang past Farris's ear, followed by another. A third struck him in the forehead, violently shaking his helm and knocking him to the ground. He quickly scrambled to his feet, as a dozen more crossbow bolts rained down upon them.

"Farris, over here!" cried Nicole, taking refuge with the others behind a thick boulder jutting out from the ground.

Farris darted over as more projectiles shot towards him, one flashing right past his eyes. As he stumbled forward, he stole a quick glance up ahead, and saw six cloaked figures standing next to the guardhouse, and more climbing out.

Wraiths!

Farris swore under his breath as he dove behind the boulder with the others. Fire burned in Fionn's hand as the mage launched flames blindly over his head, not daring to move from his hiding space. Padraig clutched a useless broadsword in one hand as Aislinn Carríga unsheathed her own.

"They've pinned us," said Farris, quickly sticking his head out to examine what lay before them. "There's no way over."

"Look up!" cried Nicole, with terror in her voice. "There's more!"

Indeed, high above them, along the icy valley walls, another group of Wraiths marched forward, crossbows in their hands.

"We need to retreat," said Farris. "Leave and regroup!"

More bolts tore through the air as Farris gave the signal to flee. Everything seemed to slow as he ran, with Nicole and Fionn by his side, the other two not a step behind. The Firemaster roared as he threw more flames behind him, though these were met with another stream of silent bolts.

"Regroup!" cried Farris. "Over here—"

From the corner of Farris's limited vision, Nicole glanced back up the valley, but as soon as she turned, a bolt struck her in the face with a sickening crack. She fell backwards, collapsing onto the stone floor with a clang of metal.

"No!"

Paying the salvo of ammunition little mind, Farris leapt to the ground where Nicole lay. A thick iron bolt extended out from her visor, barely small enough to fit. Blood poured out from the motionless helm, running down the snow-clad steel in drips.

"No," Farris whispered, desperately shaking her body. "Not here... not like this."

But she did not respond.

"Please," said Farris, shaking her again. "Don't leave me. Nicole, don't leave me!"

More bolts fell around him, one striking the back of his neck, ricocheting off his armour.

"Don't. Please. There's no one else."

Tears streamed down his face, obscuring his vision.

"No one else knew," he sobbed, bowing his head over her chest. "No one else knew me like you did."

His throat went dry, his words failed.

No one else made me feel unafraid, as you did.

A flaming arrow struck the ground by Farris's feet, followed by another.

"She loved me," he whispered. "She said she loved me, but I was too afraid to say the same."

Because I am a coward.

Farris heard voices, shouting out to him. But whether they came from his allies, or his enemies, he did not know.

He removed his gauntlets, then removed one of Nicole's. With both his hands, he clutched her exposed one. The kindness and warmth that her touch once held had already gone, lost to the cold of this dead world.

Maybe he always knew how he felt but was too afraid to acknowledge it. Or maybe he only realised it now that she was gone. There in that isolated, frigid valley, with steel bolts and fiery arrows raining down upon him, it all became clear.

"I loved her," he said. Slowly, he stood, flexing his exposed fingers. He faced the Wraiths, as more crossbow bolts bounced off his armour.

"I loved her!" he roared. His voice boomed through the canyon. A familiar fear gripped Farris's spine. The same anxiety that plagued him his whole life. The same terror that made him lie so often, to pretend he was someone he was not. But without Nicole's warm presence to quell it, the old fear thundered through his chest.

There's nothing left in this world to fight for. There's nothing left to fear.

"Do you hear me?" he cried, reaching down for Nicole's satchel. "Do you fucking hear me?"

He picked it up, checking that the ammunition was inside. They were, along with Nicole's explosive device.

I'll kill them all, he swore, slinging the satchel over his shoulder. *I'll kill them all and shove this down Seletoth's fucking throat myself.*

From his waist, he pulled two daggers, clutching both tightly in each hand. Then he turned towards the valley and *howled.* His chest strained with the outpour of grief, and whole mountain seemed to shake. In that cry, there was everything he had felt for her. Everything had had been afraid to admit. Everything she had the courage to tell him, but he did not have the same to say it back.

I should have told her first. I should have told her every hour of every day.

He roared again, but this time a cloud of flaming arrows answered. Farris raised his arm to cover his visor. Most of them missed their mark, while others bluntly struck his body and bounced off.

"She never wanted to come," he whispered, more tears forming. "She wanted to go home to Penance, to live the rest of our lives in peace. Together." He sniffed, clenching the daggers in both hands. "But you took that from her, and for what?"

Farris jumped into a sprint.

"AND FOR WHAT?!"

Through the flaming arrows and bolts of the Wraiths, Farris tore forwards, not slowing no matter how many hit him.

Her armour is made from strong stuff.

Through the thin slit of his helm, Farris focused on one Wraith standing in the centre path up ahead. The dark figure held his crossbow between his knees, frantically reloading as two of his companions continued to fire at Farris.

But the enraged Simian did not slow.

As if observing his actions from another body, Farris saw himself leap upon the Wraith, plunging a dagger into the darkness of his hood. They both fell to the ground, the cloak of the Wraith knocked askew. With a wet crunch, the blade of Farris's dagger found the centre of the Wraith's now exposed face.

Farris ripped the bloodied blade from bone and turned to the other two. Both figures balked in response, hands raised in surrender.

As anguish surged through his veins, Farris plunged forward, running both blades across the chests of the cloaked figures. The two fell easily, their hoods revealing two old, greying men.

Just men, thought Farris, turning his attention to the others, now fleeing up the mountain path. *Only men.*

Farris threw the daggers aside and reached into his holster, his fingers finding two firearms. Without a second's hesitation, he pulled both out and fired at those running, immediately dropping two, leaving one remaining.

"TELL THE OTHERS!" Farris roared. "TELL THEM I'LL KILL YOU ALL!"

Several yards from where he stood, a rope ladder hung down the cliff's face, leading up to where the Wraith's upon the higher ground had been. Farris threw himself against the stone face, pulling himself up the ladder with pained movements.

Don't think about her, Farris told himself. *Just keep on moving. Don't stop until they're all dead.*

When Farris reached the top, he was greeted with another burst of ammunition, bolts and fiery arrows bouncing from his armour. Six Wraiths stood before him, huddled together like an unarmed phalanx.

"WHERE IS YOUR GOD?" Farris roared, pointing two bloodied daggers in front of him. "TELL ME OR I'LL KILL YOU ALL!"

His vision was obscured by the helm, so he pulled it off. The blood of those he killed blurred in his eyes. Farris screamed the name the only person who had ever loved him, then charged towards the cloaked men.

Another salvo of bolts and arrows met him.

***

"Now's our chance," said Fionn. He thought it best to not show the others his fear. And his pain. "While they're distracted."

"Distracted?" cried Padraig. "She's dead. Dead! And that's all you can say?"

Ignore him, said Sir Bearach. *Just go. They'll follow. You won't get another chance.*

Fionn sprinted forward, through an arrow-littered ground. The faint footsteps of the others told him they followed.

Don't look at her, urged Sir Bearach as they passed Nicole's corpse. *You need to keep moving, or she won't be the last.*

A harrowing scream rang out overhead, and the body of a Wraith came tumbling down the valley wall. More cries rang out from above, but Fionn kept his attention focused ahead. Not on the wooden outpost, but on the road that wound past it.

"Farris," muttered Aislinn as they ran past the blood-soaked structure.

"He'll be fine," assured Padraig somewhere behind Fionn. "He's strong, that one."

Onwards, they went, leaving the scene of the slaughter behind. Fionn led the way, the snow-encrusted path taking them further up the mountain, curving towards the peak. The shrivelled remains of pine trees flanked the path, like skeletal sentinels standing tall overhead.

Farris... thought Fionn, a lump starting to form in his throat.

Not now, urged Sir Bearach. *Dwelling on it won't help. You need to keep moving.*

Fionn gritted his teeth. The dead knight was right.

I can't stop. Nobody else can do this but me.

Up ahead, a thin sliver of smoke rose upwards, like a great serpent swimming through clouds. This, joined by the sounds of faint voices, alluded to a settlement up ahead.

"More Wraiths?" asked Padraig, not too far behind Fionn. "Should we stop?"

"No," said Fionn, curtly, He brought his rings together, catching the spark they produced and igniting it. "We'll strike first."

Without giving further orders, Fionn sprinted ahead, only assuming Padraig and Aislinn followed. The path rose over a steep hill. Once Fionn reached its crest, he let the fire quench in his hand, for there would be no need for an ambush.

Before him, the path led up to a small encampment. Wooden buildings surrounded a great bazaar in the centre, in which a fire burned brightly, expelling plumes of smoke and rich odours of incense.

Dozens of figures surrounded the fire, running to and fro, but none appeared to be armed. Nor did they seem like the Wraiths from before. These instead were simply men, old men, dressed in black robes. Not unlike the druids of the Trinity, these holy men scurried throughout the settlement, worried cries and orders being called back and forth.

Fionn ran towards the bazaar, grabbing the arm of one old man running by.

"Seletoth," said Fionn. "I need to see Him."

The man stared back, pale-faced, and with wide eyes encircled with black weariness.

"None may see the Lord," he whimpered, casting a frightened glance at Padraig and Aislinn, who came up behind Fionn. "Only the Blind Ones may enter."

Perhaps unconsciously, the old man nodded towards the far end of the settlement, where the rest of the mountain rose into the clouds. At the base of this peak, a huge, crooked opening was embedded in the stone, covered with a thick, grey canvass.

"It's urgent," said Fionn. "He'll be expecting us."

"Ardha!" roared a voice. Another man, younger than the first, ran over to them. He thrusted a crossbow into the old man's hands. "I hope you remember how to use one of these," he said. "He'll be upon us soon enough."

"Who will?" asked Fionn.

The younger man narrowed his eyes. "A Simian," he spat. "Went blood-mad and killed half our garrison. He's coming for the rest of us."

He's alive!

"The Simian is with us," said Fionn. "Take us to whoever is in charge, and we'll ensure no more harm comes to your people."

The two holy men exchanged worried looks, then the older one nodded. The other man turned to Fionn and the others.

"Follow me," he said, turning away before waiting for a response. The three followed, jogging through the encampment. There must have been about two dozen other men and women there, all clad in the same dark robes as those that ambushed them back in the valley.

"Could these be Wraiths?" asked Padraig, though none answered.

The robed man brought them to the foot of the opening, and pushed the canvas inwards, slightly.

"The Blind Ones are inside," said he said. His grip on his crossbow tightened. "They tend to the Lord, but they shall never grant you access to see Him."

"For your sake," said Fionn, stepping through, "they better make an exception."

It took a moment for Fionn's eyes to adjust to the darkness inside, but when they did, he found himself in a wide, circular room, barely illuminated by tiny candles lining the stone wall, twinkling like stars in a night's sky. Stone etchings marked the floor in crooked circles.

Fionn clicked his fingers, illuminating his immediate surroundings. To his surprise, several more robed men stood along the wall, motionless in the dark. They chanted softly in low whispers, but Fionn couldn't make out their words. He pressed onwards, squinting at a nearby worshipper. This one had his grey hood pulled over his head, grey lips moving rapidly as the rest of his face remained perfectly still. When Fionn stepped forward for a closer look, he jumped back, yelling with fright.

The worshipper had no eyes.

Where they should have been, a pale scar upon thin skin lay stretched above his gaunt cheekbones. In the flames of Fionn's torch, the scarring almost seemed translucent, like hide stretched thin.

"We are the ones who have seen too much," said one voice, louder than the rest. Another robed man stood at the far end of the chamber. Both hands stretched upwards. "The minds you've reached, the souls you've touched. The One, most true..."

"Lord Seletoth," answered the others, in unison.

"Who are you?" cried Fionn, stepping towards the one who spoke. Fire raged in the mage's hands.

"We are your Sons, born to no Mother," he continued, ignoring Fionn's words. "We are your seed, One God, no other. No Lady, no King."

"Just Seletoth," came the refrain.

Realisation dawned on Fionn as he stood there, staring up at the eyeless face of the speaker. Older than the rest, this one wore no hood, but an oddly shaped headpiece, asymmetrical in its design. Crooked shapes curved upwards over another, entangled around his forehead. The reflection of Fionn's flames danced upon its steel.

"I've heard this prayer before," said Fionn. "You're Sons of Seletoth, aren't you?"

For the first time, the one who led the prayers responded.

"The Lord has graced many with His infinite wisdom, though most caught but a glimpse. We are those who have seen the Truth in its fullest form, and have come here, to Seletoth's resting place, to tend to Him directly."

"I need to see Him," said Fionn.

The old man chuckled. "None may see Him," he said, gesturing to the scars on his face. "And we make accommodations for those who must be in His presence."

Fionn took a step back. "Why? Why can no one see Him?"

A terrified cry rang out from somewhere outside, followed by a loud crash.

"Farris!" cried Padraig. Two metal clangs told Fionn that both his companions had armed themselves. But the red mage ignored the commotion outside.

"Where is He?" demanded Fionn, taking a defiant step towards the Sons' leader. "I'm the son of King Diarmuid, Third and Nineteenth, and I demand you bring me to Him."

Again, the old man smiled. "He is just beyond here, but even King Diarmuid himself would not be allowed gaze upon the Lord's face."

Another loud crash echoed through the walls, followed by a torrent of screams and shouts.

"Don't you know what's happening?!" roared Fionn. "Diarmuid is dead! Meadhbh is dead! Seletoth is our last hope in stopping Morrigan!"

Fionn caught a glimpse of a great iron door directly behind the old man. The same iron door that he had seen in his dream. In the chapel with Morrigan.

There must be a way in.

"We are aware of what has been destined to come," said the old man. "For Seletoth has shown us all. The Beginning, and the End. For even He is powerless to prevent the End."

"No!" cried Fionn, his voice rising over the commotion outside. "The Lord brought me here! I am to see Him, and I won't let you stand in my way!"

"I told you," said the priest, "none are permitted to enter. For one glance at the Lord is enough to—"

Suddenly, the large canvass at the chamber's entrance was torn open, spilling blinding light from outside over them all. Fionn turned to see Farris Silvertongue, clad in blood-soaked armour, standing before the chaos that was once a quiet settlement. The Simian wore no helm and limped as he strode into the chamber.

"You!" cried the priest. "You—"

With a crack, the old men fell backwards abruptly, a bloody round wound in his forehead. The Simian held a smoking firearm in one hand. The other worshippers cowered in fear, but with a terrifying cry, Farris fired at each one in turn.

"No!" roared Padraig, bolting towards the Simian. "Farris, stop!"

But something else had caught Fionn's attention. Hung around the priest's bloodied neck, a thin chain held a thick, metallic key. Fionn darted forward, pulling the key from it. He glanced back to see Farris collapse to the ground. He clutched his waist with one hand, as blood poured from a wound behind a crack in his armour. In his other hand, he lowered a satchel to the ground. It spilled open, and tiny black balls poured out from it, followed by one large round object of black stone. It rolled to a stop on the floor nearby. Padraig and Aislinn ran to the Simian.

Fionn, instead, sprinted towards the great iron doors. The key quickly found the lock, and as Farris's cries of protest echoed through the chamber, Fionn pushed the door open and stepped inside.

Chapter 19:
Heresy

As we forged through the Glenn, fighting against the beasts of the valley, morale among my men grew low. A reasonable response, for why would we be risking our lives to travel through such a terrible place that no native, or no sane animal would dare stray?

But what we found there challenged their faith far more than anything else we had come upon. The horror of that valley, we swore to never speak of again. A Truth so terrible that few living should ever be made to bare it. But a Truth so important that it should not be forgotten.

The Truth, by King Móráin I, AC55

***

The main hall of the Basilica was crowded, far more than usual. Dozens of Churchguards stood in silent attention against the back wall. Ahead of them, two rows of priests in white robes and druids in grey stood face to face, either side of a red carpet that stretched the length of the chamber. At its end, cardinals and high-cardinals sat upon an altar. The former wore silver robes, the latter the same, augmented with golden ornamentation around the chest and shoulders.

Before them was a golden throne, its back rising high, with an elaborate design representing leafy branches of a gilded tree. And there sat Arch-Canon Cathbad, dressed in the extravagant red and golden robes of his station, with an elaborately pointed headpiece resting upon a wrinkled forehead.

On the far end of the hall, Argyll the Silverback came, accompanied by a handful of the Sons of Seletoth. Ruairí pushed Argyll, the wheels of his new lightweight chair gliding silently along the carpet. As per Argyll's design, this had larger wheels angled outwards, leaving the seat closer to the ground. On either side of Argyll, the tops of the wheels rose over the chair, concealed beneath thin steel sheets. Argyll rested an arm on one of them.

As they moved through the hallway, the rows of priests and druids either side seemed to regard the visitors with contempt, with many avoiding looking directly at Argyll. Through a gap between two standing priests, Argyll briefly caught the eyes of Ned. But this momentary glance was enough to tell him everything he needed to know.

Everything is in place. We are ready.

As they approached the altar, Arch-Canon Cathbad rose and stepped towards Argyll. His immaculate red robes shimmered as he moved. He raised a hand outwards. His middle finger bore a ring bearing a thick, white stone. Argyll leant forward to kiss it.

"Your Holiness," he said. "We are honoured to be in your presence."

"As you should be," said Cathbad. "You seem to have chosen an inopportune time to request this audience. Tell me, why are there so many Simians gathering at Sin?"

"Because we wish to leave this land, Your Holiness. Morrigan the Godslayer has defeated the Triad's army at Dromán. We have no choice now but to flee before she returns."

"There are no lands spared by the Grey Plague," said Cathbad. "You are fleeing one danger to another far worse."

"The Grey Plague has reached this land too," said Argyll. "By your own reasoning, if those lands claimed by it are uninhabitable, why would this land by any different?"

"Because this is the land promised by our Lord!"

"Promised as it may have been, we do not share the same love for it than you do. Many Simians of Penance have agreed to leave, but we have struggled to convince those that hold the Church dearly to them to do the same. Of course, they are free to stay if they wish, but after what this city has already witnessed, surely you can admit that leaving is the best option."

"And where is it you wish to flee to?"

"There are lands beyond the Eternal Sea," said Argyll.

This answer was met with murmurs that frantically ran through the room.

"Heresy!" cried the Arch-Canon, bringing the room back to a tense silence.

Argyll leaned forward in his chair and bowed his head. "All we ask is for your blessing to leave," he said. "With so many of your followers reluctant to join us, we believe your words may encourage them to come."

"Spare me this nonsense," said Cathbad. "We all know your long-distance ships are grounded without our focus-crystals. Have you not come here to grovel before me, and ask for them?"

"No," said Argyll. "We have come to take them."

With this, the Sons of Seletoth removed their hands from under their robes, revealing firearms clenched in each of their fists. Firearms they all pointed directly at the Arch-Canon.

"Guards!" cried Cathbad. "Apprehend these heretics!"

The Churchguards, Humans and Simian among them, immediately responded, stepping forward and lowering their spears. But these, they pointed at the Arch-Canon.

"Traitors!" cried Cathbad. "I'll have you all killed for this! You'll burn in the Holy Hell!"

Ruairí strode forward, pointing his weapon squarely at Cathbad's forehead.

"Beg me for your life," said Ruairí. "Get on your knees and beg this heretic to spare you."

For a moment, Cathbad gazed at Ruairí with defiance. Then his eyes lost their fire, and they acquired a glassy look. Slowly, Cathbad went to his knees. And at the mercy of the Sons of Seletoth, the Churchguard of the Basilica, and Argyll the Silverback, the rest of the druids and the cardinals and the high-cardinals of the Church did the same.

With the firearm still pointed at Cathbad's head, Ruairí reached for his headpiece, and removed it. Trembling, Cathbad now seemed more of a weakened old man, with a pale, bald head bearing whisps of grey hair and blackened liver spots.

"Please," muttered Cathbad. "Spare me."

"I've waited so long for this," said Ruairí. "Let me relish your fear. Your pathetic grovelling. Your—"

"Stop," commanded Argyll. Abruptly, Ruairí turned around.

"Do you not want to see him dead?" he asked. "All of our preparations, was it not for this end? The end where his blood is spilled on his gilded halls?"

"I did," said Argyll. "And it was. But his life may serve a better purpose." Argyll beckoned Ruairí over, who wheeled him towards Cathbad. Argyll leaned inwards, so his face was level with the kneeling pontiff.

"Listen carefully," said Argyll. "Your Humans wish not to leave this land, due to some sort of misplaced belief that the soil here is more special than that of anywhere else. I want you to you convince them otherwise."

Argyll reached down and picked up the Arch-Canon's headpiece. "I need you to wear this, and all of your regalia and your pomp. I want you and your holy men to walk to Sin, and in front of the crowds there, ask for passage to cross the sea. There will be no gods and no kings in our new world, and you will be treated as an equal among the rest of your fellow men. You will board a ship, as an equal, and those reluctant to join before shall see that leaving Alabach is indeed their best option."

Cathbad paused for a moment, then nodded. Argyll gentle placed the headpiece back on his head, and ushered Ruairí to wheel him away.

"Now," Argyll called out to the rest of the room. "Plunder the vaults of this place but take only the focus-crystals we need for the ships. The material wealth the Church has accumulated here shall remain in this doomed land."

With this, the Sons quickly ran past them, towards a doorway to the right of the altar. The Churchguard escorted the holy men from the hall. Cathbad stood to his feet, but Argyll raised a hand.

"Oh, and one more thing," he said. "I'll need your ring."

Reluctantly, Cathbad handed it over, and Argyll clutched it in his fist. As Cathbad left, Argyll looked over his shoulder, up to Ruairí who looked back through narrowed eyes.

"I thought you'd be happier," said Argyll. "Come, let's see about this book."

***

As Ruairí wheeled Argyll through the marbled halls of the Basilica, the shouts and cries of the looters elsewhere in the building echoed overhead.

"Do you think they'll heed your words?" said Ruairí. "They've had so much taken from them; it'll be tempting to claim it all back."

"Perhaps," said Argyll. "But they'll have to leave most of it here if they wish to board our ships. If they want to stay, they are welcome to it all."

Ruairí slowed Argyll to a stop as they reached the end of the hallway. There, a steel grate in a doorway marked the entrance to a large cargo lift.

"I trust this is it?" asked Argyll. "Let's make this quick, please? There's still much to be done."

"Of course," said Ruairí. "We'll take the tome, and we'll be gone."

They entered the lift, and Ruairí examined the pulley mechanism on the far end. After some fiddling, the lift lurched into motion, with ropes pulling and pushing either side. A counterweight quickly passed by as they descended deeper into the darkness.

In silence they waited, until the lift slowed to a stop. There, Ruairí opened the portcullis and wheeled Argyll outside.

A thick door stood before them across a small stretch of marbled floor. The door bore no obvious locking mechanism, nor did it seem to have a keyhole. But adjacent to it, some three feet tall, was marbled column, one face of which was white and smooth. It bore an imprint of the three circles of the Trinity.

As they approached, wordlessly, Argyll handed the arch-canon's ring to Ruairí. The Human handled it carefully and pressed it against the imprint on the column. A moment passed where this seemed to have no effect, then slowly, with a creak and a grind, the door opened.

"Is this some sort of magic?" asked Argyll.

"A lost kind, yes," replied Ruairí, pocketing the ring, and removed a lit torch from beside the column. "And inside, we shall find a great many more lost things."

The door revealed to them what seemed like a cross between a storage room and a museum. Two silver suits of armour stood in attention at the entrance, with piles of neatly packed boxes filling shelves either side. Immediately in front of them, a parchment depicting a map hung behind a glass case.

"I don't recognise those lands," said Argyll, as they passed it.

"The Church would prefer to keep it that way," said Ruairí. "Those are the lands to the east, where Móráin was born. This vault contains a great many treasures from the time of our first king, but there is one treasure in particular I seek."

With a torch in one hand, and the handles of Argyll's chair in the other, Ruairí forged onwards, raising the torch to examine old portraits and busts on display, but he never stopped moving.

Everything he has done was for this moment, Argyll reminded himself. *Not for loyalty to myself. Not for belief in our cause. But for these treasures.*

They took a corner, passing many more shelves of many more books, when Ruairí came to an abrupt stop. Trembling now, he raised his torch up, and pointed ahead.

There, at the end of the room, was a display case containing a red velvet cushion. And on that cushion, sat a book, bound in black leather with golden pages within.

"*The Truth,*" whispered Ruairí. He let go of Argyll's chair. "Written by the hand of Móráin the First Himself."

"That's often how autobiographies are written, yes," said Argyll. Sure, he was intrigued by this Truth he had heard so much about, but it was not his greatest concern right now.

Ruairí did not respond to Argyll's comment. He left Argyll in the middle of the chamber and dashed towards the display case. He hung his torch on a nearby sconce, and with the butt of his firearm, broke open the glass. Its shatter echoed through the room.

"Finally," he said, taking the tome into his hands. "The Truth shall be known to all, and the Church shall no longer have power over us."

Argyll sighed, slightly amused by how Ruairí's body seemed to be *convulsing* with excitement.

The Human opened the first page.

"'It is against the advice of the Church that I recount the things I have seen,'" he read, "'but I do not believe truths as important as these should be forgotten. It is my wish that this account is recorded and locked away, so none may ever look upon these pages. But I do not wish for them to be lost. The truths of our existence, no matter how terrible, should never be lost.'"

"Terrible?" asked Argyll, leaning forward. "That's not what I was expecting."

"Yes," muttered Ruairí. He flicked through the pages. "He describes how he came to power among the disparate Human clans of the eastern lands, and the visions Seletoth showed him. Then he describes the voyage..." He flicked forward a few pages. "... the settlements they established and their struggles with the natives."

Argyll scoffed. "Not dissimilar from your other history books then. Now please, can we go?"

Ruairí didn't respond, seemingly absorbed entirely by what he read. Argyll went to speak again but held his tongue. This was an important moment for the Human, he reasoned, so best to let him have it. For a few minutes, anyway.

Ruairí continued to read, lips moving silently. Every so often, he'd shake his head in disbelief and flick the page. Or often he'd flick the page back, to re-read something, then move a few pages forward.

Then, abruptly, with the turn of another page, Ruairí screamed.

This was no scream of fright, or of excitement, but a disturbing, high-pitched wail that resounded through the room. With the tome still clutched in his hands, and his eyes locked onto it, Ruairí fell to his knees.

"Nooo!" he cried, prolonging that howling syllable until his voice broke. His face contorted into a twisted expression; his eyes shut tight and his mouth fell ajar. He gasped, trying to catch a breath that would not come, and when it did, he inhaled with another maddening note. Once his lungs were full, he shrieked again, louder this time, with the faint impression of *no-no-no-no* behind the inhuman screech.

"Ruairí!" yelled Argyll, still stationary and seated across the room. "What's wrong?"

But only a deranged barrage of sobs answered him, which spluttered out of Ruairí's heaving chest.

"They... found Him," he wheezed, his voice cracking. "In the Glenn...."

"Ruairí," said Argyll, in a softer tone now. He held out a hand. "This was a mistake. Put the book back and let's return to the others."

"In that valley," whimpered Ruairí. "They found no god."

"Yes," said Argyll. "It's just a book, we don't need to take it with us."

"We were created... we were created only to find Him...."

"Come on, Ruairí. Let's go."

"Only to find him, and to aid him.... He created the Tapestry... and the Godslayer... her purpose is only... only to...."

To Argyll's relief, Ruairí put the tome down. But with horror, he saw that the zealot now held a firearm in his hand.

He pointed it at Argyll.

"They *knew!*" rasped Ruairí. "This whole time... they kept this from us!"

Argyll raised his hands in submission. "Put the weapon down, Ruairí," he said. "Please, we need to return to the surface. Now."

"He is not a god," said Ruairí, with a weak, breathy laugh. "There is no god. There is no... purpose."

"Ruairí, please."

"There once was a purpose," he said, looking back at the book. He turned another page, his armed hand lowering. "But we served it. We served it long ago, and life was meant to end when we did."

"Ruairí...."

Abruptly, he aimed the firearm at the ceiling. "We studied the plans of this place, for so long. So long. Do you know what is above, Argyll? Directly above us?"

Argyll shook his head.

"The stores... the stores of focus crystals, blues and reds and greens and whites. The power to mend, and the power to break. The strength of fire, of the earth, or water and of ice.

But our people are looting those that produce ice. Those that chill the air."

Where is he going with this? Argyll frantically looked around the room for a means to help, but found only dusty old artefacts of a world long left behind.

"With the blue focus-crystals taken, we've left an imbalance... now the fire crystals above us are unstable. What would it take, to cause them to expel their force?"

"No," said Argyll. He gripped the thin steel sheets that covered the tops of his chair's wheels.

"One bullet," said Ruairí, pointing the firearm at Argyll again, then back to the ceiling. "If I shoot, the fire crystals would catch alight, and in the absence of the ice to chill the room, they'll come crashing down upon his heretical place!"

Ruairí, keeping the firearm pointing upwards, turned his attention back to the tome. He muttered as he flicked through the pages with his other hand, shaking his head in disbelief.

He underestimates me, thought Argyll. Slowly, he went to work. He reached beneath the steel sheets of his chair and undid a mechanism holding them in place. Daring not to blink or take his eyes off Ruairí, Argyll removed both steel plates, revealing the full circumference of the wheels on either side of him. They rose over his seat, just as he had designed them to. And running around the outside of each wheel, was a raised rim.

Not making a sound, Argyll stretched both hands outwards, the steel plates clenched tightly in both. He knew any sudden movement would be enough to cause the madman to shoot.

Therefore, he had to make this one sudden movement count.

Just as Ruairí leafed through the book again, Argyll threw both steel plates up into the air.

Before they fell back towards the ground, Argyll gripped the rims of both wheels of the chair, and *pushed* as hard as he could.

The chair propelled forward under his force, and Argyll pushed again. With a crash, the steel plates hit the ground, and Ruairí quickly turned towards Argyll. Upon seeing the Simian darting towards him, Ruairí pointed the firearm forwards.

But Argyll was already too close.

With one hand, Argyll pushed his body from the chair, and with the momentum he had already attained, he leapt through the air. With his other hand, he reached for Ruairí's throat.

Argyll fell upon the Human, Ruairí's neck wrapped firmly in the Simian's fingers. Ruairí coughed and spluttered and attempted to fight off his attacker, but Argyll was far too strong. He added another hand, and Ruairí's face turned from red to purple.

After a moment's struggle, Ruairí stared up at Argyll through maddened, dead eyes.

Argyll sighed, rolled off the Human's body, and crawled back towards his chair. With some effort, he re-seated himself in it, and took a moment to catch his breath.

Before making a move to leave, he looked behind him. Next to Ruairí's body was the book. *The Truth.* For a moment, Argyll considered it. Thinking first he should leave it, then second that he should read it.

Instead, he picked it up, tucked it into his coat pocket, and turned himself around to roll back towards the cargo lift.

CHAPTER 20: THE TRUTH

We are here because we have seen too much yet learned so little. Only by sharing the sights of our Seeings can we truly know the way of the Lord. Some of our brothers and sisters have gone mad from their revelations, but it is they who should feel sorry for us, for only they have seen the face of God.

Sermon of the Sons of Seletoth, from God's Blood, 4:21

***

The door closed behind Fionn with a slam. Faced with a darkened corridor, he flared the fire in his fingers, and stepped forward.

He'll help us, he thought, his heartbeat pounding in his skull. *He must.*

Sir Bearach gave no response, leaving both in deathly silence.

Fionn's flames revealed many irregularities within the cavern. Whereas the previous room had been formed directly in the mountain's body, this room seemed to be built separately, for a different purpose. Oddly shaped stone columns re-enforced the walls, pointed and jagged at strange angles.

Just like Meadhbh's temple. Fionn swallowed. Of course, it would make sense for both deities to dwell in similar structures, with architecture far removed from anything else in Alabach.

With equal inconsistency, the cavern's spaciousness changed repeatedly as he went, from walkways between walls so close together they threatened to trap him, to wide, high-ceilinged corridors that seemed to never end.

You hear that? Bearach whispered abruptly. *Your light, lad. Kill it.*

Fionn's torch quelled to an ember as he listened intently. Somewhere among his own staggered breathing and his beating heart, another pounding resounded through the caves. Though this was too irregular to be a heartbeat, and too loud to be organic.

Wraiths? Fionn conjured images of more cloaked men beating war-drums, patrolling through the caves.

With increased caution, he carried on forward, led by nothing more than a dim light. The pounding grew louder as he went, but something stranger joined it. A hum. A low, hideous hum like a voice rasping through lungs clogged with phlegm.

Don't stop, Fionn thought, creeping forward. The dim light at his fingertips revealed that the corridor had widened once more. Bright blue slabs replaced the drab stone floor, catching Fionn's embers in their reflection.

The strange noise grew to an abrupt crescendo; faster beats, louder hums. The clamour stopped Fionn in fright.

We are not alone here.

Gritting his teeth, Fionn poured his power into his hands, illuminating the great chamber. Light fell over the stone floor, the walls, and the source of the sound, in the centre of room.

No!

Immediately before Fionn, a great mass of squirming tentacles rose like a tower, each tendril writhing madly. Hundreds of feet tall, it loomed over Fionn, disappearing somewhere in the darkened ceiling overhead.

Amongst the glistening mound, countless eyes glared out, bloodshot and lidless. Their pupils dilated in the light of Fionn's torch, twisting and turning in their bleeding sockets. Further up, two giant wings emerged from the horrendous form, crooked grey feathers distorted out of shape.

The thing shook again, sending all its eyes rolling, its tentacles twisting, its wings beating, and it let out another cry. High in pitch, the sound cut against Fionn's skin like razors, freezing him with such unspeakable terror that every bone in his body could have screamed back if they could. And if they did, all Fionn would have heard was the terrible cry of this... being.

This terror reached heights Fionn had never known before, when he realised what this thing was.

Seletoth!

Taking in every inch of the shapeless mass of eyes and limbs, Fionn hardly noticed he now sat on his knees, jaw agape.

"Who?" Fionn stammered. "Why—"

A voice tore through Fionn's soul. The faceless thing itself did not speak, but some strange influence penetrated the mage's mind, leaving words that stung like insects, burrowing through his skull.

"You have defied destiny to come here. You have cast off the chains that bond you. Yet you ask only... *why?*"

"Yes," whispered Fionn. Sir Bearach remained silent. "I... We have so many questions. So—"

"And they will be answered," the thing continued. "For I am the Dawn of Creation, the Dusk of Destruction. The Beginning of all you know, and the End of all that there is. I am Seletoth, your Lord and God."

An image of darkness flooded Fionn's mind, speckled with bright stars spread amongst a void. Not unlike the star-charts of astronomers back in Penance, Fionn saw what appeared to be the night's sky. Then the image shifted, moving away from a fixed position and showing more of the sky than Man could have known. Huge expanses of darkness and light. Giant balls of fire, immeasurable in size, burned with the brightness of a thousand suns. Other circular shapes sped past; emerald and cobalt spheres hanging in nothingness.

Another shape shot through the scene. A long mass of grey and green, thin and wiry compared to the rest. If these large spheres were man-made objects of iron and stone, this was a living entity, plummeting through the sky.

"That's you..." Fionn realised. "You're—"

The voice tore through Fionn's skull once more. "I once lived amongst others like me. But I was too unlike them."

Fionn's perspective shifted once more. The stars and shapes disappeared, leaving the vague impression of Seletoth alone in the void.

"I was banished. And for a timespan beyond your meagre comprehension, I was sent through the firmament, with no direction or destination. Until I came here."

Fionn found himself back in the cave, looking up at the towering mass once more as a hundred eyes dripping red stared back.

"Why are you showing me this? What is this?"

"This," said Seletoth. "This is the Truth. The Truth your Church was built to conceal. The Truth that has driven so many of your people mad. One glimpse of it was enough to send the Godslayer on her conquest of death. And now that she has killed my Lady, the rest has been laid out before her. As it shall be laid before you now."

Everything around Fionn dimmed to change once more.

Fionn stood on top of a mountain now, but not the snow-capped peak of Mount Selyth. A beautiful valley lay before him, with a plethora of greens set against the landscape, rising and falling with each hill. A river shot through the centre, like a slender laceration through skin.

Then, a flash lit up the sky, and before Fionn's vision returned, the ground shook, and a cloud of dust rose over broken trees. When the smoke cleared, a shapeless bulk of organic matter lay in the valley's centre... unblinking eyes, gleaming appendages....

Blood seeped through its body, soaking into the ground below.

"The land adapted to the impact immediately," said Seletoth, darkness enveloping the scene once more. "But the flora and fauna took much longer. Poison replaced nutrients, and predators descended from prey. As I lay there, dying, the remnants of my might turned that valley into what you know now."

"The Glenn," said Fionn, looking back up at the Lord.

"The natives of the land avoided the region. And they would have left me there to die if I had not put in place one contingency. One final way to prolong my life."

"Contingency?" asked Fionn.

When the answer came, Seletoth spoke blankly, as if not caring for the word that thundered through Fionn's mind.

"Humans."

"Us?" whimpered Fionn.

"As I plummeted alone through Eternity, I spread my seeds wherever I could, and they quickened to Life wherever possible. Somewhere, on the far side of this world, beyond many leagues of land and seas, the first Humans came to be. It took some time, but eventually, my influence reached them. First, to a young virgin named Meadhbh."

"No...."

"And in her womb, I planted one more seed."

"No!" Fionn's hands reached up to clasp his ears. But the Lord's voice spoke again.

"Her son, the soon to be King Móráin the First, united the scattered tribes of Man. To sail to this land. For one purpose."

Fionn stood to his feet. "To... save you?"

"The natives fought with great tenacity to prevent the Firstborn from reaching the valley, for even their primitive minds knew of the power that lay within. Once my people were close enough, I blessed them with magic. And once my son was here, I lent him my power."

"The Apotheosis of Móráin," whispered Fionn. "The Church says he ascended to Godhood."

"He may as well have," boomed Seletoth. "For even an ounce of my strength is the equivalent to the greatest power the Human imagination can conjure. If a fraction of my power is that of a God, what does that make me?"

Fionn stared dumbfounded at the great being, and a question that had burned in his heart for a long time manifested on his tongue.

"But if you are so powerful... why has all of this happened? Why can't you stop Morrígan herself?"

"Because she *serves* me," roared Seletoth. "Each Human spirit is a fraction of my own, split from me as I created them. King Móráin and Lady Meadhbh, gods in your tongue, possess larger parts of my power. I weaved the Tapestry of Fate to ensure they would all return to me."

Fionn took a step back.

"As I lay dying in the Glenn, I called for my son to return to me. But when he saw my form and learned of his purpose, he turned away. Instead, his most trusted servants conspired to take me from that valley, in secret, and kept me here, far away from the throne of my lineage. Far from the tomb of his mother.

"And here I would stay. Those who knew the Truth concealed it and named themselves the Church. But the Tapestry of Fate was already woven, for I ensured I would someday be restored to my full power."

"By Morrígan," whispered Fionn.

"She is a thrall of fate, like every other Human, but her purpose is a greater one. She was destined to discover a means of reclaiming the souls of every Human and god I created, all for the purpose of returning them to me."

No, realised Fionn. *He... He did this? All this?*

Only now did Fionn comprehend how quickly his heart was beating, how short his breath had grown. Something moved along the ground at his feet. He glanced down, seeing thin, grey tendrils moving across the floor.

"Fionn the Red, shall you give yourself willingly back to me?"

"No!" said Fionn, his mind desperately trying to form a plan that wasn't there. "Morrigan! I'll find her! We... have spoken before. I think she may listen to me." He took a step back. "I can convince her to come. I–"

Something pulled Fionn's feet backwards from beneath him. He hit the ground face first. Dazed, he struggled to orientate himself, but when he did, he found that he was hanging upside-down, dangling in the air, tendrils wrapped around his ankles.

"The seeds of the Simians' chaos have reached too deep," rumbled Seletoth. "I can no longer trust my creations to carry out my deeds."

Fionn struggled, but the vine-like appendages gripping his feet only bound them tighter.

Your magic, lad! roared Sir Bearach. *Burn him!*

With blood rushing to Fionn's head, he found it difficult to focus, but sure enough, a click of his fingers brought forth a spark from his flint-rings. With a surge of the power of his soul, the spark ignited, and a plume of fire burst around him.

But the flames were extinguished by an unseen force.

"You dare use my own power against me?" thundered Seletoth. "You are but a fraction of what I am, and to me, you shall return."

Fionn fought and struggled, but the tendrils pulled him closer to the gargantuan, rubbery mass. A hundred eyes glared at him, and a thousand limbs convulsed, each wriggling and writhing like bleeding worms. Then they began to fold inwards, at the base of His body, forming a shapeless, gaping maw.

"No!" cried Fionn. "Please!"

He scanned his memory for any mote of information, any secret, any story, anything at all that could help. But he found none.

Don't give up, lad! said Sir Bearach. *Keep fighting!*

The tentacles around Fionn's feet loosened, and he fell before bulk of Seletoth's body. From that blackened mouth, more tendrils sprung, pulling Fionn inwards, legs first.

I can't, thought Fionn. *It's over.*

As his legs entered the mouth, an unbearably heavy force clamped down on them. His bones broke and Fionn howled in pain, his cry echoing throughout the cave.

Fight it lad! roared Sir Bearach. *Fight and fight and fight and fight until there's no fight left!*

Through the pain, Fionn attempted to click his fingers, but a spark did not form. The tendrils around his body shifted, pulling him inwards. With another sickening *crunch,* Fionn's lower torso caved in. Unbearable agony filled his mind, pushing out every other thought. He tasted iron on his tongue.

The walls! wailed Sir Bearach. *The floor, the ceiling, the walls, they're stone! Stone!* The dead knight's hysteric voice sobbed through Fionn's mind. *Can't your magic move stone?*

If one last attempt to placate the knight was all Fionn could do, he would make it the last thing he did. For all the time they spent together, bickering, arguing, aiding one another, Fionn would try this one last thing. For the companion he had been. For the friendship they had fostered. For the love that came with it.

Seletoth's form convulsed, pulling the rest of Fionn's body inside. Fionn raised one hand in defiance. The hand that once belonged to a brave knight, and he focused on the stone around him.

Geomancy had never been his strength, but with ease, the power of his soul touched upon the ground. Some great Geomancers could cause mountains to rise and fall, though Fionn was not one of them.

His pain reached a new, terrible height as the remnants of his legs burned to Seletoth's digestive juices.

Fionn closed his eyes; only his head, shoulders, and one arm were free. His focus now was only on the stone floor. If not for a distraction from the pain, then for the soul of Sir Bearach. The soul that begged him not to give up.

With Geomancy, he groped along the stone floor. The weight of the stone was far too much to push or pull. He moved his power away, touching upon the ground of the path that had taken him here, searching for anything that may give way, for anything that may help.

Once more, Seletoth bore his strength down upon Fionn's broken body, pulling his head inwards. Fionn's eyes burned, and his skull cracked, but his arm remained outside, his fingers touching the air, the power of his soul uselessly scrambling across the cavern walls.

Until *there*, something felt different. Not stone but iron, and lighter too. It felt like a door, which pushed open with some effort. The stone out here was different, with images etched into them. Like a blind man, Fionn used the last of his strength to trace their etchings, trying to conjure an image of what they looked like.

Fionn's skin burned, as his arm up to his wrist was consumed, but his soul still fought. Not his soul, *their* soul, searching the ground, trying to find anything to help. Even if futile, Sir Bearach deserved an end like his first, out in the fields of the Clifflands. A fight until the last breath.

Then Fionn found a rock made from a different type of stone to the rest. It was circular in shape. Smooth to touch.

With sudden realisation, Fionn flared the final strength of his and Bearach's soul. The object came hurtling through the darkened halls of Seletoth's caves.

When it collided with Fionn's opened hand and Seletoth's body, it exploded with a deafening roar that shook the cavern around them, consuming them both in a mighty torrent of blue fire and cracking the very earth itself.

CHAPTER 21:
OMNISCIENCE

As my most loyal servants and I gazed into that poisonous chasm, we learned the Truth: Seletoth is no god, but a malignant being born far from this land. Further than mortal minds can comprehend.

But still, He welcomed me like a father would a son. That terrible, rotting, pulsating creature at the bottom of the Glenn praised me for bringing His creations to this land, returning them to Him, and for a horrifying moment, something overtook me; a compulsion to give myself to this monster.

But as I stepped closer to the valley's edge, something deep within me fought back, and I steadied myself. My allies, however, were not as strong-willed, giving into that madness and throwing themselves into the pit to be devoured by the horror.

I was powerless to help them, so I fled.

For a week I dwelled upon what I had seen, urging my men to explore other parts of the valley and beyond. This I did, until I came upon the only conclusion available to me.

Seletoth had to die.

Under the cover of night, I rode out, my most powerful battlemages by my side, but when we came upon that unholy chasm, the Lord was gone.

Back at camp, I questioned my men, and found that I had been deceived. Seletoth, it seemed, had spoken directly to the minds of others who served me; those who would not hesitate to betray me. They had deserted me and found Seletoth in the Glenn. But to where they took Him, I spent much time wondering.

Many years later, when my Lady Mother died, she transcended into a beautiful goddess of blue light. With this power, She could see the fates of all who lived, who had lived, and who would ever live. She named this the Tapestry of Fate, and it detailed the actions of those who had betrayed me for Seletoth.

Those deserters had found Him and carried Him to an isolated region near the western coast of this land. There, Seletoth created a mountain in which to dwell.

When I asked why, my mother said that Seletoth only had to wait, for there would come a day when a girl, and girl she named Godslayer, would claim all the souls that Seletoth had created, including Hers and mine, and bring them back to Him.

I confess, I did not know how to proceed. I asked my mother for council, but She said that even my own efforts would cause this fate to unfold as She had seen it.

So, I lied. I lied to my wife. I lied to my son. I lied to every man, woman, and child who served me, because the Truth must be concealed.

I write this by my own hand, only to be shared with those most faithful to our cause. Our new Church of the Trinity shall conceal this Truth and spread the teachings of Seletoth as we had first worshipped Him in ignorance. As a father. As a Lord.

As the god that never was.

The Truth, by King Móráin I, AC55

***

Alone and afraid, the young mage tried to move, but his body failed to comply. He attempted to speak but found that he had no voice. As he tried to remember where he was, or who he was, his memory recalled nothing. For indeed, right now he was *nothing*. No voice, no body, but just a vague awareness of being.

Sir Bearach! he thought, suddenly recalling the name he had given to other soul that once dwelled within him. *Sir Bearach? Where are you?*

There was a time, long ago, when the mage had first used magic to reach out and touch the soul for Sir Bearach. This he did again, his power searching through the void for the familiar warmth of the dead knight. But it could not be found. Instead, the mage found something else. Something different. Another soul, far larger, and far more powerful than anything he had ever sensed before. This other soul recoiled to the mage's touch, but the mage pressed on.

As if grabbing the other soul by two hands, the mage merged it with his own.

Slowly, the names of other people the mage had once known came back to him. First was Fionn, which had been his name once. Then he recalled the Simians, Farris and Nicole. The Humans, Aislinn and Padraig. Morrígan, who had caused all of this. King Diarmuid, Fionn's late father.

But this other soul did not belong to any of those people. An incredible force surged within Fionn's own soul as it touched this other. The darkness that surrounded him seemed to cast itself aside, replaced by a deep, golden light. Abruptly, Fionn opened his eyes for what felt like the first time he had ever done so, and with this came a sudden understanding of the world around him.

Then he remembered one more name. One more important name, which had set him on this journey.

Seletoth.

***

Fionn emerged from the ruin of Seletoth's cave. He did not pay any mind to how he walked, or even if he did walk, for a thousand-thousand thoughts and memories roared through his mind in the void where Sir Bearach's soul once lay. There, instead, was a deep well of wisdom and knowledge, of understanding and truth, the thoughts and dreams and histories of every man, woman, and child that had ever lived.

The Tapestry of Fate

Fionn glided through the rubble in his new form; a body made of golden light, resembling the one Fionn wore in life, but without the arm of Sir Bearach. The crumbling cave mouth overlooked a smouldering settlement, once occupied by the Sons of Seletoth. Without realising He was doing it, Fionn gazed into the deep well of his soul.

The people of this village lived here for hundreds of years, and Fionn could see every one of their minds and memories all at once. He tried to sift through them one by one at first, but the lives and the deaths and the thoughts and the dreams of everyone who had ever been, inside and outside of this village, all across Alabach, came to Him faster and faster and faster and faster and faster and faster and faster for those in the village had once welcomed newcomers there as long as they came at the behest of Seletoth, but other times strangers came, and they had to be fought off, just like the five strangers who had come today, trekking through the snow, clad in arms and armour noticed first by Thomás who called on his brothers to rain down bolts upon them but there was one, a Simian, who fought and fought and fought without mercy and although the Tapestry of Fate did not depict a Simian bringing so much death to these peaks, Fionn could see the anguish that Simian had in his heart, and the pain and the pain and the pain and the pain that had come forth upon seeing the death of the one he had loved, whose death only made him realise that she had felt the same, and within that pain was the regret of not being able to share that love, and knowing that they could have run away together, back to Penance, away from this war, away from Fionn, to live out their days together in peace and in love but instead he was here, dead, beneath rubble, his armour broken and cracked by the force of a hundred bolts and arrows from the Sons of Seletoth but there! beneath the rubble too were two Humans that Fionn had once known to be named Padraig Tuathil and Aislinn Carríga both of whom saw the horde invade their city and slay all who they loved both of whom travelled far from their homeland, spurred on only by the honour and duty they held for those who no longer lived, but there were so many, oh so many, lives lost since then, and one by one by one their memories bore down upon Fionn, children running through street and merchants setting up stalls and engineers overseeing plans and sailors loitering by the docks and students studying in their rooms and—

Fionn tore his mind away from the Tapestry, bringing his focus back to where he was. Aislinn and Padraig were alive beneath the rubble, though barely. He raised a hand and moved the crumbling rocks aside, exposing the two broken bodies to the air. Although he was no healer in his past life, now Fionn had complete control over every school of magic and mended their bones with ease. He closed their wounds, took their pain away, and gave them the strength to open their eyes.

Padraig opened his first and cowered back in fright. This roused Aislinn too, who stared up at Fionn with awe usually preserved for coming face to face with a god.

"Be not afraid," said Fionn, unaware whether he was speaking out loud or if his thoughts were merging with theirs. "Seletoth is dead, and I have claimed His power."

Neither Human responded. Fionn noticed Padraig clutching Aislinn's hand. Finding this curious, Fionn found himself glancing back at the Tapestry to see if these two did indeed have feelings for one another, and, indeed they did, for they had grown close over this journey, and as Padraig wrote into his journal during their stay in Rosca Umhír, Aislinn came into his room and they talked about the lives they had left behind, and those they had loved before, and the grief Padraig had kept buried for Aideen of Barrow's Way, a commoner he had been seeing in secret, but after all that happened, he wondered why he felt the need to lie about their relationship but that night he told Aislinn that it was because of his stature, and his corruption with the smugglers of the Black Sail and that he just wanted to keep her safe from them but deep down Padraig knew the truth was that he was ashamed, ashamed of falling for someone born so low, of the bastard child growing in her womb, but when the horde came, this shame was made trivial in comparison to the regret he felt for sending her away to the Cathedral of St. Lorcan with the other smallfolk, protected from the horde, but only for a time before Morrígan had turned the Pyromancers of the City Guard against the city itself and burned the Cathedral to the ground, and as those inside called to their god and their king to come and save them, Aideen only called for the one she loved, but no gods or kings or lovers heard them when the burning ceiling collapsed, but when love turns to grief, and grief burns itself out, it can leave room for love to grow once more, and here, it had, and perhaps this world would not allow it to flourish, so they must find a new one, "Go," said Fionn, struggling to speak as the knowledge and history of the world surged through his mind, his voice was different, this he knew from their reactions, and perhaps his form was different, perhaps they did not recognise him, but he continued, hoping they would listen, "The Grey Plague has ravaged this land, and you will not live long here," this they seemed to understand, as Padraig looked to Aislinn, and both nodded, "But there is land, far to the south," said Fionn, as the Tapestry conjured the image of the lands, wide grassy plains with tall, lonely trees dotted throughout, sheltering herds of strange animals that roamed through it, and from the reaction both Humans gave, it seemed both could see this too, so Fionn continued, "It may take many moons to make this journey, for you will travel through harsh landscapes and over frozen seas, but it is one more journey you must make," and then the Tapestry conjured forth another image, which all three saw, of people roaming this new land, people who bore a resemblance to Simians, but appeared to be more animalistic, intelligent yet savage, primal, but with potential, these creatures were capable of using tools, but did not know how to make fire or farm, "Find them," said Fionn, "Find them and let them be your purpose."

Padraig stood now, and said something to Fionn, but the Tapestry had taken Fionn's full attention away from them. After all that had happened with Seletoth, Fionn had forgotten the intention of this journey. Morrigan needed to be stopped, and Fionn could see now where she was.

He turned away from the two Humans and their many questions, and left them alone, atop Mount Selyth, and took to the skies. He flew northwards.

Chapter 22:
Our New World

Slowly, Argyll wheeled himself through the crowds at the Tower of Sin. Many leapt aside upon seeing him, others giving him strange looks. Some looks he had grown familiar with long ago. Other looks seemed directed at his chair, which he now propelled forward himself using the raised rim of the wheels that rose over his seat. Parallel to the great staircases of the great tower were ramps for moving cargo, which Argyll took to with little effort.

On the top floor, crowds queued before three airships, docked along the open rooftop of Sin. Snow fell gently over the city now, landing upon roofs already laden with a layer of white. The gangway to *Thunder* was raised, its deck crowded with eager Simians.

A separate crowd of Humans stood aside, some red-robed Churchguards among them. They looked on towards three Humans, who spoke to each other in frantic, panic whispers. One saw Argyll and beckoned him over. On recognising this

Human as the priest from the congregation of Sons the previous night, Argyll went to him.

"Argyll," said the Human. "We have finished loading the ships with the focus-crystals of the Church. Where is Brother Ruairí? Where you with him?"

"Brother Ruairí has fallen," said Argyll. He had intended to feign grief at this, but found his voice naturally cracked upon saying the name.

The fool read a book that made him want to kill me. Why should I grieve him?

But still, he found himself dwelling on memories of times their interests aligned, and the feelings that came with them. And with a well-practiced feat of emotional acrobatics, Argyll pushed them deep down, until they were no more.

"We were set upon by guards still loyal to the Church on our way out," he said, the lie coming to him easily. "Ruairí bravely fought them off but paid dearly for it."

"May Seletoth watch over his soul," said the priest. "His final Seeing has blessed us with the wisdom of the Lord. Thanks to Brother Ruairí's fate, we now know what we must do."

"No," said Argyll. He raised his voice at this, seeing the rest of the Sons were watching him. "As Ruairí died, he entrusted me with this."

He took the tome out from his pocket and held it up high. This was met with many gasps from the crowd.

"*The Truth.* Written by King Móráin the First."

"It cannot be!" cried the priest, eyes wide with wonder. "So many of us have seen but a glimpse of the Truth. With this, we can see the world as He intended."

"And you shall. If you agree to come with us across the Eternal Sea."

This was met with concerned mutters that bubbled within the crowd. On seeing this, Argyll pressed on.

"Ruairí said that the Lord said you must stay here, but to what end, only Ruairí knew. His knowledge is lost now with his death. But if you come with us, you will have all the knowledge you desire."

As the crowd considered this, the priest turned to confer with the other two he had been speaking to. These, Argyll presumed, were priests too. After a time, the first turned to the crowd, and spoke. "If the Truth is crossing the Eternal Sea, than I shall join it too. You are all free to make up your own mind on this matter."

On seeing the others consider this, Argyll moved away, seeing is job as being done.

As long as they make their mind up, independent of any vision any fool had, I'll consider it a victory.

He moved towards a gangway leading up to *The Dreadnought*. Many Simians who had come carrying too much luggage were turned away at the threshold, given the choice of either abandoning their belongings or staying in Penance with them. Argyll boarded with nothing more than the shirt on his back, for if a lack of his own belongings meant there was room for just one more person to embark, then that was a sacrifice he was happy to make.

The crowd cheered as next to them, *Thunder's* engines rumbled, and the ship took flight. Argyll's heart soared with it.

He boarded *The Dreadnought*, and the crowd in the dock stepped aside to give him space, but no one spoke to him. This didn't bother Argyll, until he thought about those closest to him before. Farris, Garth, Nicole, Ruairí... now all dead. Was it that he truly had no one left?

This was a thought he let linger longer than he would have allowed before. Other people aboard laughed and joked with one another, sharing stories and speculating about the life that waited ahead of them. Instead, Argyll looked over the side of the ship, out across the city of Penance, towards the huge hull of *Thunder* that sailed silently over the high spires of the Steamworks.

The crowd cheered again as the engines beneath their feet came alive. *The Dreadnought* rose into the air and slowly turned to face its bow westwards. Some passengers started making their way inside the ship's massive gondola, but most stayed outside to take in this unique view of their city. The last view of their city.

But Argyll's eyes remained locked on *Thunder*, which would spearhead the journey west.

From somewhere beneath them, a bolt of fire burst forth, shooting towards *Thunder* with deadly precision. It struck the ship. The back side of its hull burst alight. A huge plume of red flame rose upwards, sending the nose of the ship pointing upwards.

Argyll's breath evacuated his lungs. Chaos erupted aboard *The Dreadnought*. People screamed in anguish and fear, but none could do anything but watch as the body of *Thunder* took flame. The flames spread over the canvas envelope quickly, as it slowly descended. Within seconds, the canvas burned away, leaving only the metal frame of the hull; a burning patchwork of iron shapes that collapsed into one another.

All eyes aboard *The Dreadnought* were fixated on the smouldering ruin of *Thunder*, but Argyll wheeled himself to the side of the ship to find the source of this destruction.

He peered over, and there, directly beneath *The Dreadnought*, was a dark, winged figure floating in the air.

Morrigan!

Desperation took hold of Argyll. He glanced around. No one else aboard the ship seemed to notice she was *there*, just below them. He quickly considered his options. Sure, there were likely some Sons of Seletoth aboard, somewhere, with the arms to fight back. But was there time to find them, to alert them?

As he leaned over the side of the ship, Morrigan's attention was still fixed on the burning ship, which now fell slowly to the ground. How long before she realised another ship was sailing above her, waiting to be burned from the sky too?

There was no time to consider these questions, no time to assess these outcomes. Before he even realised what he was doing, Argyll started wheeling himself across along the deck, focusing still on the girl. There once was a day when he trained to be an engineer and found he could estimate distances and speed with ease. He was no true mathematician, so close estimates would have to do.

Once he reached a certain point, representative of a certain distance ahead of Morrigan, with her a certain distance below, Argyll climbed from his chair. He pulled his body onto the ledge of the deck, limp legs dangling over the side. He did not know long much time this would buy them, nor how well this would even work, but without any further hesitation, Argyll threw himself overboard.

All seemed to slow as he fell. For a moment, weightless, he was free from his chair. Free from the limitations of his injuries. But he could not dwell on this freedom for long, for figure of Morrigan sped closer and closer to.

This is for my legs, he thought, balling his right hand into a fist. *For Farris and Nicole. For Simiankind.*

As he approached, Morrigan turned. Against the blackness of her clothes and her wings, her pale face shone. A face that grinned, taking joy in her slaughter.

But her smile quickly vanished at it collided with Argyll's fist, sending both spiralling to the ground.

***

Pain surged through Argyll's body. He opened his eyes, slowly, blinking through the cloud of dust that rose above him.

Where am I? he thought, raising his head slowly. He pressed a bloodied hand into the ground beneath him, feeling ragged stone pressing painfully into his skin.

Morrigan! he realised. *Where is she?*

He found himself lying inside a building of some sort. A wooden roof above him bore an open hole, from which heavy sleet fell within, on top of him.

Each movement brought him great pain, but he pulled himself from the wreckage. Slowly, he crawled out into a cobblestone street. Glancing up, with a surge of relief he saw that *The Dreadnought* was still in the sky.

Across the street, something moved. He glanced to see Morrigan in a heap on the ground, her wings bent crooked from the fall. Gradually, she stood and turned her attention to the ship overhead.

Argyll reached out his hand and shouted to try and pull her attention away, but he was interrupted by a sudden *whoosh.* Bright light bathed him.

Between him and Morrigan, a great, glowing figure landed. It shone like a golden statue, with huge, gilded wings spreading from its shoulder. It turned to face Argyll, and when it spoke, he felt a fear unlike any he felt before, burning deep in his chest.

"You have given the Simian people a chance at a new life," it said. As Argyll looked up at this figure's face, he saw the vague likeness of Firemaster Fionn in there.

"For your courage," the figure said, "I shall mend your wounds, and allow you to walk—"

"I don't give a shit!" cried Argyll. Whatever religious nonsense was going on, they could leave him out of it. He pointed towards Morrigan. "Just stop her!"

***

Fionn turned to see Morrigan stepping across the street.

"I see you have done as I asked," she said. "By killing Seletoth and merging His soul into your own, you can help me rid this world of its meaningless life. And together we can start anew."

A ball of fire formed in her hand. She looked up to the airship that glided through the sky overhead. Fionn darted forward, crashing into Morrigan and sending both hurtling into and then through a nearby building.

With great force, Morrigan pushed away from Fionn.

"Why do you fight me?" she cried. "You have seen the Truth yourself. The Lord is nothing more than a celestial monstrosity, and all that we have lived and suffered through served only to play back into His hands. This life is nothing more than a tool He created to save Himself."

"You're wrong!" roared Fionn. "It matters not where we came from, but the lives we lived." He gestured towards the sky. "Why not let them live, and allow them to forge a new life across the sea, away from the lies of the Church and of Seletoth?"

"That too will be a life without meaning!" She raised a hand and pulled a large chunk of stone from the ground below. "No life born of Seletoth can have meaning. We once believed the Eternal Sea had no limits. But we were wrong. The seas we know are but raindrops in the oceans of existence. All we know hangs in the infinite darkness of the Endless Firmament, and nothing that happens here serves any purpose."

She flicked her wrist, flinging the chunk of stone at Fionn. He lunged forward and shattered it into a thousand pieces as it came. Through the cloud of dust it left behind, he flew, approaching Morrígan.

"You were once ignorant of these things," he said. "And you found joy in life. Or have you forgotten?"

Morrígan paused. "What do you know?"

Fionn let his mind give way to the vast knowledge of the Tapestry of Fate. One memory, one life, one dream tumbled into another, then another, and another and another and another until the cascade of ideas became a huge waterfall of the lives that had come and gone, and among them there was many that Morrígan had touched, had enriched, had taken away, and he turned these thoughts outwards, so that she may see that once she sat in the back of a classroom, passing notes to the innkeeper's son while a teacher's voice droned on about letters and numbers and stories, for that teacher was himself a mage, with a lineage that traced all the way back to Móráin the First's most loyal servants who had followed him across the baren, icy lands to Alabach, but that did not matter here, as Fionn steered his thoughts back towards that classroom, to that village, to the man named Yarlaith the White, who called himself Morrígan's uncle, but in truth was her father, and he had—

"No!" cried Morrígan, leaping towards Fionn. With a surge of Geomancy, she caused a huge stone column to burst forth from beneath Fionn's feet. Distracted by the knowledge and wisdom that flooded his mind, Fionn could not react. The collision sent his body soaring upwards. Further and further up he went, until the skyline of Penance below slowly vanished beneath clouds.

***

Argyll covered his face with his hands as the two gods, or demi-gods, or whatever they were, fought on. He lowered them only after one strong assault from Morrígan sent the golden creature that may once have been, or possibly still was Fionn, hurtling into the sky.

No better chance than now, he thought. He bared his teeth as he pulled himself across the street, hands grasping the ground and dragging himself forward, one cobblestone at a time. He had once climbed many walls of many manors in his youth, a second-story burglar of significant talent. This was just like climbing, but more horizontal. Although he could not use his legs to help, at least gravity was on his side. If anything, this was easier. If not for the pain that raged within.

But this was not a fight for survival, for he had already succeeded in stopping Morrigan, at least from a time, from burning *The Dreadnought* from the sky. He was some distance away from Sin, and it was possible that *Sinfall* was already leaving. If it left without him, there would not be much lost, for if his life was what it took to give hope to so many others, then so be it.

With great effort, he reached the end of the street, which reached a main basalt road that led all the way to Sin. Without a grip upon individual stones, however, Argyll found no way to pull himself onwards.

Ironic, he thought, rolling himself forward with the strength of his shoulder alone. *That the roads of our Simian engineers replacing the cobblestones of the Seachtú would seal my fate.*

He could roll, using a significant amount of energy in the process, but he was maybe half a mile from the tower. Perhaps this was no longer a struggle he could partake in. If the other two ships could set off, wouldn't that be enough?

With that, Argyll gave up. He lay on his back upon the basalt road, his arms spread wide, facing the cloud-covered sky. The pain within him displaced his fighting spirit. Perhaps this fall, this second fall, had done irreparable damage to him. It was likely only the final wind of an animal struggling to survive had taken him this far, and perhaps there was no other option but to die here.

He closed his eyes and welcomed the embrace of death.

"It's him," came a frail voice. "See if he's alive."

Argyll didn't bother opening his eyes, for why burden anyone to save him now, if his purpose had already been served?

"He's alive, your Holiness. What should we do with him?"

No, thought Argyll. *Don't bother.*

"See if you can carry him," came the first voice. "All of this was his idea, after all. It wouldn't be right, to leave him behind."

It doesn't matter. Just leave me to die.

"Come on," said the second voice. "I'll need a few hands to help. Let's see if there's a healer aboard."

Argyll struggled to open his eyes and saw the distorted shapes of a dozen or so Humans surrounding him. He could not make out their faces, only blurs that suggested robes, of silver and gold and grey and red. The effort it had taken him to open his eyes left him, and he drifted out of consciousness again.

For a time, Argyll had a vague awareness of what was around him. The air was cold, for some time, but the breeze that brushed his face subsided, indicating that he was indoors. Around him, he heard more voices, and more hands touched his body, and he felt himself moving faster than before.

When he felt the cold wind blow against his face once more, he opened his eyes. This time, the image was clearer.

He was aboard an airship, presumably *Sinfall*, and was surrounded by Humans. Strange faces all around smiled with glee upon seeing him conscious.

"He's alive!" one voice called. "Quick, get him to a healer!"

They lay him down on the wooden floor of the deck, and Argyll felt the rumble of engines beneath. Were they already flying?

He turned his head to the side and saw two Humans in the white robes of healers rush to him.

A crowd had gathered now, Humans all, looking to steal a look at the Simian who once would have seen them all dead, only to give his own people a place to call home.

Among them, one Human was dressed in a bright red cloak, with a golden stole draped around his neck.

Upon seeing him, Argyll laughed, for this Human did not bear the all-too-familiar dour expression of the Arch-Canon, but instead smiled warmly.

"Thank you, Argyll," he said, approaching the Simian's side. He took off his headgear and laid it on the ground next to him. "If not for you, the Sons would have killed us all in the Basilica."

"Outside," Argyll said. "I need air."

Quickly, the healers took him out to the deck, where other Humans looked on as they carried him out.

"The gunnel," he grunted, gesturing to the edge of the ship. "Sick...."

The healers didn't hesitate to bring him to the side of the ship. They allowed Argyll to lean over it, where he saw the foaming waters of the Eternal Sea flowing far below.

Expecting him to throw up, the healers politely looked away. On seeing this, Argyll feigned coughing and retching, and reached into his coat pocket as he did. When he was sure nobody was looking, he tossed *The Truth* overboard and watched as the tome splashed into the sea.

"Thank you," he said, turning up the healers. "I feel much better now."

***

High in the sky, Fionn turned around to face the earth. With Hydromancy, he parted the clouds, and saw the landscape beneath. Alabach was covered in snow, from Elis Point to Gorán. As he surveyed the land, the dark shape of Morrígan came flying towards him. But this time he was ready.

He surged the flame of his soul, which burned brighter than all the stars of the firmament, and pulled upon every mote of vapour from the surrounding clouds. With a glance towards Morrígan, he sent a torrent of icy water at her, slowing her ascent.

"You were brought up to never learn the truth of your birth," roared Fionn. "The man your mother was married to knew all along, but he kept his feelings inside him, lashing out at you and your mother whenever he drank."

"What are you doing?" yelled Morrigan. "Why are you telling me this?"

"Because it means something to you."

Fionn tore downwards towards Morrigan, and pulling upon the air, sent them both plummeting to the ground, away from Penance, away from the Simian ships.

Somewhere in the Midlands they crashed, sending the earth all around them upwards, forming a crater in the ground.

"Why would that matter?" said Morrigan, pressing a hand into the earth. With a burst of energy, a huge fissure formed between them. The land parted, and Fionn leapt backwards to avoid the dark chasm that opened.

"Because you once lived with purpose," he said. Somewhere far to the north, the sound of running water rumbled. Fionn glanced towards the source to see the High Sea itself bend to Morrigan's command. It came flooding through this fissure, bursting forth and consuming all in its path. Fionn quickly took flight as the water rushed beneath him.

Desperately, he let his own thoughts quieten and allowed the knowledge of the Tapestry of Fate rush forth as he reached out towards Morrigan, hoping she would see, hoping she would understand, and all of those lives she had touched upon came forth and her life was laid bare before them *If our ancestors claimed this land from the Simians, what use was an axe and a shield?* thought a girl as she watched her mother's coffin being carried through the chapel, and how untidy her hair was, if only her mother could have helped tidying it this morning, as she had done so many times, for Aoife Ní Branna loved nothing more than Morrígan, and her husband did too, despite knowing the child was not truly his.

"Stop!" said Morrígan, covering her ears, "Don't show me this!"

But Fionn gave in more to the Tapestry, and it showed all those mornings that Aoife and Cormac Ní Branna had just stayed in bed together, letting the hours of the morning turn to the hours of noon and even into the evening, doing nothing but playing with the baby Morrígan, as Cormac would hold her under her arms bouncing her body over their laps, both parents taking so much joy in talking nonsense to her, and how Aoife would warmly grasp Morrígan's foot saying, "that's your foot!" and then her arm saying, "and that's your arm!" and the two would take so much joy from the baby's reaction for hours and for hours and for hours and they would smile as she would smile back, for despite the fights they had before, despite how deep down Cormac knew Aoife had sought Yarlaith's bed, in this moment, and in many moments afterwards, everything was perfect was perfect was perfect was perfect and safe for surely if a child was to grow and develop surrounded by so much love, they could overcome every hardship and failure and disappointment life could throw at them, no matter what, and even though the love between Cormac and Aoife was to fade and turn to something worse, the love for that child was still there, and even if Morrígan was to grow, and fight with her parents, they could never bear anything close to hatred towards her, for how could any parent ever hate a child that once bounced upon their knee and responded to their funny faces and their silly voices with a wet gummy smiles and high-pitched giggles and gurgles and—

"No more," said Morrígan, tears in her eyes. "I... I cannot remember this. I... I don't believe this. The man who named himself my father was a drunkard, and—"

"And still he loved you," said Fionn. "He knew you were not of his blood, but still he loved you, for despite where you came from, you were worthy of love."

Fionn readied himself for another attack, but Morrígan reacted by falling to her knees. She held a hand to her head.

"You were his purpose," said Fionn, stepping forward. "The circumstance of your birth had no bearing on his love for you."

Then Fionn reached towards the Tapestry of Fate, and showed Morrígan more, so much more than either could have ever comprehended before, for there once was a captain of the Cruachan City Guard who loved a low-born woman, and they spent many hours lying together, eyes locked upon eyes, despite never telling another soul about the love they shared, because nothing else mattered to them but moments like that, and they longed to make more, and an innkeeper's son, who once bore feelings he could not understand for a neighbour, but just when he was mature enough to understand what he felt, she was gone and he searched and he asked and he wanted nothing more but to speak to her and tell her all that he had ever felt, but she was gone, alone, in darkness, coping with her own grief in a terrible, profane way that left no room for growth, for strength, because the death of a parent is a terrible thing that befalls every living person fortunate enough to not die young, and one thing that makes Humans who they are is their ability to deal with grief with the help and the support and the love of those around them who have experienced the same, if through conversations or through relationships or through the rituals of their religious beliefs, every person who has ever lived has gone through that pain and has come through the other side, not stronger, not without that pain, for that pain never fades, but through the other side with the knowledge that they must cherish every coming moment with every other person they come upon even more than before, and this force named love must be appreciated and respected and sought no matter its form, no matter where it comes from, and perhaps that child who dissected bodies in the darkness of those caverns could have healed and learned to love again, stronger than she ever had before, if she confronted her grief instead of hiding away from it, fantasising about a reunion that would never come, for others around her did love her, if she did not see it, and

Taigdh and Sorcha and Darragh had all lost things themselves, but each loved Morrígan enough to share their own pain to let her overcome her own, but she pushed them away, she pushed them away because she saw a chance to circumvent the cycle of life, to conquer death, but instead of conquering death, she conquered only her own humanity, and this is why she saw the life created by Seletoth as a mistake, not because He created life for His own selfish purpose, but because she denied herself a process of healing so ubiquitous, so commonplace, so *Human* that no one can ever live a life with any real purpose without having once gone through that loss, for to the parents who spent a day in bed playing with a child with so much tenderness and so much care and so much laughter, and the Simian who lay next to his love, unaware that she felt the same, with the same feelings hidden so deep within that he could not recognise them himself, and the regret he felt when they left that one place he could be himself, and the unspeakable pain he felt when she was taken away from him; if they were all to learn that the life they were given was never intended to have any meaning, would that even come close to nullifying any of those feelings? No, for if one were to interrupt any of those moments, between Aoife and Cormac or Farris and Nicole or Padraig and Aideen and tell them how their lives have no purpose because of Seletoth this or Seletoth that, they would not care, because they have found something else to care about, something that renders the Truth and their origin and the true nature of Seletoth and the vast black void from which He came irrelevant in comparison.

As if struck by a force stronger than Fionn could muster even now, Morrígan fell to the ground, whispering to herself as Fionn caused more images to pass through her mind; the quick glances Taigdh gave her in the inn, the way he clasped his hand into Sorcha's, the way he pushed through the crowds at Sorcha's mother's funeral, desperately searching for Morrígan, for it had been so long since he had seen her.

"No," Morrígan wept. "They… they didn't understand what Yarlaith, what my *father*, sought to do. They feared the power they could not understand. They…."

"And out of fear they killed him," said Fionn. "But from your own lust for revenge, you killed far, *far* more. You sought the power of the gods, but would you have done so if you knew the Truth of Seletoth's nature? Would you still endeavour to become like Him?"

"No…" whispered Morrígan. "I… I just wanted to feel… something."

"And you could have," said Fionn. "If you had broken away from Yarlaith and embraced the love of your friends in Roseán, you would have felt far more than what you do now. You had a chance."

Then Fionn conjured another image, the day Morrígan and Yarlaith succeeded in raising Aoife Ní Branna from the dead, but before Morrígan went downstairs to help, she tended to Darragh, who had injured his hand with a meat cleaver earlier that day, and Morrigan healed it and he thanked her and gave her a necklace, and from this gesture, Morrigan regained some humanity, a mote of compassion, for Darragh shared with her the loss of his own mother, and Morrigan recognised for a moment that circumstance of his loss may have been worse than her own and for a moment she forgot about the catacombs and the experiments and the Necromancy, but then she remembered, she remembered the sanctuary she sought from grief, and in seeking it she left Darragh alone, and later that night, Darragh took his mother's necklace back from Morrigan with the last of his dying strength, as Morrigan's undead horde burned the village and slew its villagers.

Morrigan looked up to Fionn. "Darragh… I'm sorry. I don't know what to do now…."

"The Simians are sailing across the Eternal Sea," said Fionn. "They seek a new world to the west. Two Humans are travelling south, far from here, there are creatures that someday may form a civilisation. If we want to give them a chance of ever flourishing, of ever doing better than we did… we must leave them."

"Yes," Morrigan said, standing. "I hold the souls of Meadhbh and King Diarmuid. And you, that of Seletoth. If we cannot die, how can we let these people live their lives without this terrible power?"

Abruptly, Fionn lunged forward, and embraced Morrigan. She buried her face into his shoulder, and he felt the dampness of her tears upon his skin. Fionn bent his knees and launched them both upwards.

"We keep going up," he said. "As high as we can go. Until we can't go any higher."

Realisation dawned Morrigan's face.

"To the firmament," she said, aloud. "To the void from where Seletoth came from."

Both of their wings unfurled, and both accelerated their ascent to the skies above. Wisps of clouds streaked past, and the air around them quickly grew thinner.

Once the last of the clouds vanished, Fionn turned around, to stare down at the land he was leaving behind.

He recognised Alabach straight away. Warped and broken, with a great crack in its surface from north to south, the kingdom he had once known well now seemed so tiny and insignificant amongst the rest of the world. To the west, the Eternal Sea did not go on forever, but ended at a landmass far larger than Alabach. To the south, unfamiliar lands stretched all the way to the far end of the earth. Grey ice covered the majority of the land, but further on, to the land that he had directed Padraig and Aislinn to, plains of gold and green prevailed.

"This is it," whispered Morrigan to Fionn. As they went upwards, the air grew thin and colder than anything the Grey Plague had brought. "If we keep on going, we won't be able to return. We'll have no control of where we go. And like Seletoth, we'll plummet blindly through Eternity."

"I know," said Fionn, as darkness surrounded them. The world now seemed so small; a tiny disk of blue surrounded by darkness. "But Seletoth eventually came upon a world, our world, which he brought life to."

"And if we come across the same, will we do as He did?"

"No," said Fionn, embracing Morrigan as the dim light of the world vanished behind them. "We'll do so much better."

***

As the two gods departed, They spoke to those who still lived. Both voices entwined boomed like a song from the heavens, and all who heard Them rejoiced. It brought encouragement to two Humans who were setting on a frightful journey south. It brought hope to the hearts of the Simians and Humans sailing westwards, and they cheered and prayed and sang along with words of their own.

Though one lone Simian did not open his heart to the music, for his eyes remained fixed eastwards, on the land he was leaving behind. He looked on at the smoking ruin that was once Mount Selyth, and he wept for all of those he lost.

As powerful as the Tapestry of Fate was, there was one who had always evaded its threads. And he did so even now. The departing gods assumed him dead, but who were They to assume anything, after all that had happened?

And the lone Simian who did not sing to Their song saw something even They could not see. Perhaps it was a secret magic of his people, or perhaps it was something stronger and more ancient than even Seletoth Himself. But this lone

Simian *saw* something among the smoking ruins of that mountain. And he was sure of it.

He frantically called for help, and even as the others aboard let the melody of the gods fill their hearts with so much courage and so much joy, Argyll the Silverback hoped they still harboured some fear in there for him. For it would take the fear he used to wield in Penance to turn this ship around.

Because his friend still lived.

Epilogue: Journal of Padraig Tuathil

Dearest Journal,

It has been far too long since I last put a pen to your pages. After all that has happened, I am still the same man that filled the space between your covers with complaints about the City Guard. About the love I had and lost for Aideen. About the night the horde came to Cruachan. And all the insanity that followed afterwards. When I last left an entry here, we had reached Rosca Umhir, but the Lady Carriga interrupted my entry. After this, we climbed Mount Selyth, but Nicole and Farris died in the ascent. As we tended to Farris's injuries, Fionn went to Seletoth's chamber to request the god's help. But before he emerged, a great explosion tore through the chamber, and indeed the peak of the mountain was blown asunder.

Knocked unconscious, myself and Lady Carriga awoke to see Fionn appear as a god, who told us to travel far south to seek a new world. He did not answer our questions, and fled northwards instead.

Collecting what we could from the remnants of the mountain settlement, we started on our journey south, on horseback, across a frozen sea. And when the horses couldn't go on, we went by foot. First, we came to a new land that had also fallen to the Grey Plague, but we carried on south. And alas, just as we were about to give up hope, the ice retreated. We found ourselves in a land of wide plains and tall trees. As alien as this landscape was to us, one thing was for certain: this was a place capable of sustaining life. Our arduous journey had come to an end. But what we found next proved more challenging than anything we had come across before.

Fionn spoke of Simians to the south, and we found a band of them soon enough. We observed them from a distance at first, nomads travelling across the grasslands, hunting and gathering in packs. When we were certain they were not a threat, we introduced ourselves.

They are a simple people, far more primitive than the Simians of Alabach, communicating with a very basic dialect. Fortunately, by standing before them, unarmed, with my palms spread wide, they recognised that we meant no harm. They also must have identified that we're like them in many ways, as despite the language barrier, they welcomed us into their tribe. If 'tribe' would even be the correct word.

Much time has passed since then. We've grown quite close to these Simians and have managed to break through the barriers of communication. Aislinn speaks to them about the Trinity, and about the Love of the Lord and the Light of the Lady, but I wonder how much actually gets through to them. Though, it has been a long time since I saw another Human, and these people seem to become more like us with each passing day, from the way they walk, to the manners of their grunting speech. If Aislinn has aimed to teach them what it means to be Human, she's done an astounding job. Hopefully, they don't take on our worst traits, and learn to live without greed and misery. We thought them other practical things, like how to create a fire, how to cook food, and most importantly, how to farm. Although it required much patience from both us and them, when these primitive people saw that they could create food from the ground itself, they no longer needed to roam. With them, we settled, exchanging hide-yurts for wattle-and-daub huts, growing their community from a mere few dozen to the population of a village, for so many others wanted to come and learn of these strange ways.

Our new life is not without pain, however. Aislinn has taken our burden with a significant amount of grief. What I mean is, we're both all too aware that we are the last. The final two. If our kind were ever to propagate once more, it would need to start here. At the bond between a man and a woman.

But we have tried. So many times, we have tried. Sometimes driven by love and passion, but often out of pure duty. Each time, Aislinn is certain that my seed will hold, but at the turn of each moon, we learn that we have failed. Now, when we lie in bed at night, I hear her weeping. I'm aware of how a woman's mind work: she blames herself. And she sees herself as failing not only her own desire to bear children, but of all Humanity as a whole.

I constantly try to re-assure her that it may not be her body's fault but....

But I know that my own seed is strong. Aideen, back in Cruachan, was bearing my child the night the horde came. Perhaps the fault really does lie with Aislinn....

No. I can't blame her. Gods, writing this, it's the first time I've recalled the details of that terrible night in Cruachan. I can still hear them, the dead, as they first came over the walls. The scent of burning flesh is still fresh in my nostrils, and I can still taste the king's thainol on my lips. The drink we shared before the undead broke into the keep. What was it he said, a gift from Farris? From Penance?

But I digress. It never fails to surprise me how such a minute detail like the taste of alcohol can over-shadow such terror. I must not dwell on the past. This shall be my last entry. I'll live out the rest of my life amongst these Simian-like beings, and maybe someday, when the Grey Plague has gone, we'll return to Alabach. Until then, I'll stay by Aislinn's side. We'll keep on trying. To bear the first child of this new and frightening world. I believe this is the only thing that's keeping her going, and I fear that it may be our very last hope. For if we fail, all memory of Alabach and all the people who died will vanish for eternity.

No. We will not fail. If the world is just, and the Lord's love for us was ever true, we will not fail.

The End

GUIDE TO ALABACH, HER PLACES, AND HER PEOPLE

AC: After Conquest. The Thralls of Fate begins in AC403.

Aislinn Carríga: Lady of Keep Carríga, Rosca Umhír, sister of Sir Bearach and Cathal Carríga.

Aldrich Canal: Simian-built canal connecting the Rustlake to Móráin Sea.

Aoife Ní Branna: Morrígan's deceased mother. (*Ee-fa Nee-Branna*)

Ardh Sidhe: One of the Seven Seachtú of Alabach. (*Ard Sid-heh*)

Argyll the Silverback: Leader of the Simian dissident movement in Penance, formally the head of the Guild of Thieves.

Borris Blackhands: One of the Triad, the governing body of Penance, along with Cathal Carríga and King Diarmuid Móráin III, XIX.

Cathal Carríga: One of the Triad, the governing body of Penance, along with Borris Blackhands and King Diarmuid Móráin III, XIX. (*Ca-hal Carry-ga*)

Cormac O'Branna: Father of Morrígan.

Divine Penetrance: Also known as the Gift of Immortality, this is a power passed from father to son through the Móráin line, ensuring the royal bloodline stays intact.

Dromán: Capital of the Woodlands of Alabach, home to the Academy of Mages. (*Dro-mawn*)

Dustworks: A residential sector of the city of Penance, home to Simians of low social standing.

Earthmaster Seán: Master of Geomancy, based in Penance.

Elis Point: Northernmost point of Alabach, where the Simian Elis Highwind tested the world's first airship.

Eternal Sea: Sea to the west of Alabach, with no known land beyond it

Farris Silvertongue: An agent of the Triad

Fionn: A young Pyromaster. (*Fee-un*)

Focus-crystals: Crystals encrypted with magic. Allows for use of magic without the need for a mage.

General-Commander Plackart: General of the Triad's Army in Penance.

Geomancer: Mage capable of manipulating the earth and Her fruits

Grey Keep: Residence of King Diarmuid Móráin, Third of His name, Nineteenth Incarnate of Seletoth

Grey Plague: Mysterious force that the Firstborn fled 400 years ago. Some speculate it was a sickness, others claim it was a supernatural blight on the earth.

King Diarmuid Móráin: Third of His Name, and Nineteenth Incarnate of Seletoth. Son of King Flaithrí IV, Diarmuid spent his reign attempting to bridge the gap between Man and Simian. (*King Dear-myid More-ain*)

Lady Meadhbh: One of the Trinity of Alabach. Called the Mother, the Lady, and the Weaver of Fate. Said to have determined the destiny of every living soul in Alabach. (*Lady Mayve*)

Lord Seletoth: One of the Trinity of Alabach. Called the Father, the Lord, and the Creator. Believed by some to be the One True God, rather than one of three as the Church teaches.

Móráin I: The First King of Alabach, also known as the Old, or the Great. Instead of accepting true divinity from the Lord, he chose to be with his wife. As a compromise, Seletoth bestowed upon him Divine Penetrance, in order to ensure that the Móráin line would never be broken.

Móráin Sea: Sea on the east coast of Alabach

Moray Head: Headland north of Point Grey

Morrígan Ní Branna: Daughter of Aoife Ní Branna, and niece to Yarlaith the White, Roseán. (*Morry-gan Nee Branna*)

Mount Selyth: A lone peak said to be the residence of Lord Seletoth, though no person has climbed the mountain and returned to confirm the myth.

Padraig Tuathil: Captain of the City Guard in Cruachan. (*Pad-rayg Twa-hill*)

Penance: The home city of the Simian people following the Final Conquest; named by Lord Seletoth following the Fall of Sin.

Plains of Tierna Meall: Human version of an afterlife, with rolling green hills and summers that last forever. (*Plains of Tear-na Myall*)

Point Grey: Capital of the Clifflands of Alabach.

Pyromancer: Mage who manipulate fire.

Pyromaster: An expert in all things pertaining to Pyromancy, recognised as such by the Academy of Dromán.

Resonance Crystal: Crystals that, when paired with another, can be manipulated by a crystallographer to relay messages over long distances.

Rosca Umhír: Capital of the Midlands of Alabach (*Ros-ka iv-er*)

Roseán: Small town in the Clifflands of Alabach, adjacent to the Teeth of the Glenn. (*Row-shawn*)

Seven Seachtú: Provinces of Alabach. (*Seven Shock-two*)

Simian: Native people to Alabach, holding science and technology to a hire esteem than faith and magic.

Sin: The name given to the remnants of a once great tower in the centre of the city of Penance.

Sir Bearach: Knight of Keep Carríga—deceased. (*Sir Byar-ak*)

Slaíne the White: Healer of Dromán—deceased.

Terrían: Capital of the Godlands of Alabach. (*Terry-Ann*)

The Academy of Dromán: Educational and academic institute based in the Seachtú of Dromán. Thrives on research into the Nature of magic and training young mages. (*The Academy of Dro-mawn*)

The Black Sail: A smuggling group operating in Cruachan.

The Churchguard: Elite soldiers charged with guarding the Basilica of Penance.

The Clifflands: One of the Seven Seachtú of Alabach, its capital city is Point Grey.

The Dustgate: Entrance to Penance via one if its residential districts.

The Dustworks: Residential district of Penance, home to the Basilica.

The Fall of Sin: An event in the history of Alabach where a tower built by the Simians was cast down by Lord Seletoth for exceeding the height of Mount Selyth.

The Firstborn: Early Humans who conquered Alabach 400 years ago.

The Glenn: A valley separating the greater Penance region from the Alabach's Seven Seachtú. Uninhabitable as all flora are poisonous, and all fauna, carnivorous.

The Glory of Penance: Airship built for long-distance travel. Decommissioned and used as a trade vessel. Crashed in the Glenn.

The Goldgate: Entrance to Penance via its commercial district.

The Goldworks: Commercial district of Penance.

The Kinglands: One of the Seven Seachtú of Alabach, its capital city Cruachan houses the seat of King Diarmuid III, XIX.

The Rustlake: Lake adjacent to Penance.

The Saltgate: Entrance to Penance via one if its residential districts

The Saltworks: Residential district of Penance

The Seven Seachtú of Alabach: The kingdom's seven provinces. They are (capital cities in parentheses): The Clifflands (Point Grey), The Godlands (Terrían), The Midlands (Ardh Sidhe), The Woodlands (Dromán), The Wetlands (Rosca Umhír), The Floodlands (Tulcha), and Cruachan (Cruachan).

The Steamgate: Entrance to Penance via its industrial district

The Steamworks: Industrial district of Penance

The Steel Mountains: Mountain range that surrounds Penance

The Stonegate: Entrance to Penance via one if its residential districts

The Stoneworks: Residential district of Penance

The Triad: The governing body of Penance, comprising of Borris Blackhands, Cathal Carríga, and King Diarmuid III XIX.

The Trinity: The three Gods worshipped by Humans in Alabach, comprising of Lord Seletoth (The Father), Lady Meadhbh (The Mother) and King Móráin the First (The Son). The current ruler of Alabach is said to be an incarnation of King Móráin.

Tulcha: Capital of the Floodlands, one of the Seven Seachtú of Alabach. Named after the river that runs through it. *(Tul-ka)*

Wraiths: Mysterious cloaked figures, agents for the Church, but rumoured to be affiliated with Lord Seletoth directly.

ACKNOWLEDGEMENTS

Well, there we go.

It's been a very long journey since I first opened the empty Word document in 2013 that would be the first book of this trilogy. There are so many people who've helped me between then and now, that I can only make a weak attempt here to thank you all.

First off, thank you to everyone from the Ubergroup who helped me along the way, especially those of you who taught me how to actually write. Also, thank you to everyone who read the first two books and constantly pestered me to finish this third one. Again, thank you to my excellent editor Lauren Humphries-Brooks, who has now developed a keen sense for my poor writing habits, the symptoms of which are fortunately absent from this version.

Big thanks to Cornelia Yoder as usual for the map, and to MiblArt team for the beautiful cover art.

And that's it. Like all indie authors, a review on Amazon or Goodreads would be very much appreciated. It's probably the best way to ensure I get cracking on more work!

About the Author

Alan was raised in the seaside village of Rush, County Dublin. He began writing fiction at the age of ten, starting with short stories about each of his classmates being eaten by dinosaurs. Fortunately, this behaviour was encouraged by both parents and teachers, allowing him to grow as an author.

Alan's first novel was *The Thralls of Fate*, written while studying for his PhD in Dublin City University. During that time, he also wrote a thesis on genetics and molecular biology.

Today, Alan works for the pharmaceutical industry, and spends most of his spare time playing Dungeons & Dragons and Magic the Gathering. He recently started running, but he doesn't enjoy it very much.

Twitter: *@AlanHarrison*
Instagram: @TheRealAlanHarrison
Email: *AlanHarrisonAuthor@gmail.com*

* 9 7 8 1 8 3 8 1 3 2 8 4 2 *